The Lotus Blossom Chronicles

Book 2

by
J.M. Jeffries
Dyanne Davis

Lotus Blossom is an imprint of Parker Publishing LLC.

Copyright © 2008 by Dyanne Davis, Miriam Pace and Jacqueline Hamilton

Published by Parker Publishing LLC
12523 Limonite Avenue, Suite #440-438
Mira Loma, California 91752
www.parker-publishing.com

ISBN: 978-1-60043-045-9
First Edition

Manufactured in the United States of America
Printed by Bang Printing, Brainard MN
Distributed by BookMasters, Inc. 1-800-537-6727
Cover Design by Jaxadora Design.

The Lotus Blossom Chronicles

Book 2

Dirty Little Secrets

By
J.M. Jeffries

Books by J.M. Jeffries

Dedication

For Dyanne Davis: thank you for writing to our rescue.
For Patty Sorensen at royaldandie.com: thank you for your kind
assistance in bringing Mojo to life. You made our swine divine.
For Deborah Burke at antiquedress.com: thank you for letting us
'play' in your cyber closet. You made Elle gorgeous.

Dirty
Little Secrets

by
J.M. Jeffries

1

"YOU WANT FORTY GRAND TO HACK my computers?" Mike Patterson screamed into Elle Walker's ear. She pulled the phone away and let out a long breath. First he'd wanted to hire her and now he's questioning the price. She was easy, but she wasn't cheap.

"I'm the best, Mr. Patterson. Trust me it's a bargain." Snow fell gently across the warm hood of her Jeep Liberty and then melted. When she'd first moved to Maine, she hadn't thought about being cold and having snow blanket the ground for most of the winter. But she found herself loving winter. No wonder she was the only black woman crazy enough to come to Maine. She cranked up her car heater another notch and covered Mojo up to her snout. Her Royal Dandie pig sighed or what Elle thought was a sigh. With a Royal Dandie she just never knew.

Patterson was still screaming. "I got a guy who will do it for twenty G's."

She wanted to tell him he'd get what he paid for. Cheap didn't always mean good and Elle was the best in the business.

She watched the road wondering when the tow guy would arrive. Having a flat tire in the middle of a blizzard was not particularly fun. "My left pinkie toe on a bad day has more skills than Phillip Blackstone."

Patterson sputtered into silence and after a moment he said in a more normal tone, "How did you know I talked to him?"

What the hell was taking the tow truck so long? As soon as she got Mr. Cheapskate Mike Patterson off the cell, she'd call Lee's Garage again. "Blackstone always underbids me," she explained, "and when he's done and you find yourself compromised by some pimply faced geek in Hoboken because Philly Boy's work is crap, you'll have to call me again. Then you're out sixty G's. Why not just pay me now and have the job done right." Phil was good, but Elle was better. She was the best internet security specialist in the United States. Forty thousand dollars was a bargain compared to what Patterson could lose if someone infiltrated his system.

"Why are you trying to hose me?" Patterson said gruffly.

She didn't bother to answer that question. "Barry Foster gave you my name, didn't he?"

Another long pause and then he said, "How did you know?"

"Six months ago you hired his security firm to travel with you to Iraq and Afghanistan to survey your company's weapons systems in action. He had your back there and I have Barry's back here. Barry and I are old friends." A friendship that went all the way back to the days when her hacking was highly illegal and Barry, an FBI agent at the time, busted her when she hacked into the DOD's mainframe on a bet. She'd won the bet and almost ended up doing time at Club Fed. On Barry's recommendation she'd got probation and a job with the government. He'd been her mentor ever since. When he hung up his badge and opened his own security firm, he hired her to freelance. "If the number one private security firm in the country trusts me and will happily pay my fees why can't you? Barry and his people guard royalty, dignitaries, and rock stars. You think he messes around with the B team?"

"But forty grand..." Patterson made one last ditch effort to force her price down.

What a whiner. Elle checked to see if the tow truck had arrived. No such luck. She pressed an icon on her laptop and pulled up Patterson's info. He needed proof of her abilities, so she'd give him some. "Mr. Patterson, the last four numbers of your social security number is 2698. Wednesday you ordered a five carat canary diamond ring for your wife from Harry Winston for her birthday next Monday. She'll be forty-seven, but she tells everybody she's forty-two. You purchased an antique ivory handled riding crop from Christie's for twenty-five grand via secret auction, which I find very interesting because you don't own a horse, but you do however keep a pretty blonde 'stabled' at Trump Towers."

The line went totally silent. She could feel him sweating all the way from New York. Elle forced herself not to snicker. "Mr. Patterson, are you still there?"

Of course he was. "How did you find out this information?" His voice came out garbled as though he were strangling.

She kissed the gloved fingertips of her free hand and planted them on the screen of her laptop. "It took me less than ten minutes to get all your personal info. I have your life story from the time you were a twinkle in your daddy's eye in St. Louis while he and your mother lived in a three story walk-up in Clifton Heights. Want to know who Mike Jr. is boinking at Yale on your nickel?"

Another pause and then burst out, "Jesus H. Christ."

"If He was alive today, He would give me some competition."

The fight went out of him. "Where do I wire the money?" he asked wearily.

Ka-ching. She had him. "I'll send you a secure email with all the info."

"How long is this going to take?" He sounded more than exasperated. Did she detect a tiny hint of fear?

Next week she was on a plane to Santa Inez, Florida for two weeks to help her parents celebrate their anniversary; she would probably break into Patterson's system as soon as he sent the money though she wasn't about to give him a specific time. "Sometime within thirty days of receipt the payment I'll hack your system and then we talk about how much it's going to cost to get you up to snuff."

He yelped. "I gotta pay more?"

Duh! She didn't fix for free either.

"W9867408728."

"What the hell is that?" he said, his tone more than uneasy.

To think she could pry into people's lives and still get paid. Her life was better than a soap opera. If she would have known at age sixteen, that ten years later she'd be rolling in the millions, she would have gone legit a hell of a lot earlier. "The serial number on your blonde's boob implants. Doctor Cochran's security is pathetic. You might want to give him a call and recommend me. He can afford me."

"You're raping me," he growled.

"You contacted me to test your security, not be to be your girlfriend. That is what I've done."

Again, he sounded resigned. "Barry called you the microchip

mafia."

Good ole Barry. She liked that. "From you that's a real compliment." Mike Patterson was a shark who didn't play nice in the world of big business. She wasn't going to play nice with him either.

"This is illegal? Hell, its blackmail."

Who is he going to tell? "I keep secrets better than your priest, Mr. Patterson. I'm just proving a point."

"All right, do it. The money will be in your account within twenty-four hours." And he slammed the phone down.

Of course she was hired. She had ole Mike by his jewels, his wallet and his secrets. She closed her cell and reached over to pet Mojo on her head. "Baby, momma's gonna buy you a whole bag of Blood Oranges when we hit Florida and I won't even make you share with me." She could afford her own bag. Mike Patterson's company held the number twenty two spot on the Fortune 500 list. She'd hit the big time and a bottle of '98 *Perrier Jouet Belle Epoque* was in her future. That and the oranges would make great Mimosas. Now if she didn't have to head to Florida to visit her parents she'd be peachy.

Mojo raised her little head and snorted. Then her little black and pink head dropped back down on her blanket. Elle gently ticked her under the chin. "We'll be back home in no time," she said as she opened her internet browser. Fortunately, the blizzard wasn't wreaking havoc with her connection.

Elle browsed her way to her favorite wine brokers and quickly ordered herself a bottle to be sent to her parent's house. It would arrive just about the time she'd need a stiff drink to get her through the trauma of family time.

A knock sounded on the window and a man with a bushy beard peered through the glass. He looked kinda Chinese which meant he was Mr. Lee's son. Finally, the tow truck had arrived.

His dark eyes trained on her as though he could see right through her. She found her heart racing, which was weird because she didn't normally go for the rugged and ready type. He looked like he could run with the Hell's Angels or eat chains. She preferred Goth geeks like herself--the type of man who was as smart as she was, but totally non-threatening.

She couldn't move and just sat there staring at him. Her mouth went dry. Snowflakes clung to his hair and eyebrows. His face had a steely quality to it like he could spit nails and swill beer at the same time.

He pointed his index finger down.

Then it occurred to her he wanted her to roll down her window. She pressed the auto button. The window slid smoothly down and cold air along with a few snowflakes rushed inside.

"Elle Walker?" he said.

His deep masculine voice sent her blood pressure into overdrive. She just got a twinge in her special place and was that a squeak coming out of her mouth?

"Are you Elle Walker?" he repeated.

"Yes." This time her voice sounded a little more normal.

"You need a tire changed?"

She nodded.

This guy was all man. He had to be about six feet tall or so. And it was hard to tell under the navy blue parka, but he looked like one of the healthy straplin' boys who ran around in the woods communing with Mother Nature and firearms. The guy was all about bringing on the sexy.

"You need to turn off the car."

"But I'll freeze."

His almond shaped, brown eyes stared at her. "Like I am now."

She bit her bottom lip; she normally was just rude on purpose. "I'm sorry." She turned off the motor.

"Go wait in the truck. The heater is on. I should be about twenty minutes."

She closed her laptop and secured it in its case, then gathered Mojo in her arms, tucking the blanket tightly around her.

"What's that?" he asked, his eyebrows raised in surprise.

"My pig." She hugged Mojo to her chest.

His eyes widened as if he'd never seen a pig before. "That's one tiny piglet."

"She's not a piglet, she's full grown and nearly two years old."

"Is she a runt?" His head tilted to side as he studied Mojo as if she were some lab experiment.

"She's a Royal Dandie, they're bred small." Elle pushed open the door and stepped out into the snow. Wind swirled around her face as she sneered at him.

"Not raising her for bacon?"

Elle whipped her head around and glared. "Mojo's my pet."

❦

Merrick Lee wanted to pull those words right back into his mouth as soon as he said them. Ms. Elle Walker's beautiful dark eyes narrowed and her full lush lips compressed into a hard straight line. A little gold nose ring jiggled against her copper brown skin and her body vibrated with anger. If laser beams could shoot from her eyes he would have been fried. As a matter fact he hadn't seen a look that lethal since leaving Iraq six months ago. He gulped.

He watched as she planted her pink Doc Martens on the white snow, the pig held tight against black jacket covering her chest. Damn she had little feet. "Can I help you carry something?"

"Thanks."

He'd gotten a good look at her laptop before she'd put it away and was impressed with her hardware, but then his dad said she worked at the Coop with the rest of the eggheads. The Coop was a small government run place where no one knew what anyone did up there, but it was guarded 24/7. In other words major government voodoo was happening behind those fifteen foot fences--his tax dollars hard at work.

She turned and bent her petite body over and her black jacket rose up to reveal an ass crafted by the hand of God himself. Two perfect rounded globes were outlined beneath the black fabric of her low riding jeans. Merrick had to pull back his hand because he just wanted to touch such perfection one time in his life. Then she wiggled her hips and he wasn't cold anymore. Nope, he was on fire.

She stood again and handed him her laptop. She checked her pig so tightly wrapped in the blanket all he could see was a pink and black snout peeking out. She took a step toward the tow truck and started to slip. He grabbed her arm and yanked toward him and the pig hit in him in the chest and let out an ear piercing squeal. Had that sound come from that little thing?

"Easy, baby," he said in a calm 'I just got accepted to Cornell Veterinary School' voice. "I'm not going to hurt you." He reached out and touched the little head.

The nose started twitching and he let go of Elle Walker's arm.

"She wants a kiss." Elle said.

He drew back, startled. Kiss a pig! Was she crazy? "I have never kissed a pig before." And wasn't going to start now, no matter how cute the owner might be.

Elle shrugged. "I do it all the time."

Which was probably as close as he was ever going to be to Elle Walker's luscious lips. "Do you French your pig or do you just give her a little peck?"

Her lips quirked, but just a quickly stilled. She wanted to laugh and he wanted to make her laugh.

"This is your first date, I don't want you to think my girl is easy, so no tongue."

"I'm okay with that." He bent down and kissed the pig's head. And actually the pig smelled kind of nice, like oranges. "You smell nice."

"Thank you."

He took a second discreet whiff. Elle smelled pretty nice, too, like sweet peas and violets. "You're welcome."

She stared at him as if she knew he was lying. "You meant Mojo, didn't you?"

What did a man say at a moment like this? He tap-danced as fast as he could. "I can neither confirm nor deny that your pig smells better than you."

This time she did laugh. "I take her to work with me so I can't let her smell like a barnyard. Not that she's ever seen a barnyard in her life."

As they walked to his truck, he realized he liked her laugh, it was almost musical. "You take your pig to work?"

"Mojo's very social. She's the office mascot. She even has a picture with Dick Cheney when he came for a tour of the Coop."

So the geeks knew what the town people called the place. "Vice President Dick Cheney?" Dick Cheney didn't seem like a 'love the pig' type and he wondered if the V.P. had kissed the pig.

Her head bobbed up and down. "The Big Dick himself."

"That sounds like a vaguely disrespectful name to call the V.P." He fished in his pocket for the keys.

"Take it any way you like it."

Merrick suspected she was a "take it or leave it" type of woman. He opened the door and stored her laptop on the passenger seat. Then he helped her up into the truck. For a second he wanted to climb inside with her and keep her talking, but that flat tire needed changing.

She was the first woman who had sparked any interest in him since his return--at least mentally. He hadn't been lacking for bed partners, but he had missed finding a woman who generated any interest in his brain. With her beautiful face and gorgeous ass she had looks, but the sassy tongue was what reeled him in every time.

He removed the spare tire from the rear of the Jeep and rolled it to the side of the road.

He glanced back at the truck and found Elle Walker staring at him a look of interest in her eyes. Maybe he'd found himself a playmate until he left for school in June. Frankly he didn't mind wiling away the long winter nights with such a hot woman. Maybe his life was going to be not so dull after all.

2

MERRICK STOMPED SNOW OFF HIS boots before entering the kitchen of his parent's house. His mother, Candace, stood at the stove stirring a large pot of something that smelled really, really good. He was starving.

His dad was setting the table. When he looked up, he said, "Well?"

"I got Elle Walker taken care of." But Merrick knew that's not what his dad was talking about.

Charles Lee frowned over the line of his reading glasses. "You know what I'm talking about. What did the letter say?"

"What letter?" Merrick pulled off his gloves and stuffed them in the pocket of his parka.

His mother turned around giving him a slightly annoyed look, a lock of red hair falling over her blue eyes. "Stop teasing your father, Merrick."

Just before he answered four Great Pyrenees dogs raced into the kitchen to greet him. The big white shaggy dogs were his mother's other children. She bred them and adored them beyond all reason. Merrick squatted down and gave each dog a good scratch on their back. "Oh, that letter."

His father put the last plate down. "What did the letter from Cornell say?"

Merrick looked up and smiled. "The same as the one you got from Harvard the other day."

"They want you back." His dad had been the head of the Math Department eight years ago when he decided he wanted to find his bliss being a garage mechanic instead of the high pressure world of academia. From his dad he got his brains, from his mother he got his love for animals.

Merrick stood. "It seems so." *Vet school, here I come.*

His mother hurried over and hugged him and then his father did the same.

"I'm so proud of you, son." His mother clutched his face in both her hands.

"Thanks." A few months after he graduated with his bachelor's degree he turned down vet school to join the army and fight in Iraq, he hadn't regretted his choice. He made it into the Rangers and later into Delta Force. He grew up in the army and became a man. Now he was ready for a life.

"We need to celebrate." His mother gushed.

All he wanted was a beer, some dinner, a shower and his bed. Actually, he wanted to be alone with his fantasy of Elle Walker dressed in a French maid's outfit.

The garage phone rang interrupting any further thoughts.

Merrick disengaged himself from his parent's arms. Picking it up, he answered. "Lee's Garage, Merrick speaking."

"Hi, this is Elle Walker."

Surprised, he almost dropped the phone. Speaking of the sexy temptress, "Is your car all right?"

"Yeah, I was wondering…" Her sultry voice trailed off.

"Yes?" She was going to ask him out on a date. *Sweet.*

There was a long breath on the end. "Well actually…"

Come to daddy baby; make him be a naughty boy. "Ms. Walker, is everything all right?"

She paused and then blurted out. "I have a business deal I want to talk to you about."

A business deal? He was hoping for monkey business. Damn, he'd read her all wrong. "Sure." He tried to keep his lack of enthusiasm out of his voice. Besides, he was a little curious. What could she want with him that would be strictly business?

"Can you meet me? Say in an hour."

"No problem. Where?" Not that there was much in Swenson to do on a Monday night. Well at least outside of the bedroom. Long cold Maine nights were built for sex.

"My house, 1432 Snowdrift."

Anticipation settled in the pit of his stomach. He found himself getting a little hard. It was a nice feeling. "No problem, I'll be there in about an hour."

"Thanks." And she hung up.

Merrick turned and found his parents watching him curiously. His mother's eyebrows rose and his father smiled broadly. "Do you have a date with Elle Walker?"

Not really, but if he charmed her enough it could turn into a date. Or an orgy fest. He was definitely in favor of the orgy and the thought of his hands on her tight little ass jump-started his breathing again. "I'm not sure."

"She's nice." His mother smiled and went back to her cooking. "A little odd. She dresses in black all the time and has black fingernails and black everything."

"Called Goth, mom," Merrick said. On Elle Walker, Goth looked good.

Charles poured coffee into his mug and took a small sip. "She has a pig for a pet. That's odd."

"Maybe," Merrick said, not certain how he felt about the little pig even as cute as it was.

Candace banged her spoon on the side of the pot. "Charles Lee, you kept crickets in a cage in your office for years."

Charles shrugged. "I'm Chinese. Crickets are good luck. Pigs are for dinner, not company."

"You were born in Brooklyn." His mother poured the contents of the pot into a soup tureen, stirred one last time before sliding the ladle in and putting the lid of the tureen and setting it on the table.

When his mother's voice got heated Merrick could hear her thick Maine accent come out. God, he had so missed hearing his mother's accent and hearing his father bait her. How a red-haired, blue eyed Irish woman got together with a Chinese man from Brooklyn was a total mystery to him. His mother opened the oven and the heavenly yeasty smell of fresh made rolls wafted out. Merrick's mouth started to water. "How about we celebrate my acceptance at vet school tomorrow? We'll drive to Caribou and I'll treat."

"Of course, dear." His mother set the tureen on the table, turned and kissed his cheek. "You go have yourself some fun."

She wouldn't have said anything if she hadn't really liked Elle. He'd have to pump her for info later.

Charles held out his mother's chair for her to sit. "I'm not sure I like you dating a woman who wears handcuffs for a belt."

He hadn't noticed the handcuffs. Now that could be interesting. "If I'm not home in the morning you can call the sheriff."

"Merrick Lee!" His father grunted.

"What?" He started walking to the stairs so he could slip into a hot shower and find a pair of easily removable pants--just in case. He always believed in being prepared--the most important lesson the military had taught him.

That and how to escape a pair of handcuffs.

❧

Elle sat on the edge of her overstuffed ottoman chewing on her black-tipped thumbnail. This had to be the craziest idea she'd ever hatched in her life. And that was saying a lot. Nervously, she bit the inside of her cheek, wondering how Merrick Lee would react when he found she wanted to rent him. Rather rent his presence as her boyfriend. He was just what she needed, just unconventional enough to intrigue her parents without being too much of a redneck, though she didn't know how someone who was half-Chinese could pose as a redneck.

If mom and dad had someone else to focus on, maybe she'd be free of the intense scrutiny that went with every visit to her parents. Would he go for it? She was ready to open up her check book, since she didn't expect him to pose as her boyfriend for free. Why did her dad suddenly decide to run for mayor of Santa Inez? Why did her parents decide to have a re-commitment ceremony to kick off his campaign? Why did she even need to attend?

The list of things she'd have to get done to be ready was ginormous. She would have to get her hair relaxed and dyed back to its natural dark brown color. No blue, purple, and green Bantu knots for her. The last time she de-Gothed was when the Secretary of Homeland Security came for a visit so she wouldn't shock the old boy down to his wingtips and stop his commitment to keep the funding coming.

Mojo chased her ball around the hardwood floor of the living room, her little hooves clicking. When the door bell chimed, Mojo pushed her ball under a chair and followed Elle to the front door.

She opened the door and resisted the urge to sigh. Stud Muffin was in the building. And he just stood there, all six feet of broad-shouldered, lean-hipped man. This man was a walking talking icon for her personal global warming. The cocky grin that curved his way too pretty mouth just shot straight at her 'I've been a lonely girl' zone. She wanted to bite her bottom lip and drool.

Mojo squealed in recognition and started dancing around his feet.

A slow smile spread over his full lips, his dark brown eyes brightened with pleasure. "I think your pig likes me."

She had never seen a man with such a pretty mouth. Those lips just screamed kiss me all night long. "She never forgets a face and she's just friendly that way." She held her arm out. "Come on in."

He stepped over Mojo with his big feet, then took off his black leather jacket and hung it on the coat rack. "So what's on your mind, Elle Walker?"

She really like the way he said her name in his rich sexy voice, which was so totally wrong. "Have you eaten?"

"I grabbed a quick bite at home."

Damn, he looked good in his black turtleneck sweater and just right fitting jeans. He walked passed her and she zeroed in on his butt. His jeans loved his tight high ass, too. "How are your parents?" All those years of finishing school and she could do polite chit-chat with the best of them. Beside one had to build up to will you be my rent-a-stud slowly.

"Intrigued."

"About?" As if she didn't know. Why was the queen of Goth squad calling their son?

He gave her a lazy grin that just about ignited her insides. "Your intentions regarding my virtue."

"You have virtue?" Okay that was a classic smart-assed Elle remark. Polite conversation was officially over. Thank God.

"I'm ex-military. Not much remains."

"Hmm." She walked to her overstuffed sofa. "Can I get you something to drink? I have beer, wine, juice, water, and tequila." She was hoping he'd go for the liquor, it would lower his inhibitions enough for him to not reject her proposal out of hand.

He sat down and stretched his mile-long legs out. He knew how to make himself comfortable. "A beer's good."

She went to the kitchen, poured herself another glass of cabernet and got him a beer. She set his beer in front of him and then sat down. Mojo sat on the floor next to his chair and was staring adoringly at him. She'd retrieved her ball and nosed it at his booted feet, an open invitation to play.

He took a long drink of the beer and then looked her up and down in a way that told him he was prepared for anything. "What kind proposition do you have for me?"

That sounded so dirty, not dirty in a bad way, but in a fun way. She mentally slapped herself; she didn't have time to play in the gutter with him no matter how tempting he might be. "Can you take two weeks off to go to Florida with me?"

He paused as though thinking over her question, his dark eyes studying her intently. He took a pull of beer. "Why?"

"I want to hire you." Cool, she didn't sound too bad. Maybe she'd get through this.

His head tilted to the side. "For?"

She rolled her eyes. Okay this wasn't going to be easy. "It's complicated."

"Complicated ain't cheap." One of those big feet crossed over the other. His father was a smallish man, how did Merrick turn out so big and tall and muscular.

"Neither am I." She took a sip of wine for courage. "I need a date."

For a couple seconds the room was perfectly silent accept for Mojo's heavy breathing.

"A what?"

"I want you to come to Florida as my date for two weeks and I'll pay you ten thousand dollars." She rushed forward, her words almost falling out of her mouth in her desire to get them out before she chickened out.

His eyebrows rose and his lips quirked. "You want me to be your date? What do you think I am, a Chinese-American Gigolo?"

She waved her hands denying his accusation. "Not the sex part." Okay she did think about the sex part, but not for money.

His eyebrows rose higher. "You don't think I'm attractive?"

"I think you're attractive." How could she not? One look from his dark eyes and the lazy grin on his face melted her from the inside out.

He clasped hands in his lap studying her, an odd light in his eyes. "But?" he coaxed.

How did she explain this? "You're too...too. Too..." He was just too much man for her.

He leaned forward and trained those all knowing eyes on her again. "Too tall? Too Chinese? Too what?"

Damn, he really had that 'see into your thoughts' glare. For a couple of seconds she felt under interrogation. And she hadn't felt like that since her illegal days. "Too alpha male." There she said. God she hated when people made her tongue-tied.

He seemed to pondering her answer and she opened her mouth to kind of gentle it down again when he asked. "Why is that a bad thing?"

Because. "It's great in a romance novel, but not real life. I like someone's who a little more... low key."

Merrick picked up his beer. "You have pig you take to work, you wear pink combat boots, have a hoop in your nose and have purple, blue, and green hair. Low and key are not two words I'd associate with you."

Elle splayed her hand on her chest. "I like geeks, like me. And there is nothing vaguely geeky about you." He made her body purr with just one look. He was dangerous and maybe asking him to go with her to Florida was not smart at all.

He took another pull of beer. "Then why do you want me to be your fake date?"

She took a deep breath and launched into her explanation. "Because my parents have probably lined up ten respectable men to squire me around and for the two weeks of hell they are forcing me to attend. If I show up with someone like you, not only will they see I'm involved, they'll be too irritated to think about me." And that was the truth. She sank back almost relieved to finally get the words out.

"Because I look like a mechanic bum?"

He was a big boy he could take the truth, she wasn't going to beat around the bush. "Well, yeah."

"I see." His face went blank.

She squirmed in her chair, her stomach was in knots. He didn't look like she'd hurt his feelings, but with that glint in his eyes she couldn't tell. "Don't take it the wrong way. My family is all about appearances and I'm kinda the black sheep and they are always trying to reform me and I'm going show up looking as normal as I can be without hacking up a hairball and I'll pay you fifteen grand."

"That's a lot of cash."

She was ready to offer him twenty thousand. It would be worth if it chaffed her mom's hide and made them leave her alone. "You're worth it."

He gave a low whistle. "They pay you that well at The Coop?"

And she was worth every penny. "I have another gig." And a very serious trust fund from her adoring and free spirited Grandmother Elizabeth, who was a woman who knew how to live and say the hell with the world.

"What?"

Asking questions meant she hadn't screwed up her chances just yet. "I can't really talk about it."

"I understand."

She waited a few second letting him work things out. "Will you do it?"

After another long, appraising look, he said, "Do you want me to be rude, too?"

Just showing up with his bushy beard and mechanic hands would be enough. She didn't want to go overboard or her wily mother would suspect something. "Just be yourself."

"How do you know I'm not an asshole?"

"Because your mom is a total doll." *Whom Mojo loved to no end.* "I think I make your dad nervous, but he is always polite to me and has never ripped me off."

"I'm not sure…"

Scooting to the edge of chair, she said. "I'll buy your clothes, too."

"I have summer clothes."

"I'm sure you do, but you know Maine only has three days of summer and we have a full itinerary of events." Somewhere she had the schedule. Her mother had been kind enough to let her know what would be happening during the two weeks and the clothes required for each event.

"What kind of events?"

"Cocktail parties, a tea party, a garden party, a ball, a polo match," she ticked off each event on her fingers, "and a cruise around the Keys on my father's new mega yacht, the re-commitment ceremony and the speech with my father declaring his intention to run for mayor. We're going to be busy." She looked at him hopefully. *Please say yes. Please say yes.*

He frowned. "Seems like a lot of work."

Boy did she know it. "My mother throws brouhahas like Busby Berkeley musicals."

He smiled. "I don't have polo clothes."

"I've got you covered." He had a nice smile to match that glorious mouth. Not too much teeth--just enough mischief to make the smile interesting, but sincere enough to lead a girl astray and not make her feel bad about giving in. He must do well with the ladies. To be honest he was doing well with her. She'd have to watch herself around him. "I can have an entire wardrobe Fed Exed immediately." Thank God for the Internet.

Rolling the beer bottle between his long supple fingers, he seemed to thinking about his answer.

Please. Please. Please. She couldn't bring one of her fellow geeks from the Coop, her dad would run him off and then a few days later, they find his half eaten body in a swamp. Then she'd have some explaining to do. Merrick looked like he could handle himself, even against her parents. No small feat indeed.

"You're not making this easy to accept."

She pointed at Mojo who was now standing on her head trying to get Merrick's attention. Her baby really liked him. "I'm bringing my pig."

He gave the pig a surprised look. Mojo dropped back to all fours and trotted over to him, her little snout in the air, her eyes soulful as though begging him. "How can I resist a cutie like you." He scratched Mojo between her ears. "Okay, I'm in. But half in advance and half once we arrive."

She nodded, relieved.

He lifted his beer bottle and toasted her. "To fun in the sun."

Poor man. What he didn't know wouldn't hurt him, but her family was the world biggest fun killers in the South.

Elle slumped in her chair. Thank God. Now she just had to get through the trip and she'd be fine. Wouldn't she?

3

AS HE WAS TAKING ONE LAST look in the mirror of his hotel room, Merrick heard the door to their hotel suite open and shut. He rubbed his hands over his smooth cheeks almost forgetting what he'd looked like under his bushy beard.

Wow! He looked respectable.

"Honey, I'm home."

"I'm ready when you are."

Elle was going to pop a gasket. He knew she wanted him to look like the bum she thought he was, but he couldn't do that because he badly wanted to shake her up.

She fascinated him. The money was great and he could use all the new clothes she bought him, but he just wanted to get to know her better. That and get into her panties. Damn she was hot and for some strange reason she just tripped his trigger.

They hadn't spent much time together after he agreed to come to Florida with her. He only gotten a call to make sure that his clothes had arrived and that Mrs. Lancaster had taken care of all the alterations. Which considering they had been done in a matter of days, this must have cost her plenty. For a woman who sported grunge and Goth clothes she had taste in menswear. And she had money. Money she didn't have any problem spending.

"Give me five minutes to get dressed and I'll be ready to rock and roll."

After she had spent the last five hours getting ready she was going to be dressed in five minutes. That he doubted.

After spending the entire day in the spa, he knew what 'getting ready' for her really meant. She'd told him she needed to get her hair done, a mani-pedi (which after his trip to the men's spa he now knew what it was,) waxed, and her make-up done. She'd also gotten her butt buffed, her words not his, even though he'd gotten a total body exfoliation, too. But he would slit his own throat before he admitted how much he'd liked it. Although the lady at the spa frowned at his decision to skip the body wax, but Merrick had every chest he had, he was keeping it. He did feel relaxed and kind of sexy. So this is what they meant by being metro sexual. He studied his manicured nails, how that woman got all the grease out, was miracle. And Elle paid for everything. Even the tips, which must have been stellar because every time he'd whipped out his wallet everyone smiled and told him. "Ms. Walker has already taken care of us."

He left the bathroom and picked up Mojo's harness—a designer Louis Vuitton harness. The pig sat patiently as Merrick buckled the straps. He was surprised the pig had traveled so well. Of course she did have her own first class seat. The airline people were a bit miffed until Elle whipped out a letter from Doc Griffin claiming the pig was her emotional support pet, and that Elle couldn't get on a plane without her. After about thirty minutes into the flight, Mojo had everyone charmed including a cranky five year boy. So it worked out for the best.

"I'm ready--" Elle said and came to a sudden stop as she stared at him, mouth agape and pointed a finger with her face was all scrunched up like she'd eaten a lemon. She'd had fake nails put on. "What happened to my scruffy date?"

He studied her as he ran a hand through his newly styled, blow dried and product (the hairdresser's word, not his) laden hair She looked good. She looked damn good. "The woman in the salon said I needed to look more Miami Beach."

She put a hand on her hip and tapped one of her muted gold stiletto feet. With the other hand she fanned her face with her gold purse, which was looked like a large gold envelope. "Now you look like Keanu Reeves, only...only...better. That's not what I wanted."

What the hell does a woman put in a purse that size, he wondered? "So you're saying I'm too good looking to be your date?"

Her lip glossed mouth compressed into a thin line. "Pretty much."

"Then why not let me wear my oil-stained overalls instead of buying me all this." He backed up, arms spread.

She frowned as she studied him. "Okay, maybe there are a couple flaws in my plan."

"Only a couple."

"I had the idea you blended in a little. Not be too much...too much..." her voice trailed away as she floundered for a response.

"...like a bum." Merrick finished for her.

"I guess I didn't think it through completely."

"That seems a little out of character for a self-professed geek like you."

"I was distracted," she snapped at him.

  "By what?"

She simply glared at him and wouldn't answer.

Merrick scanned her body. She wore a big black coat that reminded him of Zorro. She just needed a sword and she'd be ready to go. He shrugged. "I suppose one will take notice of me with you wrapped in that blanket."

Her sherry brown eyes narrowed. "This is an opera coat. The height of chicness in the fifties. I have a cocktail dress on under it. I just want to show up in this to get my mother's motor running."

Honey this ain't the fifties, he wanted to say, but with that look on her face, he didn't have the balls. She would have hurt him bad. "Tell me it's not that pink leather milk maid dress you showed me on the Internet." She had told him she'd bought it and his eyes nearly rolled back in his head. He was getting on plane ASAP if that was what she was wearing. He didn't need to show up with Pepto pink Heidi no matter how much she was paying him.

A finger came up and she glared at him with one hand on her hip. "First of all I love that dress. It's vintage Alexander McQueen. And it's Florida in January. It's like eighty degrees outside. I'm not wearing leather to prove a point, even if my mother would have had a fit and make me go home."

Rolling back on his heels he studied her. She was all whipped in a frenzy and looking way too sexy. He wondered if she got that way in bed, too. He'd like to find out. "Isn't that being a little mean?"

"Wait until you meet her."

His gut clenched. Maybe he could go play tag with the Taliban again? At least they would kill him quick and his misery would be over. "Then let's get this over with."

She took Mojo's leash from him and headed for the door with the little pig trotting on her heels. "Is the luggage in the car?"

He hurried to open the door for her. Luckily she was short and he could out walk her. "Yes, but do we have to stay at your parents?"

She stepped across the hall to the private elevator. "Part of the mom's plan. We'll be out in the pool house, so we won't be tripping over them."

They got into the elevator and the door closed. "Does she know you're bringing a pig?"

Her full mouth tilted up into an evil smile. "Don't think I didn't send her that letter from Doc Griffin, too."

Doc Griffin was about honest as they come, how did he go about lying for her. "How did you get him to write that?"

"I helped him get his website fixed after his son totally messed it up."

Damn this woman could corrupt a saint. God knows she was making him do things he would have never thought he'd do. And making him like it. "You are sneaky."

"Yes I am, but going back to the original subject. How come you went all glam on me?" she sounded almost plaintive.

"Because I want to look respectful, that way when they get to know me it will be more of a shock. I thought you'd appreciate that more." Damn, he was pretty sneaky himself. If he could manage it without her seeing him, he'd pat himself on the back

Elle looked as if she didn't believe him. "I have to think about that."

He sounded sincere; he knew he had the right look on his face. The tone was perfect. Time for them to move on to something new. "You really think I look like Keanu Reeves?"

"Better."

She may not want to admit it, but she liked him. And maybe he could use that. Deep down in the place he didn't like to think about that's the real reason he was here, he wanted her. That was his little secret at least for the moment. "Thank you, Elle."

He could swear that he heard her growl.

And he found that very, very sexy.

As the limo drove to her parent's beach house along a narrow highway bordered by flowing palm trees and a canal on one side with boats tied up to slips that looked more like mansions that boats, he couldn't help but wonder what she wore under that coat. He had to think about something other than the Arctic breeze coming from the air conditioner. She looked positively elegant with her newly dyed, long dark hair dipping across one eye and falling over her shoulder. She reminded him of a forties movie star. He just wanted to touch it, play with and feel it trail all over his body. Damn he was excited. She thrilled him on a level he forgotten he'd had.

In Iraq, sex had been a form of release from the tensions of combat, and home it was a way to pass the time. But looking at Elle he wanted her on a completely different level. He wanted to spend hours touching her, kissing her, talking to her. It bothered him that he got all caught up in her in such a short time. That wasn't his style at all.

Mojo stood on the seat, her nose pressed against the dark window to watch the traffic. Her little tail whirled like a windmill.

Elle reached into her purse, took out her cell phone and made a call. "Hi mom, we'll be there in about ten minutes." She snapped her phone closed and stuffed it back into her sequined evening bag. "It's on." She looked out the window at the fading evening sun that cast long shadows on the ground.

Merrick raised on eyebrow. "What's on?" Fear settled in his gut.

She smiled. "The ten minute warning. She'll be at the door waiting for us."

He rubbed his hands together. "You are enjoying this way too much."

Elle held up her hand. "This is self defense. My mother is going to spend the next two weeks trying to fix everything about me. I've tamed the hair do and spent a fortune on clothes. I have to bring some part of the real me to this shindig, or I'm just going to pop. Okay? Why my dad needs to be the mayor of Santa Inez is beyond me."

"What does he do?" He did know her family owned the hotel they stayed at because one of the maids had let it slip.

She sighed as though she was in pain. "He runs the family business."

"Which is?" he prodded.

"Walker International has a lot of concerns from agri-business, hotels, real estate and banking. What everybody doesn't know, which is the dirty little secret of the Walker clan, is that my great-grandfather James made a ton of cash in the bootlegging business."

So little Ms. Goth was really an heiress. No wonder money ran through her fingers like water. Though he had to admit the change in her was refreshing. She looked enticingly beautiful and he couldn't stop a piercing vibration that swept through him. "Interesting."

"But no one talks about that. The whole sordid affair embarrasses my brother and my parents. I love them madly, but they are such tight asses."

"So you're cool with the bootlegging thing."

She giggled like a school girl. "Hell yeah. Wouldn't you be? Why be uptight about something that already happened over seventy years ago. The family's legit now."

One of his father's grandfathers had been a general in the Imperial army for the last Chinese emperor. Yes, it was nice to have that type of lineage and he respected it for what it was worth, but to be honest Merrick didn't think it had that much to do with who he turned out to be. Besides, like Elle said, the man was long dead what difference did it make who he was or what he did. "I'm not surprised."

A devilish smile appeared on her lips. "Well, I'll have to work on that."

Be afraid, Merrick Lee, be very afraid. "I heard all the nuts roll down to Florida, how come you left?"

One of her newly plucked eyebrows arched. "I'm almost insulted."

But he couldn't resist baiting her. It was so fun. "Why did you leave?"

She seemed to be considering her answer. "I had an offer I couldn't refuse."

He shifted in his seat. So Elle had a shady past, too. This woman was a whole box full of secrets. And he wanted to discover them all. "You worked for the mob?"

"Nothing so exciting." Elle shook her head and her hair danced around her slender shoulders. "But then again working for the Feds is almost the same thing."

She didn't seem to have a lot of love for authority. "Explain that to me." Not that it surprised him. She liked to flaunt her unconventionality, which was very attractive to a man whose whole life was about following the rules.

She fanned her face with her envelope shaped purse again. "Well, since I've technically concluded my court mandated obligation to them three years ago, I guess I can let you know a bit about my shadowy past. I hope you won't be shocked."

Jack and pot. A woman, who was willing to give up her secrets, was about a step away from giving up the other stuff. He could almost taste her now. Elle would be his. "This is getting better all the time."

"I had a choice. I could go to work for Feds or do hard time for them."

Merrick let those words float around the ether for a few seconds, because he wasn't sure what to make of them. "What did you do?"

She held up her fingers and pretended to type. "I liberated some classified information from the DOD."

"Damn!" She was a hacker. Now that was impressive.

She leaned back on her seat and crossed one shapely calf over the other. "Once upon a time I was a very naughty girl."

He loved naughty girls, but he suspected Elle's naughty was different from the kind of naughty he liked. "Not in the fun, get naked way I take it."

She rolled her eyes. "Until the FBI came a knockin', I was having a blast."

"So they gave you choice?"

"I didn't think incarceration was in my best interests. And neither did my parents."

The limo stopped in front of a pair of elaborate wrought iron gates. Elle rolled down her window. Moist air flooded the car as a tough looking white guy with a shock of black hair with grey streaked through it stuck his face in. He looked around, his light blue eyes pausing on Elle and he seemed to go a shade paler.

Elle smiled. "Hi Steve."

The man smiled back, but Merrick saw a glint in the world-weary blue eyes that he interpreted as fear. Mojo whirled and stared at the man. She made a squeaky noise and Elle gently patted her.

"Ms. Walker," Steve said in a calm voice, "it's a pleasure to see you again."

Elle clapped her hands. "I'm thrilled beyond belief." She didn't sound thrilled. "Anybody I should know about here?"

Merrick had to wonder what kind of things Elle did at these parties that would cause Steve to look so nervous. Merrick wondered if he would need a lawyer.

The older man shook his head. "It's spit and polish time."

Elle sighed with just a touch of drama. "I'll be on my best behavior."

Steve looked relieved. "Snoop Dawg and his crew couldn't make it?"

Elle batted her eyelash. "Those were the days."

Merrick looked at the guy's face. He'd been around the block a time or two, maybe even ex-military. And this pint-sized woman promising to behave had the guy looking so happy made him wonder what she could do to upset the balance so much. Suddenly, the bodyguard winked. "You know how much I like dull."

Elle smiled. "Just for you, I'll be nice."

"Thanks Ms. Walker. Have good time."

As he watched, Elle gave the man a quick wave and the limo driver rolled the window up. The gates opened slowly and the limo eased through following a long drive bordered by green grass, huge urns filled with flowering plants of some sort and the ever-present palm trees that swayed with the ocean breeze.

Merrick said, "Who comes to your parents parties?"

She leaned back in the seat. Mojo jumped into her lap. "My parents invite the rich, the powerful and the terminally boring."

A couple of minutes later they pulled around a huge fountain with water spurting out of the mouths of a number of fish. Lilies dotted the water. The driver jumped out, and ran around to open the door. Merrick stepped out and reached in to help Elle out of the car.

Merrick stood and looked up at the imposing façade of three story Mediterranean style mansion with the stucco painted a pale cream. Mosaic tile lined the stairs leading up to the arched portico that appeared to go completely around the huge house. Arched windows dotted the front to either side of the huge wooden doors that looked like they belonged to a castle.

Elle's parents were loaded. Merrick was doubly impressed. He slid a glance at her. She was bent over adjusting Mojo's leash. She glanced at him and he could see a hint of something in her eyes, he couldn't quite interpret. Mischief, maybe?

An elegant looking woman in a flowing green gown and with dark hair piled high on her head stepped out the front door and stood waiting, studying Elle with a look that only a mother could manage.

Elle plastered a wide smile on her face. "And here's my mother," she whispered through clenched teeth as she walked up the steps and across the tiled floor to the front door.

The woman stepped up to Elle, a tight look on her face. "Ann-Elizabeth, you look ..."

Elle glanced at him, a warning in her eyes. He mouthed the words Ann-Elizabeth and she glared. How did she come up with Elle? He just had to find out.

The woman frowned not only at Elle, but at Mojo who squeaked happily as she nosed at the flowers in a terra cotta pot. "I was hoping you would wear..."

Elle handed Merrick the leash and stepped back. She unbuttoned her coat and whipped it off her shoulders, revealing an orange dress. A very bright orange dress. His eyes nearly fell out of his sockets, the silky material skimmed her body showing off her slender curves and firm butt. A deep V with some kind of netting over it let the world know she was a girl in all the right places. She tossed him her coat and twirled. The back of the dress was secured by a little bow that seemed to hold the whole thing together. If he reached over and tugged the bow open, he had the feeling the whole dress would fall off.

Merrick couldn't breathe and his palms began to sweat. He had no idea that hidden behind that encompassing coat was a woman of unusual charm and fashion. Damn, she was more than beautiful, she took his breath away.

Elle's mother covered her mouth for a couple of seconds, then her hands dropped to her side. "You're so beautiful." She sounded almost wistful.

"Thank you, Mother." Elle struck a model pose. "It's vintage Oleg Cassini."

Her mother smiled. "He also designed for Grace Kelly and Jackie Kennedy."

Merrick knew who Grace Kelley and Jackie Kennedy were, but didn't understand why this bit of information was important and he really didn't want to know.

Elle kissed her mother's cheek. "I knew you would approve."

God knows he did.

"Thank you, Ann-Elizabeth." Relief and something else, something more furtive, flooded the older woman's face. She turned to Merrick. "Who is your young man?"

"Merrick Lee, this is my mother Patricia Walker." He held out his hand hoping his calluses would offend her. He was sure Elle was hoping he'd drool or something, but this woman was all gracious class no matter how tight-assed Elle thought she might be.

"How do you do, Ma'am? Ann-Elizabeth," he found himself stressing the name, "has told me so much about you."

She gave him an appraising look that told him she knew exactly what Elle had probably said. She gave him a slight flirting look. "And you still came to my party. You are a brave man, Mr. Lee."

He slid a sidelong glance to Elle and saw her scowling. Good, let her sweat for a while. "I've been looking forward to meeting you." Damn he was smooth.

Patricia slipped her arm through his and through the front door to the huge foyer beyond. "You must tell me. How did you two meet?"

He grinned and tossed a glance at Elle. Mojo trotted at her heels. "I changed her flat tire."

"How kind of you."

"It's his job." Elle said from behind them.

Her mother's eyes widen, but her face didn't change otherwise. This woman was good. "You're a ..."

"A mechanic," he responded. Suddenly he wanted her to know he wasn't a bumbling idiot. "I've been working for my father since I came home from Iraq."

Her face brightened up. Patricia was a soldier lover. "A soldier? You are a surprising man. I'll introduce you to Colin Powell, he's around somewhere." Patricia turned to Elle. "Why don't you walk your pig before you join us? I don't want *it* to have any accidents on my rugs."

Merrick tried not to laugh as Elle turned and marched back down the stairs to the bushes. So the mom gave as good as she got. Maybe this wasn't going to be so bad after all.

4

THE BALLROOM LOOKED LIKE A floral display with arrangements in giant vases situated throughout the huge room. On one side of the room was the buffet with every conceivable delight available from Beluga caviar to the finest cheeses. Across from the buffet was the bar with fine wines. People milled in groups while a three piece chamber group provided the background music—nothing loud enough to force the guests raise their voices to be heard, but soft enough to still be heard. Even though the evening had turned cool, the French doors overlooking the formal garden were open to let in the cool ocean breeze bringing with it the tang of salt.

Elle sipped a glass of champagne. Mmmm, if she wasn't mistaken this was a Krug *Clos de Mensil Brut '95*. The honey and ginger notes gently tickled her nose. Her mother was sparing no expense for this shindig. Speaking of which, she spotted the old girl flitting from group to group being the perfect, cordial hostess. Elle studied her mother. There was something off about her tonight. She seemed a bit frantic in a nervous way that was so atypical of her. Usually her mom was in her element as a party hostess seeing to the comfort of all her guests. Elle found that rather strange and wondered what was bothering her?

Elle saw her old friend, Barry Foster, near a potted palm talking into his sleeve. He winked at her as she lifted her glass to him, glad her father had hired his firm for added security especially with so many dignitaries here. Merrick was talking to Colin Powell and a few of her father's other cronies. The governor just fed Mojo a strawberry after she stood on her head then she launched into her famous pig shuffle to the delight of her audience. Damn Mojo was the belle of the ball. Who would have thought everyone would take to a Royal Dandie pig with such class.

A hand touched her shoulder and Elle turned. "Georgina!" she said at the sight of her tall, TV star cousin who leaned down to kiss her cheek.

"Elle, I didn't recognize you. You're a girl." Georgina wore a candy apple red sheath that caressed her voluptuous body. Unlike Elle she always looked glamorous.

"A hot one," came from behind Georgina as Dante Mayweather, Georgina's fiancé bent over to kiss Elle on the cheek.

"Soon to be cuz-in-law," Elle said, "Mom didn't tell me you were coming."

"With the writer's strike, I'm temporarily out of work." Georgina touched Dante's hand. "and loving it."

"You look terrific," Georgina said fingering the russet lace netting across Elle's bodice. "I love your outfit. I'd give up my boobs to get in that dress. It's sublime."

Dante raised his hand. "Excuse me. That's my playground."

Elle laughed. She was thrilled to see them. They'd met about four months ago when Dante had rescued her in the Iraqi desert and it was mad love for the both of them.

Georgina walked a circle around her. "Vintage?"

Her cousin knew clothes like Elle knew code. "Oleg Cassini."

"Sexy and classy rolled into one." Georgina sighed. "Where did you get it?"

Georgina was seven inches taller than her and had a real woman's body while Elle was a short glorified boy. She'd love to be able to fit into her cousin's wardrobe. "Deborah Burke at antiquedress.com will hook you up. She has the best closet on the eastern seaboard."

Dante rubbed his forehead. "If you two are going to talk about dresses some more, I'm leaving before my testosterone dries up."

"Weatherman?"

Elle heard Merrick's voice behind her.

Dante's eyes widened and he smiled as Merrick approached.

For a second they just looked at each other. Then shook hand and slapped each other on the back.

"Dragon," Dante said, "what the hell are you doing here?"

Surprised, Elle could only look at them wondering how they knew each other. To her knowledge, Dante had never been to Maine in his entire life.

Merrick put a proprietary arm around Elle. "This is my girl."

Her skin sizzled with sudden head as he touched her and Elle nearly dropped her glass. "How do you know Dante?"

Merrick grinned. "We served together."

"You were Delta Force?" Elle was surprised. She'd worked with the military every day and knew Delta Force was the military all stars--the best of the best. Bums didn't make it there. She found herself glaring at Merrick.

He shrugged as if it was nothing. "Elle, did you want to say something?"

"Delta Force is the best of the best." God did she sound pathetic. Although she didn't mean to be insulting, she couldn't believe he hadn't told her. She should have investigated him a little harder, but she'd been so enthralled with her plan she hadn't gone beyond the obvious.

Merrick kissed her forehead. "What's your point, Ann-Elizabeth? I'm that good."

Elle felt her knees go weak at Merrick's closeness. Her stomach was doing all kinds of crazy things and she was really turned on. She liked the way he touched her skin.

Dante smiled. "And he was an officer."

Well of course he was. Why would he be just a dumb minion-type grunt? She looked at her cousin as though Georgina could help her in some way, but Georgina just shrugged. Obviously she was as clueless as Elle. "Where did you go to school?"

"Cornell," Merrick answered a sheepish grin on his face.

An Ivy League man! Her father would do a jig. Merrick was so perfect it just had to be wrong. Okay, she was turned on and feeling stupid. "Isn't that nice?" she said knowing her response anemic and ungracious.

Dante took a sip of his wine. "I can't believe you are dating Georgina's cousin."

Georgina tilted her head and studied Elle for a second. "How did you two get together?" her tone held a hint of incredulity as though Elle wasn't in the same league as Mr. Ivy League, Delta Force Commando Lee.

Elle's lips scrunched up. "He's my auto mechanic." One time

did qualify him as hers.

Dante's mouth dropped for a second. "Man, what happened to vet school?"

Merrick's fingers massaged her upper arm playing with her as if he had a right to. "I'm back at Cornell next June."

Oh, how wonderful and he loved animals. No wonder Mojo was crushing on him. He was her pig's kind of people. "You're going to be a veterinarian, too? Isn't that nice." Her words came out strangled, as though her throat had closed. She's spent so much time looking for Mr. Wrong to keep her parents off her back and she ends up with the cream of the crop, Mr. Right. How did she get herself into of this mess?

Merrick grinned. "I have a few years before I can hang Doctor on my name."

She hated to be one-upped. Normally she was the one who was full of surprises. She just didn't know how to react to Merrick's revelation. She hated being impressed by people, but he was just that. "Damn."

"You didn't know?" Georgina asked her, a knowing look in her eyes.

Duh, because she didn't ask. She didn't think she had to. "Merrick is certainly full of surprises, isn't he?" Again her words sounded strangled. She thought she'd gotten a troll and ended up with a prince. How shitty could her luck be?

Merrick moved his hand down her arm and patted her on the hip. "Keeps you coming back for more."

Before Elle could open her mouth again, her father slid an arm around her and kissed her cheek. "Ann-Elizabeth, you look lovely." Relief shone in his dark eyes.

Elle took a deep breath. She couldn't send Merrick home now. He was here, she would have to make the best of it. "Thanks, Daddy. You're looking pretty spiffy yourself."

Her father was tall and slender, his dark curly hair only slightly highlighted with silver. He looked every inch the lord of the manor. "I came to meet your friend."

Elle held up her hand. "Lawrence Walker this Merrick Lee." She could barely keep the sarcasm out of her voice.

Merrick held out his hand. "A pleasure to meet you, sir."

Her father took his hand and shook it. "You're not what I expected."

At least Merrick had the decency to look surprised. "Is that bad?"

Her father chuckled. "Not at all."

Next time she was bringing home a biker with tattoos and beard that went to his stomach. Take that, Daddy.

She imagined a thought bubble over her father's head with the words, *you're so normal*, highlighted inside. "Oh please." She pointed her glass at Merrick. "Let's get this off the table. He graduated from Cornell. He served in Iraq with Dante in the Delta Force. And he's going to vet school this fall. At Cornell. And he knows how to fix cars. Are you happy?" Even to her own ears she sounded like a sulky, surly five year old.

Her father eyed Merrick for a moment then he rubbed his chin. "Why are you dating my daughter?"

With a completely straight face, Merrick replied, "It was the pig, sir. I always knew I wanted a woman who had her own swine and when Ann-Elizabeth fell into my lap, it was love at first sight."

"Boy, you're a smart-ass." Her father started to laugh. "I like that."

Elle's sucked on her bottom lip so her mouth wouldn't fall open in disbelief. She got in trouble for being a smart-ass and Merrick just got away with the same thing. This wasn't her real father. Who replaced her tight-assed dad with this too amiable guy?

"I do my best, sir," Merrick said with an answering grin.

"Suck up," she mumbled.

"What did you say, Ann-Elizabeth?" Merrick raised one of those sexy jet black eyebrows.

"Nothing, Merrick." She gulped her champagne. She had to get away and think for a few minutes about this turn of events. "I need another drink."

Her father grabbed her upper arm. "That sounds like a good idea, if you'll excuse us for a moment." Her father led her right past the bar, out of the ballroom into the foyer and down a hall to his office.

Oh no. Now was not the time for one of their father daughter-chats. They hadn't had one in a long time. And she couldn't think of what she had done to warrant one of their infamous 'talks'. "What did I do now, Daddy?"

"You and I are going to have a chat. Have a seat." He pointed to a wing-backed chair next to a giant stuffed goat he'd bagged a few years ago on one of his hunting expeditions.

She ran her list of recent sins through her head and couldn't come up with anything interesting. To her everlasting determent, she'd been a well...a good girl. Had she turned boring? Oh no!

"Well?"

Her father poured two snifters of brandy and handed one to her. "How long have you been working for Randall Greene?"

She never discussed her side job. "Excuse me." How did he find out? "How do you know?"

"Randall is retiring and his sons don't want to run the trucking company so he's selling out. Your name come up during due diligence." He sat down across from her and crossed his legs. He held the brandy snifter in both hands and stared at her over the rim.

Now that was a surprise! Lawrence was running for mayor and still trying to rule the business world. "You're buying a trucking company?"

His eyes narrowed. "When did you start doing private computer security?"

Elle's palms started to sweat. She didn't want to stain her dress so she rested her elbows carefully on the chair arms. "Since the end of my probation."

Her father looked stern. "Randall can't say enough good things about you. I'm disappointed." He said that like he was surprised she could do something right.

"I'm perfectly legal," she quickly added. Okay, maybe she'd had a wild moment, or two, or three, but she'd turned her life around. She was on the straight and narrow now and thought she was doing a pretty good job.

"Why didn't you let me know?" He put his drink on the coffee table. "I would have hired you."

Elle replayed his words in her head. He wasn't mad at her. He wanted to hire her? Was he drunk? "Daddy, be real. You don't trust me." Besides, she didn't want to work for him. That was the whole point of doing what she did. No one could accuse her of getting all the lucky breaks because of who her father was.

"I want to hire you," he said.

Elle was stunned. "I'm not going to give you a discount because you're family." She didn't mean to say that, the words just rushed out of her disbelieving mouth.

"You'd better not." He chuckled and took a sip of the brandy.

She fought the urge to stand up and run out of the room. This whole visit wasn't turning out the way she'd envisioned. "Well, okay."

He took another sip of his drink. "So you like what you're doing?"

"Yes. I love my job. I think I really found my calling. I get to be bad, get paid a whole lot of money, and I'm on the right side of the law." *For a change.* She didn't think her father would dispute that.

"Why are you still working for the government?"

That was an odd question. Her daddy never asked questions he didn't already have the answers to. He was crafty that way. "You tell me why you want to be mayor after running a multi-billion dollar empire. What are they going to pay you, thirty grand?"

He chuckled. "Twenty seven five."

Elle shook her head. They were actually having a real conversation that didn't involve her shaming the family. "Mom won't be able to get her shoe collection into the mayor's official residence. She'd have to re-model."

He seemed to get a bit choked up. After a few seconds he said. "I want to give back. I want to keep my town safe and productive. Things are changing here and I want to make sure the town stays ahead of the curve."

"Doesn't everybody in Santa Inez work for you in some way? I'd call that keeping the town in the green."

He took a long breath. "I think I might run for national office, I want to have some experience. You haven't answered my question, yet. Why do you still work for the government?"

She sipped the brandy and it burned going down. "About seventy five percent of my private clients come from government contractors and their buddies and they pay well. Besides I discovered I like doing good for my country. Last month I nabbed a major arms dealer and never left the comfort of my cubicle."

His eyes widened. "How did you do it?"

Her family hadn't known how the government put her illicit skills to work. All they had cared about was keeping her out of jail and out of the papers. She considered her answer because a part of her job was classified. "He kept his arms dealing very low tech, but his kiddie porn was easy to trace. And when they caught up with him, they told him he'd be tried as a pedophile, so he cracked. Better a terrorist serving a life sentence then Chester the child molester spending a couple years in prison. Those guys in the general prison population have a shot life expectancy."

Her father nodded, looking impressed. "And you helped catch him?"

Elle would die before admitting to her father how important her job had become to her. Now that she was a few years older, she realized she liked not being thought of as the family fuck-up.

Oh my God, she was growing up and becoming responsible. When had that happened? For a second she couldn't breathe. Finally, she said, "Mostly I work on national security, but I get loaned out to all the alphabet agencies."

A companionable silence fell between them. Elle kept waiting for the other shoe to drop. Having approval from her dad was rocking her world, especially after so many years of not having that approval. She felt strange sitting here talking with him adult to adult.

"By the way," her father said, "your boyfriend is impressive. I like him."

She held up one hand in supplication. "Can I pick them or what?"

Her father chuckled. "To my everlasting surprise."

This conversation was starting to make her nervous. "Let's go back to the party." She stood and set her snifter on the bar.

He drained his snifter and stood. "I know how you feel, Elle. This conversation is a little strange for me, too."

"You'd really hire me?" She wanted to make sure he wasn't messing with her head. Getting Walker International would be a major, major coup. Even if her dad and brother ran the company, she'd earned the invitation. And she could say she had just cracked the top ten of the *Fortune 500*.

He smiled. "Randall Greene is the hard man to please. If he's happy with you, then you'll do well for me."

He made it sound so easy. "But I'm the bane of your existence quote unquote."

Lawrence smiled. "I told you that when you were seven years old and you tried to drive my new Rolls Royce to McDonalds and crashed into a palm tree."

She remembered that day. If only her legs had been a little bit longer, she would been home before anyone missed her. "But--"

Her father let out a long breath. "Let it go, Ann-Elizabeth. You're an adult."

She bit her bottom lip. "Are you sure?"

He palmed her cheek and smiled. "You have turned out to be a responsible, hard-working adult. I'm going to take full responsibility for that."

Wow! All she'd had to do was bring home the right guy and all is forgiven. Too bad she hadn't figured that out sooner. She laughed as they reached the door together. She wasn't certain how she felt about the new territory her relationship with her parents was going, but maybe it was time to be less abrasive and a lot more understanding.

The phone on the desk rang. Her father checked his watch and a look of panic crossed his face.

What the hell was going on with him? And her mother? The two of them were so on edge.

He turned back to his desk. "Excuse me; I'm expecting a call from Tokyo. I need to get that." The smile on his face was too forced, too strained.

All of Elle's red flags went up along with every storm warning she'd ever weathered in her life. "I'll see you back at the party."

He stood next to his desk, glancing at the phone each time it rang, yet still watching her. She figured he needed her to hit the road, not wanting to share what was bothering him. Maybe her brother knew. She made a mental note to talk to her brother and find out what was going on.

Elle stood outside her father's office door. The huge palm plant in a brass pot next to the door tickled her nose. She pushed it out of the way just as one of the waiters opened the hall closet door and stepped out. He glanced around, not seeing Elle, who shrank back behind the palm. He adjusted his pants as he sauntered back to the ballroom.

Elle waited. Behind her she could hear her father's muffled voice as he spoke on the phone. The closet door opened again and Elle saw her sister in law, Vanessa, step out. Against Elle shrank back against the palm, but Vanessa never even looked in her direction. Instead, she headed back to the ball room as she shifted the strap of her tissue thin, black slip dress.

That bitch! Elle thought as she watched the woman enter the ballroom and slip into a group of people joining the conversation as though she'd been there all along..

What the hell! Elle felt sadness. Obviously, Vanessa was cheating on her brother? Elle stalked across the foyer, entered the ballroom, and went in search of Merrick.

5

MERRICK STOOD ON THE BRICK walkway leading to the pool house. The night breeze off the ocean had turned cool. The water in the lighted pool showed a clear blue. The pool was the most amazing thing he'd ever seen with a variety of fish and cherub statues at the four corners, a spa at each end large enough for ten people, and a dolphin squirting water from its mouth in the very center of the pool.

He bent over and kissed Patricia's cheek. "Good night, Mrs. Walker--"

"Patricia," she interrupted her dark eyes sparkling. "You're part of the family now, Merrick."

He gave her his best meet-the-mom smile. "Patricia, I had a wonderful time. Thank you."

She dimpled as if he just handed her the world. "You are just so polite, you're parents must be so proud."

"I'm sure I've given them my share of problems."

The wind pushed around her dress around her slender body. "Are you sure they can't come down for a few days? I'd be happy to send the jet for them." She looked hopeful.

He wasn't sure if his parents were ready for this kind of lifestyle. They had made a great living as professors, but they were basically uncomplicated people who wanted to do nothing more than read a good book and play with their dogs. "I promise I'll give them a call in the morning." And he meant that.

Her eyes shone in the bright light from the lanterns lining the walk. "How did a Mathematics professor from Harvard end up in Maine as a mechanic?"

He'd often wondered that himself. "My mother's family is from Swenson originally and my father put himself through Columbia working as a mechanic. He always loved fixing things and when he and mom decided they were done molding young minds they bought a shop so they could be close to her father without being too far from his family."

Elle stepped onto the veranda from the ballroom leading Mojo on her leash and saw them. She hesitated on the steps leading down to the pool, eyeing Merrick with one eyebrow raised.

"Being close to family is important." Patricia glanced at Elle. "Well, I'll let you two settle in. And don't forget, tee off is at nine sharp. I know golf isn't your sport, but I'm sure Tiger will be happy to give you a lesson or two. Sometimes he even lets my husband beat him."

As Elle approached, Merrick could detect a slight frown form on her lips. Little Ms. Ann-Elizabeth wasn't a happy camper and he wondered why. Her parents were nice people, nicer than she'd led him to believe. He even liked her older brother, Darrin. The guy was wound a bit tight but he was very friendly. The only person in her family who gave him the willies was the brother's wife, Vanessa. She eyed him like he was ice cream and she'd been on a year-long diet. He made a note to stay away from her. She had sexual predator written all over her.

Patricia gave him a peck on the cheek and turned around. He watched her give Elle a kiss good night, bend down and pat Mojo on the head, then sashay off up the steps to the veranda and into the house.

Merrick steeled himself as he entered the pool house. Elle was a southern girl and he could see she was about to have a hissy fit. He felt along the wall until he found the light switch. Light flooded the living room and Merrick glanced around. He wasn't certain what he expected of the pool house, but the elaborately furnished interior was a lot more than the name pool house suggested.

Wicker furniture painted white with colorful pillows was arranged about a large glass-topped table. Ferns with long willowy fronds hung from hooks in front of the windows. Two

closed doors led to the back of the house, presumably the
bedrooms. A large kitchen, off to the side, gleamed white with a
tiled island and chrome stools pulled up to one side of it.

Merrick stepped into the living room and unbuttoned his suit
jacket waiting for Elle. Elle entered and he felt an Arctic breeze hit
his backside.

She slammed the door. "I have bone to pick with you."

He turned to face her steeling himself. "I'm sure you do, Ann-
Elizabeth."

Her delicate eyebrows drew together in a fierce frown. "Don't
call me that."

He liked her name. It was classy and a bit old fashioned. He
liked the name Elle, too. It suited her, but Ann-Elizabeth got her
goat and that was worth the price. "It's your name isn't?"

"It's my slave name."

Looking around the opulent room, he wanted to disagree. "If
this is the slave quarters sign me up."

"Don't push me."

Merrick put his hands in his pocket. "How did you come up
with Elle?"

"I was named after both of my grandmothers. Ann-Elizabeth
sounds like someone's grandma who wears gloves, has tea
parties and grows roses. Do I look like an Ann-Elizabeth to you?"

In a perfectly cordial voice, he said, "I like it."

Elle snapped, "How dare you charm my parents and be
so...so...so perfect?"

Please don't let me laugh at her, he thought, she'd kill him. "I
just can't help myself."

She poked him in the chest. "You deceived me."

"How did I do that?" It's not as if she didn't have her own
secrets.

She threw up her arms. "You aren't the person I hired and you
made my parents like you."

He stuck his hands in his pockets, trying to keep a straight face.
"What can I say, I'm a real diamond."

She clenched her fists. "My mother is already planning our
wedding. If you're not careful, we'll be married by Tuesday." She
shook her finger at him. Agitated, she stalked around the living
room looking like a cat on the prowl.

"You could do a lot worse."

She stopped pacing and glared at him. "That's what I thought
I was getting when I hired you."

He'd had a good time at the party, but baiting Elle was just plain fun. She wouldn't get this worked up if she didn't like him. Right? "You're not seeing the big picture."

"Who the fuck do you think you are? Monet?"

Even when she was talking trash she was sexy. Merrick pointed to Mojo. "Not in front of the baby."

She tilted her head. "What big picture?"

"Look at it this way. We play the game, pretend to be happy with each other, then we argue and separate. Tell your mother how I broke your heart and your family will hate me. Then you'll be in the cat bird's seat. They'll love anyone you bring home after me, even if he's some earring-wearing, peacenik communist slacker."

Elle looked thoughtful. "I wanted them to--"

He knew exactly what she wanted. She wanted her parents to not like him. For a second he didn't like her. What did she have against her parents? They were nice people. He could see how her parents wanted to mold her into their image of what a daughter should be, but that was pretty much every parent's wish. He'd been a good boy until he ran off to play G. I. Joe. He'd never forget the look of disappointment in his father's eyes when he told him he'd enlisted, but their relationship survived and in fact grew stronger. If she'd only give her parents a chance, she'd discover a whole new aspect to them.

"I am who I am," he said quietly. "When you set down the ground rules you didn't include the rule that said I had to look like a bum to piss your parents off. I'm sorry I had good home training."

She glared at them. "You're one of them."

Why was that a bad thing? "Tell me when I'm supposed to be insulted."

"I paid you to be..." she stopped just short of saying something he knew she would regret.

"Fine, I'll leave and you can find someone else to play the part of your bum boyfriend." The panicked look on her face was priceless. He loved tossing his trump card on the table. Now she was backtracking.

"Don't threaten me," she hissed at him.

"Have you asked yourself why I'm being so perfect?"

Elle's head tilted to the side and she studied him for a moment. "Why are you?"

Merrick crossed the room in a few steps until he was standing right in front of her. "Maybe I want to impress you."

"Why?" Slowly she took a step back and licked her bottom lip.

She got it. He snaked an arm around her and pulled her to him. "I. Want. You."

Her mouth opened and he kissed her.

The second his mouth touched hers, he was lost. His lips moved over her closed mouth, but he could taste her sweetness. Champagne and chocolate. Her lips opened and that was all the invitation he needed. His tongue slipped inside and he sank his other hand into her hair.

Elle gripped his jacket sleeves, but didn't try to pull away. In fact, she seemed to be trying to get closer and was kissing him back. He heard her moan and his entire body tightened to a hard and throbbing need unlike anything he'd felt before.

Her slender body was perfect.

Suddenly she pushed hard on his chest. His brain demanded he let her go, but his body had other ideas.

Elle shoved one more time and he stepped back. She stumbled away and as he reached out to steady her, she jerked away. With shaking fingers covering her mouth, she stared at him, her eyes wide and startled.

She took a hard deep breath. "Don't ever touch me again." She turned moving toward one of the closed doors, her tight little ass swishing with every step.

Mojo snorted and followed, her little hooves tapping on the tile floor.

Now the pig was mad at him, too.

Elle pushed through the open door and slammed it behind her. A second later she came out of the room and stomped to the other door, Mojo on her tail. "That's your bedroom." A moment later the second door slammed.

That went well he thought.

6

THE GARDEN PARTY WAS IN FULL swing. Dozens of Santa Inez's most influential movers and shakers stood on the bright green lawn in their summer finery sipping a variety of wines and cocktails. Every man and woman who was somebody in Santa Inez was at this party, the political jump start to Elle's father's formal campaign announcement. Her father stood in a group of men chatting amiably. Every once in a while, he'd glance at Elle and she'd grin at him. Her mother flitted around being the gracious hostess to the political elite of Southern Florida.

Elle sipped tepid tea as she watched Merrick chatting up Cleo Masterson, the grand dame of the Black Orchids, a posse of wealthy black matrons who ran Santa Inez' high society. Despite her age, Cleo was still beautiful with glossy black hair threaded with just the faintest bit of silver, hair left natural to add accent to her high-cheekbones and almond shaped eyes that hinted at Indian blood in her. Cleo was from a family able to trace its roots back to escaped slaves who intermarried with Spanish settlers and Seminole Indians. And Cleo was deeply proud of her heritage.

Although her father could buy and sell the Black Orchids five times over, he wanted their endorsement. The fact that they showed up for the garden party and her mom wasn't even a member was high praise indeed, which put Elle was on her very best behavior. Although the ecru sleeveless A-line Battenberg lace dress was a tad short for the occasion, Cleo who was a secret Anglophile deemed the Edwardian pattern a hit. She was deeply impressed that someone as young as Elle would have an appreciation for old world style. If only Cleo could have seen her the last time she'd wore the lace dress. Elle had paired it with ratty black fishnets and steel toed combat boots for a Linkin Park concert in Boston. Today she'd left off the stockings for a classic bare leg look and peach colored peep toe wedge with ivory satin laces. With the floppy peach hat on her head, she was garden party ready. Her mother had nearly fainted in relief. Of course the fact that Elle had presented her mother with a Valentino designer dress custom made for Queen Noor of Jordan with the Queen's custom name tag inside hadn't hurt a bit either. Her mom even told her that a couple of the Orchids made her show them the tag with the Queen's name on it.

Cleo leaned toward Merrick and giggled. Elle gritted her teeth. While she was still angry at him for kissing her, she was angrier with herself for liking him and the kiss. Cleo glanced at Elle. Elle returned a smile.

Mojo gave a discreet grunt and Elle saw Merrick and Cleo wandering over her way. She plastered a smile on her face as if she really wanted their company.

"Young lady?" Cleo called every woman under the age of fifty 'young lady.' Thank God no one else was in the general area or they might have been confused. "Yes Miss Cleo?"

Cleo's pink hatted head bobbed as she talked. "Your young man is quite charming. Frankly, I'm surprised."

Surprised at what, Elle thought. That she had good taste in men? Or because she didn't? Why couldn't Merrick stop being so charming. He was ruining Elle's bad girl reputation. "Yes, he is." Elle kept the annoyance out of her voice.

Merrick grinned at her and she glared at him, hoping he'd get the hint.

Cleo leaned forward and studied Elle over her gold rimmed glasses. "When are you two getting married?"

Merrick's eyes went wide with surprise.

"I beg your pardon?" Elle gripped her teacup so hard she was afraid she'd snap off the delicate handle.

Cleo beamed at Merrick. "You seem such an ideal couple, and I must say, he has done a great deal in taming your high spirits."

They did? He had? She stared at Merrick and he shrugged an

unreadable expression on his face.

"We haven't discussed marriage yet, Miss Cleo," Elle said trying to keep the tremor out of her voice. Everyone, but everyone, adored Merrick. She hadn't planned on that. Maybe it was time for her to ditch the high fashion act and get back to being a Goth. That ought to shake the old matrons down to their conservative pedicures.

Cleo removed her glasses with a theatrical gesture. "And why is that?"

Elle swallowed. "You would have to ask him, Miss Cleo, he's supposed to do the asking." Hah! She'd thrown the ball into his court. She leaned back waiting for his answer.

Cleo turned her head nearly hitting Merrick with the wide floppy brim of her hat. "Well, young man?"

Merrick gave her a bemused smile. "We've only started dating." He looked a little dazed.

Cleo slapped his hand with her white gloved one. "Nonsense, it's plain to everyone here how you feel about her. Don't dawdle. Marrying Ann-Elizabeth would be a social coup. You could do much worse." With that she moved on with a regal shake of her head.

Merrick opened his mouth and Elle held up a finger. "Don't say a word. Not one word."

Merrick held up his hands, grinning. "I'm not asking you to marry me. Considering that you got all bent out of shape when I tried to kiss you, marriage is the last thing on my mind."

Why, because she wasn't marriageable! For a long moment, she just watched him, knowing she was going to be angry at herself for a long time. "I'm still mad at you."

He took a step closer pinning her against the buffet table. "You were right there with me."

Taking a quick look around to make sure no one was paying any attention to them, she jabbed him in the chest. "You manhandled me." She tried to ignore the thrill of pleasure that radiated up and down her at his closeness. He smelled of forest and pine needles. She tried not to inhale, but the woodsy scent started her blood racing.

His dark eyebrows jiggled. "Let's be honest. I want you. You want me. It's not complicated."

His voice was so low and husky and sensual, shiver after shiver went down her spine.

"What do you have to say, Ann-Elizabeth?" He gave her a wicked look that sent her adrenaline soaring. Dammit! Why did

she have to ask him to come to Miami with her? How could she
have made such a radical error in judgment?

Elle poked him again desperate to push him away from her.
He was confusing her and making her want things she wasn't
ready for. "This is a very complicated matter and this is neither
the time nor the place to talk, no matter how I feel. I have to
dazzle the Black Orchids today and that's enough pressure as it
is."

Merrick didn't back away. "These old girls are harmless."

Elle sighed. He didn't understand Southern ladies and the
power they held in their dainty gloved hands. Florida was
another world. "With the exception of the 'chad' thing in this
state, those women have championed every president all the way
back to Kennedy. If they don't like you, you can't even get a dog
license in this end of the world."

He chuckled and said in a dismissive tone, "They are not that
powerful."

"You're from Maine," she said quietly wondering how in the
world she could explain the Steel Magnolias concept to a
northerner. "And yes, they are that powerful. Nobody gets
elected in this state without their approval. No approval, no win.
Period." Pity the poor bastard who came to Florida and never
understood why they lost the state.

He eyed her quizzically, "What happened to the punk rock, I-
hate-authority, CIA hacker Elle, I've come to know and love?"

Elle shook her head. "She's back in Maine on ice." Where she
belonged. Where she should have stayed.

The look in his eyes said he didn't believe her. "Making a good
impression here is really important to you isn't?"

Elle sagged against the table. She couldn't believe it herself.
Her dad wanted to be mayor so desperately and who was she to
say he shouldn't have what he wanted. After all, despite all her
teen-age angst years, he'd done what he could to give her what
she wanted. "I didn't know how important all these functions are
until I had a talk with my dad last night. I'm gonna be good girl
until the plane lands in Bangor. I don't care how much it kills
me." After all, she owed her father.

"I'm impressed."

"So am I."

Merrick moved back as step that wicked mischief back in his
eyes. "So how do you feel about me, Elle?"

"Not talking about it." She said in a sing song voice, lifting a
hand and waving at her mother across the lawn. Hopefully she

looked she was having the time of her life.

He leaned over next to her ear. "I want to lick every inch of your skin."

Elle let out a shaky breath and her hand dropped to her side. She'd love the same thing. "Not listening."

"I want you to scream my name when I make you come." He licked to top of her ear.

Elle told her feet to move, but they weren't listening, probably because her toes wanted in on the licking action. "Stop it."

"I'd kill to know what your lips feel like on my--"

"Don't go there," she half screamed, heat flooding her like her own personal summer. Her stomach clenched in anticipation. She wanted him to keep licking her ear and not stop until he found his way down...not thinking about that, she ordered herself sternly. "Merrick!"

"Yes Elle?"

His voice was silky smooth in her ear, his tone was a sensual purr that made her half faint with need. But she couldn't be tempted. Not here not now. "If you don't shut up right now, I'm going to kick you in your...." She glanced at his crotch lest her meaning be unclear, because she was unable to say the word in this rarefied place.

He grinned, his eyes brimming with delight. "You want me."

Elle squeezed her legs together to stop the trembling. She wanted to know all those things too, but she wasn't going to give into temptation. She was going to be a good girl. She had him come down here to mess with her parent's heads and it backfired. They loved him. And that made her feel good, yet annoyed, yet still good because she wanted them to like him even though she'd never admit it to anyone.

"You're strangely quiet," he said softly, his mouth inches from hers.

That's because her imagination was running sex vignettes through her brain. "I'm thinking."

"About how much you want to jump me?" He blew a warm stream on air on her neck.

She tried not to shiver, but the volcanic sensations inside her wouldn't stop. "No."

Merrick ran a finger down her arm. "I think you are?"

She pushed him away. "How did you fit that ego on the plane?"

He just grinned. "Ann-Elizabeth, where are you manners and what would your mother say if she heard you being rude?"

Her chin lifted. "You think calling me that is going to get a reaction out of me, well you're wrong." She smiled. "I can play Ann-Elizabeth here." She started to walk away, but he grabbed her arm and swung her around.

"You and I are a long way from done." He gave her a quick hard kiss.

Elle swayed against him, her legs turning to rubber, her eyes closed. One hand crept up his arm. Suddenly, Merrick let her go. Elle glared at him, gritted her teeth, and walked away with as much dignity as she could muster.

She forced herself to meander through the throng of guests, stopping to talk to everyone she knew, hoping Merrick was watching her. She did know how to act in polite society.

She nodded to her parents' guests, but finally decided she'd had enough. She found her mother and complained of a headache. One of the servants opened the door for her and she slipped inside and headed for the nearest bathroom for a moment of privacy. As she passed her father's study, she heard the sound of angry voices. She couldn't understand what was being said, but she did hear her brother Darrin's voice. Without knowing why, she knocked. The arguing stopped and she opened the door. "Hey big brother, I've been looking all over for you."

Darrin and Vanessa stood in the center of the study. Darrin looked furious, while Vanessa studied her expensive manicure as though nothing out of the ordinary was happening. Darrin stepped back from his wife. "What do you need, Elle?"

Elle watched them. "Can I have a moment of your time? Vanessa, you don't mind, do you?"

"Of course not, Ann-Elizabeth." She fluffed her hair and hurried out of the room.

Elle had to stop herself from growling. She'd never really cared for her former beauty queen sister-in-law, whom she suspected of being cold and mercenary. But she did love her brother and even though Vanessa's physical perfection was so blinding, Elle had to give him credit. Vanessa was the ideal of what a successful man's wife should look like—beautiful, poised, sophisticated and ultra-fashionable, in much the same way Elle's mother was. But for all Patricia Walker's incredible beauty and perfect poise, she had character and an incredibly generous heart. Vanessa was only skin deep. If she had anything of character beneath the surface, Elle had never seen it.

Elle poured herself a glass of wine and took a little sip. "I'm assuming you heard the news?"

Darrin poured himself a hefty glass of bourbon. "That you are going to be checking our computer security systems." His frown said it all.

Only three years older than Elle, Darrin had been an old man by the time he hit five. The only thing he did that ever surprised Elle was marry Vanessa. Somehow the fact that a stunningly beautiful woman would pay any attention to him had confused him no end and he'd fallen for Vanessa hook, line, and cleavage.

"Don't look all overjoyed or anything," Elle half growled.

"Sorry, I have a lot on my mind." His expression was apologetic. "Dad's turning the company over to me."

Elle wasn't the least bit surprised. Who else would their father trust his company to? "So you're going to be 'the man'."

He glared at her. "You don't think I can run the company, do you?" Lines of weariness made him look older, even more dignified.

Following in their father's footsteps would be a Herculean task, but he could do it. Darrin has been groomed since the day he'd been born to run the empire. "I think you'll take Walker to the next level. You were born for this." Elle didn't envy him.

He looked at her strangely. "You mean that, don't you?"

"Yes." She loved surprising him no end. Always did and always would.

He scratched the back of his head. "I don't know what to say."

Now was the time to slip it in. "You can tell me what's going on with the family? Something's not right. Something I can't quite put a finger on." Like her mother's hectic pace and her father's nervousness.

"You care?"

"Yes, I do." Bam. Again with the surprise. She was three for three. Why did all three of them think she'd didn't love them--just because she wanted to be herself, and not the perfect corporate wife they all wanted her to. Every family had to have a rebel. Okay, usually it was the younger son, but Elle had always stretched the rules. "Mom is a nervous as a cat in the dog pound. You look like the world is on your shoulders and dad wants to be mayor. I've been in my bubble for too long."

He ran his hand through hair that had already started to thin on top. "It's difficult."

She raised her hand. "Arrested by the FBI, difficult I can handle."

Darrin paused, thinking. He shook his head, "I told Dad to tell you, but he didn't want to upset you."

"Tell me what?"

Darrin put a finger to his lips. He walked to the door, opened it and looked up and down the hallway. Then he closed the door carefully and drew Elle to a far corner. In a barely heard whisper, he finally said, "Mom and Dad found out they aren't legally married."

Elle's mouth fell open. She stared at her brother. Of all the secrets in the world, this was the one she'd least expected and she'd been expecting the worst. *Not married! Her perfect parents weren't married!* She ran the words over and over in her head to make sure, she'd heard right. She clapped a hand over her mouth to stop herself from bursting out into laughter. When she was able to control herself, she said, "Our mother and father have been shacking up for thirty-two years?" O.M.G. "I don't believe it."

"Believe it," Darrin said grimly. "Once upon a time our parents were a couple of crazy, impulsive kids. They were married by some roadside preacher in South Carolina. Two months ago the preacher got arrested for performing unlicensed marriages."

"How did they even find out?"

Darrin loosened his tie, took it off and stuffed it into the pocket of his jacket. "Stroke of luck. One of the Attorney General's assistants is an old friend of mine from college."

Where was the tequila when she needed it? Her by-the-book, family-value-spouting parents were not legally married. That was the kind of news that rocked the tabloids. "So this is the reason for the re-commitment ceremony."

"Exactly," Darrin said. Sweat had popped out on his head and he mopped at with a snow white handkerchief. "Can you imagine if the press got wind of this."

"What's the big deal?" She held up her hand. If nothing else, all they had to do was ask her to hack into the state's computer system. She could doctor the record and no one would ever know.

She stifled a giggle. She and Darrin were illegitimate. How funny! But from the look on his face, her brother wasn't going to appreciate the humor of her thought.

Darrin gave her a long, contemplative look. "You know what mom and dad are like. This is the kind of news that will shame the family back to Adam and Eve."

"Is that what you and Vanessa were fighting about?" Did her brother know about Vanessa's activities? He could have done so much better in the wife department. Elle longed to tell him what she'd seen, but he didn't look like he had anymore room on his plate.

Darrin simply shook his head.

"Then what's going on with you two?"

He pinched the bridge of his nose. For a second he looked like a lost little boy. "She's cheating on me," he finally said, all the hurt he was suffering in his tone.

Thank God, now he could give her the boot. "You signed a prenup, dump the bitch."

Darrin rubbed his hands over his face and scrubbed at his eyes. "I can't until after the election."

"Why not? Dad's campaign will survive your divorce."

Darrin looked pained and Elle realized Vanessa had a stranglehold on him. "She knows about the bogus wedding ceremony."

Elle frowned. She got it. Vanessa was using it against him. Fucking bitch. "So you're going to stay miserable for the time being while she has her little side action. She's a skanky ho."

"She said she'd be discreet and I can't risk Dad's chances. He wants to be mayor."

Vanessa wasn't that hard to get rid of. "Pay her off and call it a day."

Darrin shook his head. "She said she'd fight me for custody of the boys."

"She knows that the two of you have kids?" The best thing Vanessa ever did was get a nanny so the boys were being brought up properly.

Darrin sighed. "I didn't know she was such a bitch until Dad decided to run for Mayor. She can make me out to be a lousy father."

"I think she'll have a harder time than you think. I have every email James and Lawrence Jr. have ever sent me. You are Mr. Dad to them with all the coaching you've done for their T-Ball team and all the fishing trips. I know you skipped a U.N. economic summit for L.J.'s first day of kindergarten. I don't care what she's threatening to do; you don't have to spend one more minute being unhappy just because of mom and dad. I know they wouldn't want you to."

Darrin looked away, but not before she saw the shame in his eyes. "They don't know."

Elle touched his arm caught between rage and sadness.

Her brother was in pain. She'd been so happy being the bad daughter and the embarrassing baby sister and now she had to be the responsible adult. "Tell them and see what happens. I think

Dad will understand more than you think."

"I'll tell them. Just not right now." His eyes pleaded with her.

"Dirty little secrets will bite you in the ass every time, big brother. Trust me. I'm an expert."

"Vanessa is tight with Angela Hawkins, a reporter from the KTYO."

In other words, Vanessa had added blackmail to her little store of tricks. Take the kids, ruin a political career. A plan began germinating in her head. She fell quiet as she turned the idea over and over trying to see any loopholes, any weaknesses. She owed her family and she intended to save them.

Darrin eyed her suspiciously. "What are you thinking, Ann-Elizabeth?"

"Nothing," she said in an innocent a tone as possible. She tried to look bland and uninteresting.

"That's not a 'nothing' glint in your eye."

She needed to have a pow-wow with Barry. "Don't take this personal, big brother, but you are too honest, so don't ask and I won't tell. Plausible deniability is a good thing."

"Ann-Elizabeth," he said in a quiet, almost pleading tone, anxiety showing in every line of his haggard face.

Elle shrugged. "I don't know yet." She wasn't lying. She didn't know exactly what she was going to do--yet

"Ann-Elizabeth," Darrin said, "you've been caught once. Tell me what you plan to do."

She hadn't been as sneaky then, as she was now. "You went to law school. And you know rule number one. Don't ask a question you don't already know the answer to." And if she did get caught, she was too valuable to national security to get more than a hand slap. Sometimes it was good to be the keeper of secrets.

Darrin stared at her for a moment as if he was thinking about what she said. "Are you that good?"

"Yeah I am." She kissed him on his cheek.

7

MERRICK DUG HIS TOES INTO THE sand as he ran along the beach. The sun had just begun to rise. The song of the waves pounded in his ears. Normally a good hard run cleared his head, but after three miles he still didn't have answers. Elle was messing with his head. And just when that started he hadn't figured out yet.

She confused him. She excited him.

Three days had passed since the garden party and no matter how he tried to tease her, she would look at him as though he wasn't there. In front of everyone she acted the adoring girlfriend, but when they were alone, she disappeared into her bedroom with her laptop and Mojo and didn't come out until the next required function. She was totally preoccupied with something and despite the hope he was the focus of her preoccupation, he began to realize something else was occupying her.

Behind him he heard someone running behind him. Turning his head he spotted his former commanding officer, Dante, following behind. Merrick slowed his pace to allow Dante to catch up.

"How many more miles do you have left?" Dante asked falling into the same rhythm as Merrick.

Merrick wasn't sure if he wanted company. "Done three already. I'm probably going to keep going until I can't think anymore." And then he wouldn't have to think of Elle sitting in her bedroom doing whatever she was doing. Merrick tried not to worry that she was doing something illegal.

Dante lifted an eyebrow. "Mind if I tag along?"

It sounded like a question, but Merrick knew it wasn't. They were about to have man talk and the subject was one he didn't want to talk about. "You think you can keep up?"

Dante laughed. "No problem."

They made it about a half mile before Dante asked him the first question.

"Why are you out here running when you have a perfectly beautiful woman waiting for you back at the house?"

Merrick gave Dante a sidelong glance without breaking his pace. "Asked by the man who hooked up Georgina Landry."

Dante grinned. "I'm a lucky man."

"You always were."

They ran in silence for another half a mile. "You didn't answer my question."

Merrick shrugged. He didn't have an answer and he wasn't about to tell Dante about Elle's preoccupation.

"How serious are you about Elle?" Dante persisted.

Here we go. "Why are you asking?"

Dante began to pick up the pace. "Because Georgina told me if you hurt her, I'd have to kill you."

Ouch! He'd seen Dante in action. The man was a relentless and efficient killer. "You can try." Merrick knew they were evenly matched but that didn't mean he wanted to get on Dante's bad side.

"Trust me; you want to deal with me and not her." Dante didn't look at him to see his reaction.

Okay he tried to sound casual, but he did remember seeing her kick the crap out of some guy on *TMZ* about four months ago in Iraq and it had been the lead story on the news for a couple of days afterwards. "I'm shaking in my shorts."

Dante laughed. "You should. Georgina seems like a cream puff, but she took down Freeze."

Merrick remembered the four guys who'd tried to pull Georgina off the poor guy she'd been beating on. Freeze was a big Alaska boy who wrestled polar bears for fun. "Your woman is hardcore." Now he was getting a little nervous.

"So what are your intentions?"

What did Merrick say? Should he explain he was Elle's paid date? Dante would kick the crap out him, and then toss him to Georgina. "I like her. I don't why, but I do." And that was the honest truth. Thirty years from now he probably still wouldn't understand his attraction to Elle.

Dante chuckled. "She's not your type."

"This ain't the 'she's too short me' thing is it?" His friend couldn't be going where he thought with conversation. That had never been an issue.

"Hell no." Dante looked shocked. Then he picked up the pace of the run. "When you first arrived, I could see the sparks between the two of you, but something is off now and Georgina is concerned."

Merrick slowed and finally stopped. He bent over to stretch and catch his breath. His whole freaking life was in a mess because of one short woman and the lame ass plan he'd been so willing to go along with simply because he had the hots for her.

Dante stopped and then ran back to him. "We've bled together. I want the truth."

Merrick straightened and started to walk. The ocean was blue-gray and calm. A few early morning trawlers chugged somewhere, their nets hanging from cranes. Before his brain could engage, Merrick found himself telling Dante everything from the flat tire to the proposal to their arrival.

Dante had a sympathetic look on his face as if he understood his pain. "I say we skip the run and find a bar."

"It's not even time for breakfast."

"So we'll drink our breakfast." Dante pivoted and started jogging back to the house.

◈

Something poked Merrick in the chest and he could feel a wet spot on his thigh, which was odd because he didn't remember getting naked or near the water. Something poked him in the chest again.

"Get up," Elle said.

His head pounded and his mouth was bone dry and something was moving in his shorts.

Something bristly rubbed against his leg and he propped himself up on his elbows.

Elle stood over him wearing a white robe and big pink hair rollers in her hair. "Get. Up. Now!"

Merrick couldn't focus. He'd only been asleep for an hour. "I was just taking a nap."

"For seven hours!" She started taking the hair rollers out of her hair and stuffing them in her robe pockets. Her fat curls fell and bounced on her shoulders. "You've slept all day. What's wrong with you?"

His eyes followed the bouncing curls and his stomach was getting queasy. "Nothing's wrong with me, and I haven't slept all day."

She put her hands on her hips. "I'm not going to argue with you. You have a half an hour to get ready."

His head fell back on the pillow. He was too hung over to move, and the room was still moving in waves. "For what?"

She tossed a curler at him and it barely missed his head. "Have you forgotten the sunset cruise?"

His stomach was in no shape to take a cruise, sunset or otherwise. He tried to raise his arm, but it was too heavy. "What time is it?"

"A half an hour until sunset." She had this big 'duh' expression on her face as he squinted at her.

His shorts grunted and moved and he sat up. He saw Mojo's butt sticking out of the leg of his cargo shorts. He forced himself not to grab his dick and see if it was still attached. Pigs were omnivores after all. "Jesus, there's a pig in my pants."

Elle snickered. "Not from what I saw."

She'd checked him out. God he hoped she was impressed.

"It's an anaconda." Then she blew him a kiss.

Thank you, he sent up to the heavens. "When?"

"I looked while you were passed out drunk." She headed to the door. "Thirty minutes. Get a move on."

He eased Mojo out of his shorts vowing to never drink rum again. He was not man enough for the Mojito. That shit snuck up and smacked a person upside the head.

He was so drunk he'd let a pig cop a feel on him. As he eased out of the bed, Mojo squirmed back, yawning and sat at the foot of the bed eyeballing him.

Merrick reached Mojo, and put the pig on floor. His head started to spin again. Carefully he made his way to the bathroom. He turned on the hot water and stepped into the football stadium sized stall. Multiple jets of steaming water hit his skin and as the water sluiced off him, he felt his tension ease. After ten minutes, he stepped out of the shower stall to find a couple of pieces dry toast on a plate on the sink, two tablets and a large glass of water. His navy blue suit with a light blue shirt and silver tie hung on the back of the door. At least Elle was taking care of him.

He dried off, dressed and ran a blow dryer over his damp hair. He stepped out of the bathroom with five minutes to spare.

He stopped short when he caught sight of Elle. Her long hair was piled on her head in loose, fluffy curls. Her full lips were painted with a come-get-me red. She wore short white dress with little bows at the thin straps. The deceptively innocent dress wrapped itself around her slender body as though it had been made specifically for her.

He wasn't hung over anymore. "Wow."

She smiled and tilted her head graciously. "Thank you."

"And who are you wearing tonight, Ms. Elle?"

"Designer unknown," she replied as she stood and modeled the dress. "This is a white satin wiggle dress with a jacquard pattern circa 1954."

"What is a wiggle dress?" As if he was supposed to know.

"A dress that is fitted in such a way that when you walk, you wiggle." She spun and sauntered across the room.

Tottering on sparkly red stilettos, her butt swung back and forth like a pendulum. Merrick was totally mesmerized. What that dress did for her should be illegal in every country of the world. He was so hard by the time she turned around he didn't think he'd be able to leave the room. "I like."

"Feeling better?" she asked, with one eyebrow raised.

That dress could make a dead man feel good. "I'm vertical. I'm good. Who do we need to impress tonight?"

Elle rolled her eyes. "The Florida contingent of the Young Republicans, so you'll be among your own kind."

He laughed even though it hurt. "How did your parents end up with you as a daughter?"

She picked up a red bag that matched her shoes and draped the strap over her shoulder. "If I didn't have my father's face slapped on my head, I'd swear to God they found me in a cabbage patch."

Which led to a question he'd wanted to ask her for some time. The liquor finally gave him courage, and because he was already in pain if she hit him it wouldn't hurt so much. "Would you vote for your dad?"

She sighed. "Thank God I'm registered in Maine. My dad truly cares about people, but some of his opinions are right out of the dark ages."

"Do you like your parents?"

"Until this week," she said, "I think I would have had to think long and hard about the answer to your questions, but over the

last few days, I've changed my mind. Yes, I do like my parents."
She sounded surprised. "My mother is going to spend Dad's
money, trying to fix the world ills. She's a one-woman-charity-
foundation. Walker International is always voted one of the best
companies to work for in this big national survey and from what
I hear he's a great boss who knows the name of everyone working
in his headquarters. He's not the tyrant I always made him out to
be and he wants to hire me to work for him. And I've decided I'm
going to take the job. Not just for the cash, but to be a part of the
family business. Does that make sense?"

"I get it." And he really did. He liked this new Elle. He wasn't
sure how but she'd grown up in the last few days and seemed to
make peace with her family.

There was a knock at the door and one of the house staff stuck
their face in the door. "Ms. Ann-Elizabeth, I'm here to baby sit
Mojo."

Merrick smiled. Couldn't leave the baby unsupervised.

"Come on in, Maria." Elle plastered a big smile on her face and
held out her hand to Merrick. "It's show time."

෨

Elle watched Merrick twirl some hot blonde woman in a too
short black dress and jiggling boobs on the dance floor. A four
piece band supplied the music and a fairly decent baritone
supplied the lyrics.

Merrick and the woman looked good together. That man had
moves that would make Fred Astaire jealous.

Grandma Elizabeth, a sprightly woman nearly eighty and
barely looked a sexy sixty, who'd flown in from Sedona for the
recommitment ceremony, sat between Georgina and Elle. She
sipped a glass of wine white while watching the dancers. Across
from them Vanessa gazed at Darrin, a tight almost angry
expression on her face. Darrin danced with a particularly pretty,
cocoa skinned woman dressed in a flowing chiffon gown that
complimented her curvy figure.

"Grandma Elizabeth," Georgina said, "what do you think of
Ann-Elizabeth's beau?"

Grandma Elizabeth's steel gray braids framed a practically
unlined face and dark brown eyes that were alert with the kind of
mischief only a grandmother excelled at. "Your Merrick is very
nice." She licked her lips. "More than 'very nice'."

"He's alright." Elle said, trying to be non-committal.

Her grandmother laughed and slapped the table with a

slender, heavily ringed hand. "He's one damn fine piece of man flesh, Ann-Elizabeth." She was always blunt and a bit of a trash talker like Elle and Georgina. Elle adored her.

Georgina burst out laughing.

Elle shook her head. She definitely got her smart ass attitude from her grandmother Walker. "Grandma, no trash talking in front of the Republicans, it will scare them."

Grandma Elizabeth rolled her eyes. "I'll behave. Where did you find him?"

"On Hot Asian Men dot com," Elle replied saucily. Across the table Vanessa glanced at her, startled.

"I'll have to get my laptop," Grandma Elizabeth said as she ogled Merrick. "So tell me, Ann-Elizabeth, is it true what they say about Asian men."

Elle covered her eyes with her hand. From what she'd seen today, he had penis to spare. She should feel bad about taking advantage of him while he was passed out, but couldn't help herself. "Isn't there an old wives tale that says you can tell a man's...ah...abilities by the size of his feet? Merrick's are gun boats."

Georgina giggled. "So you're letting him hide his dragon in your crouching tiger?" She fluttered her eyelashes at Elle.

Troublemaker, she wanted to yell at her cousin.

Georgina gave Elle an innocent look. "My Dante can kill with nothing but a raisin and a piece of tissue paper, but he can't keep a secret from me and Merrick can't keep a secret from him."

Merrick had blabbed to Dante, and Elle was so going to hurt him.

Grandma Elizabeth leaned across the table. "Ann-Elizabeth, you aren't tappin' that?"

Nothing coming out of Grandmother Elizabeth's mouth surprised Elle, but it did make her nervous. There was a rumor that the old girl had once traded sheet time with Frank Sinatra and few other members of the Rat Pack. She was doing what came natural. "Did our grandmother just utter some slang?"

"Cuz, answer the question," Georgina demanded.

Fortunately for Elle, the music stopped. Merrick smiled at the blonde and headed over their way. He stopped in front of the three of them. Thank God they couldn't talk about sex anymore.

Merrick put a hand on the back of Elle's chair and ran his finger along the bare skin at the back of her neck, sending a shiver a lust down her spine. She'd brought him to keep her parents off her back and here she was lusting after him like a high school girl.

"Ladies," he said, "I hope you don't mind, but I just have to ask the most beautiful woman on this boat to dance."

Vanessa glanced at him, plastered a smile on her face, pulled herself straight and began to stand up.

Merrick held out his hand to Grandma Elizabeth. "Miss Elizabeth, would you do me the honor."

Georgina snorted and turned a nasty smile at Vanessa. Elle grinned and Vanessa looked stunned before hurrying off as though she meant to do that all along.

Elizabeth hopped up, took Merrick's outstretched hand and half-pulled him out onto the dance floor. Elle smiled thinking the sweetest thing any man could do was make time with a woman's grandmother.

As the pair walked to the dance floor, Grandma Elizabeth patted Merrick's ass.

Elle caught her breath.

"Did our grandmother just grab your man's ass?" Georgina hooted with laughter.

"Yes, she did." Why Elle was surprised was a miracle itself.

Georgina shook her head. "What a hussy."

What did a girl say after her grandma felt up her man? "For real." Elle couldn't keep the admiration out of her voice. When she grew old she wanted to be just like her grandmother.

Georgina sighed. "She's my hero."

"Mine, too."

Georgina turned to her. "So now that we're alone, tell me why you aren't on that man?"

"Because..." her voice trailed away, the question unanswered because she had no answer.   Georgina frowned. "If I didn't have Commando man, I'd being playing with Merrick."

Elle planted her elbow on the table and leaned on her balled up fist. What the hell, she might as well tell Georgina. Her cousin would find out eventually. "I paid him money to act as my escort. Tapping him would be a felony. Been there done that."

Georgina took a sip of her wine, surprise in her eyes. "You paid a man to be your escort! What the hell were you thinking?"

Elle signed. She'd figure out how to stop global warming before she'd answer Georgina. "At the moment, I'm not sure." Yeah, she was sure just unwilling to share with her cousin. She was lusting after that man like there was no tomorrow. She closed her eyes against the pounding need that filled her. Merrick was just...just...too much man. And the way he made her skin tingle, left her breathless and wanting more.

Georgina turned her chair around to face Elle, a shrewd look in her eyes. "Do you want him or not?"

Elle pointed to her cousin's purple satin mules. "More than I want those Jimmy Choo's your wearing."

Georgina sighed as if she understood. "More than shoe lust, you got it bad."

"I know." So bad it hurts.

Georgina inclined her head toward the dance floor as Merrick dipped her grandmother. "So go for it."

"No."

Georgina slapped Elle's arm. "Why the hell not?"

"Because I could go for him in a big way and he's leaving to be Doctor Doolittle and the last thing I need is a broken heart." As tempted as she was, Elle knew a fling with Merrick would be more than a fling.

"Take a breath." Georgina held up a hand.

"I know he wants me, but I'm not looking to be some guy's booty call." She trained her eyes on his muscular body as he twirled her grandmother on the dance floor.

"Have some fun. Enjoy each other. That's what I'm doing." Georgina gazed at Dante, but the look in her eyes told Elle she wasn't just having a fling.

Georgina was a great actress, but Elle knew her too well. As soon as she could, she was dragging Dante Mayweather to the altar. "Says the woman who's so crazy mad in love with her man she can't see straight."

"I'm not going to deny it." Georgina's face lit up. "He's the man of my dreams. But I didn't expect him to come along at this point in my life. I thought we'd have a hot and heavy time and then I would go back to my real life."

"But you got lucky."

Georgina patted Elle's knee. "What makes you think you can't be lucky, too?"

Because she had a swimming pool of bad karma to work off. "Nothing."

"Or more importantly why is that you think don't deserve to be lucky?"

She hated when her cousin saw right through her bullshit. "I don't know. I guess I'm going to have to think about that."

Elle took one more look at her grandmother and Merrick. They were standing next to her parents slow dancing and talking with them. God, she wished she was in his arms, though she liked the fact he was getting to know her family so well. She stood up. "I need to get some air."

Georgina smiled at her. "Think about what I said."

Elle knew she would. She just wasn't sure she liked where those thoughts would lead.

8

THE OCEAN WIND WHIPPED ELLE'S hair around her face as she stared into the dark night. The drone of the ship's engines was a background to her thoughts. She gave herself about ten more seconds before the breeze destroyed her hair and she'd end up looking like a hot mess. Crossing her arms over her chest, she took a deep breath. When had her simple plan become the mother of Godzilla?

The full moon glinted off the water. The yacht barely bounced against the waves. The stars twinkled above her head in the night sky. As much as she loved her life in Maine, she really did miss Florida sometimes. he even missed her family.

With all of their conservative world views, they loved her. They had been going through a major crisis and hadn't called her to help, or even let her know what was going on. She did care.

Damn, she'd pushed herself into a tight corner. Here she thought she was having her big, grand rebellion and instead she was being a selfish, petty bitch. She was going to make this right. She was going to fix Vanessa's little red wagon, too.

Behind her the sound of shattering glass interrupted her thoughts. She headed toward the noise hoping one of the drunk young Republicans wasn't about to fall overboard. That would be bad for her father's political ambitions. As she reached the door leading to the internal hallway she heard voices.

"Take you hands off me," Merrick said in a furious tone.

"You want me," Vanessa purred.

"Lady, why would I want you when I have Elle."

Elle paused in her rapid walk along the deck. Stop the press! Did she just hear Merrick turn down Vanessa the 'ho? Elle moved closer to the voices.

"All she has going for her is her father's money." Vanessa's voice took on a whiny quality. "I'm a real woman."

Elle balled her fists.

"I killed the last person," Merrick said in a still deadly tone, "who touched me without permission."

Vanessa gasped. "Are you threatening me?"

Elle rounded a corner and saw Vanessa with one hand on Merrick stomach. He didn't look like he was having any fun.

Merrick grabbed Vanessa's wrist and took her hand off him. "I don't threaten."

"You slant eyed mother fucker. You should be thrilled that I even noticed you." She tried to slap Merrick.

Elle grabbed Vanessa by her hair. "You don't talk to my man like that, bitch."

Merrick smiled as Vanessa struggled in Elle's grip.

"Are you here to rescue me?" he asked, pushing Vanessa away.

"Nah, I'm just taking out the trash." She pushed Vanessa toward the door leading to the salon. "I'll deal with you later, 'ho."

Merrick leaned back against the wall. "That woman is scary."

Elle watched Vanessa stumbled down the hall. "You don't know the half of it."

Merrick fixed his tie and ran one hand through his hair. "She had her hand down my pants."

Elle really didn't want to know the graphic details. "And you turned her down?"

"I feel violated."

Elle started laughing. That was like the sweetest thing any man had ever said to her.

"It's not funny." Merrick actually blanched as if he'd eaten a really bad lemon.

Elle forced herself to stop giggling. "I'm not laughing at you, but the look on your face is absolutely fabulous." She touched his cheek gently. "Most guys wouldn't turn down Vanessa."

Merrick placed his hand over hers. "I'm not most guys."

"I think I finally figured that out." Her thumb caressed his bottom lip. Heat spiraled through her. Her whole body hummed at the look on his face. "Did you mean what you said?" He had the most beautiful mouth. She remembered how it felt on her skin and she wanted him to kiss her again. She wanted him to do a thousand different illicit things to her whole body. Oh, she had it so bad.

"About feeling cheap?" His body shuddered. "Hell yes."

"No, I mean the part about not wanting her when you have me."

"I don't really *have* you." Merrick pushed himself against her, trapping her against the wall.

The heat of his body surrounded her. She just wanted to sink into his warmth. "More so than you might think." Elle slid her hand across his taunt stomach. She thrilled at the thought of this man being hers. She closed her eyes and let the feelings flood through her. She'd never felt like this before. He was delicious and all hers.

His lips brushed against hers. "What are you saying, Elle?"

"I guess I'm not showing you enough. I. Want. You." How much clearer could she be?

A slow smile curved his full mouth. "You have me." He rubbed his body against hers.

Lust, desire, passion consumed her. She opened her eyes to study his face. She could tell he was playing with her and she liked it. "I haven't yet." His erection pressed into her stomach telling her how much she had him. She ran her tongue over her bottom lip. He smelled so good. He felt so good. "But I intend to."

He twirled a strand of her hair around his finger. "You're not the first time, up-against-the-wall type, are you?"

"This is a three gazillion foot yacht. There are staterooms. Twenty of them." And she knew where they all were.

His eyebrows rose over his desire filled eyes. "Really?"

Elle rubbed harder against him. She felt herself getting damp. She was on fire for him. "With locks on the doors."

"Locks?"

She nipped his chin. "And beds." He tasted salty and warm.

"Beds do come in handy." Merrick slipped his hand over the curve of her butt.

She liked the way his big hand cupped her. She heard herself moan. "Big beds."

"Ann-Elizabeth, are you wearing panties?" He gave her cheek

another gentle squeeze.

She licked his chin. "Ruins the line of the dress."

He closed his eyes and his other hand cupped her other cheek. "God bless the wiggle dress."

Her nipples were so hard that with a little more attention from him, she would come right now. She had to get him to room and soon. She held up one crooked finger. "If you follow me, you can see me without panties."

"I thought I wasn't your type." His words were whispered low.

He was teasing her, so she didn't feel insulted when he brought up the conversation they'd had. "Did I say that?"

"Too alpha male. I believe were your exact words."

She slid her hands up his chest, the silk of his shirt warming her. "Whatever was I thinking?"

"Now you sound like a southern belle."

She grabbed his tie with one hand and pushed him away with the other. She started walking down the hall to the staterooms. "Do southern belles turn you on?

"Not as much as much as Goth girls from Maine."

She stopped and turned around, but didn't let go of his tie. "Don't like my new look?"

He gave her a sexy smile. "I liked your old look and I like your new look." He gave her a gentle push to get her walking again. "I wanted to jump you when you were wearing your black tent.

"I didn't bring it." Had she only known!

"Good."

She opened the door to one of the staterooms and walked in still pulling him by the tie. The room was lush in peacock colors and a Persian rug on the floor. She pointed to the big king sized bed across the room. "See a bed."

Merrick closed the door behind them and flipped the dead bolt. "A big bed."

She let go of him, smiling in approval at the locked door. "And a lock on the door."

Merrick reached up and untied his tie. "A good lock." He pulled the tie free of his neck and tossed it on a chair.

Elle dropped her evening bag next to his tie. "I think we have everything we need."

Merrick reached into his jacket and pulled out his wallet. He opened the flap and pulled out three condoms. "We have to have party favors."

She wiggled over to the bed, knowing he was watching her every move. She turned and gave him a sultry look. "You were that sure of me?"

"Nope. Your grandmother was."

She sat on the bed and planted her palms behind her. "I know I should be shocked, but I'm not."

He took off his jacket and hung it neatly over the back of the chair. "If she hadn't felt me up, I would be."

"I'm so ashamed of her." Elle crossed one leg over the other and swung her foot.

Merrick shook his head. "No you're not."

"Okay you're right I'm not." Elle stood up.

Merrick tossed the condoms on the bed. "Sit down."

Elle's eyes widened. "Bossy."

"I'm an alpha male. It's how I roll."

Instead of sitting down, Elle wiggled away from him, her hips swaying and her eyes half closed. She wanted to purr. "Want me to do a strip tease?"

"No, I want to take your dress off." He kicked off his shoes and removed his socks. He had almost fine-boned, narrow feet.

The way he looked at her started a flame that crashed over her like a hurricane—that flared from the tips of her fingers all the way down to the Pradas she wore. "Okay."

He unbuttoned his shirt methodically, his long slender fingers making easy work of the pearl buttons. He put the cufflinks in his pants pocket and then slowly pulled the shirt apart revealing his broad chest.

Elle caught her breath. Lean hard muscle covered by golden skin was a treat to see. His perfectly toned abs rippled with each move. He had a smattering of black chest hair over his smooth skin. She placed her palm against his flat stomach and his muscles contracted beneath her hand. She sucked in a deep breath. Alpha male was all good. Lowering her hand she was surprised when he grabbed her wrist.

"Not yet."

She was so wet. "Just hurry."

"What about foreplay?"

"Not now. Later"

One of his eyebrows rose.

He looked oh so sexy. "I'm cooling down here." She picked up a condom and tore the covering off.

His pants hit the floor.

Flaccid he was impressive, but rock hard and ready, Elle couldn't speak. His boy just stood there at attention like a perfect soldier ready to go into combat. "Oh my."

"The words should be 'all mine'."

She reached out and gently touched his cock. She worked her hand up and down his hardness. He trembled. She didn't have time to wait. She wanted him now. Her hands were shaking as she slipped the condom on. He was watched her with intense dark eyes blazing with passion.

She reached behind and unzipped the dress. "We'll try slow next time." Then she pulled the straps from her shoulder, down her arms and let the dress pool at her feet.

He reached up and thumbed her hard nipple. "I knew your breasts would be perfect."

He flicked the nipple again. Elle wound her arms around his neck, and circled her legs around his waist. "Do it now."

Slowly he pulled her toward him and entered her damp heat. Elle buried her face in his neck. "Oh God."

Merrick thrust into her warmth, silken core burying himself to the hilt. For a second he couldn't breathe as her tight wet heat clenched around him and his muscles started to spasm. Her nails dug into his skin and for a moment he thought he would come, but he squeezed his eyes shut and forced the urge to let loose inside her. Damn, he'd barely been inside her a second and she had him wanting to shoot his load. Calm down, boy. Make this good for her, too.

"You feel so good," she whispered.

She rubbed against him making him forget what he'd been thinking. He was afraid to say anything that would distract him. He stroked inside her slowly. She half sat up so he could reach her breasts. She squeezed her muscles tight around his cock. "Jesus, Elle."

"Do you like that?" she purred in a low, sultry tone.

He could come just listening to her talk. So he kissed her to shut her up.

Elle writhed against him and he felt himself sink deeper into her. He pulled her to him, her breasts crushed against his chest, her mouth open against his, their tongues entwined. Another hard slow thrust and he felt her internal muscles grip him.

"Harder," she whispered.

And that's what he did. He pushed hard deep thrusts into her until he thought his heart would burst out of his chest. Fire coursed through him. Her hands slid down his sweat slick body leaving a trail of fire. He thrust up and her back arched. Merrick took her hard nipple into his mouth tasting the hot salt on her skin.

Elle ground her hips down on him and sank her fingers in his hair. Her whole body shook as he pushed up harder. He grabbed her waist to hold her still and he just kept pumping inside her until she started milking his cock. Her body stiffened and a deep, keening moan as she spasmed over and over again. Merrick felt his balls tighten and he gave her one more hard powerful thrust and let himself go inside her.

At that moment he knew in his pleasure clouded brain everything had changed between them, forever.

9

MERRICK SLIPPED MOJO A PIECE of cantaloupe under the breakfast table. This was the big day. Elle's father was holding a press conference at the compound to announce his intentions to run for mayor. Reporters from every major network in the state were covering the story. He heard Elle humming in the bathroom as she finished getting ready.

Dirty Deeds Done Dirt Cheap started blasting in the room. He knew that was Elle's cell phone ringing. She said all the important people in her life had AC/DC ringtones. He'd earned the coveted *You Shook Me All Night Long* ringtone three days ago after their night on the yacht. Her brother was *Squealer*, her mother's ringtone was *Problem Child* and her Dad's was *Money Talks*. He was honored by his ring tone. Over the last couple days he'd just call her up, because she said it got her juices flowing.

She ran out the bathroom, grabbed the phone, and returned shutting the door hard. He figured this was the guy she'd asked to get her info on Vanessa's reporter friend. She'd told him the entire story about what was going on with her parents, and frankly he liked that she wanted to fix it for them.

"You rock!" came from the bathroom.

Merrick glanced down at Mojo who nosed the cantaloupe rind around the floor as though it were her ball. "Sounds like good news."

The pig grunted, abandoned the rind, and sat down to beg for more melon. He was having major love for the pig. Mojo knew what was important in her life. He gave her more melon and she sprawled on the floor to munch at it.

Now that he was firmly on the mom's and the pig's good side, he began thinking about the future. Despite the great sex, in fact the best sex he'd had in his life, his feelings about Elle were mixed. He wanted to be with her, but one of them would have to give up their life. Expecting her to follow him, just because he was the man, was wrong. He needed to...before he could finish his thought she walked out the bathroom with a big grin on her face.

His head tilted to the side as he studied the dress she wore. It was a white, fifties dress with the words IKE in red letters all over the dress. "What are you wearing?"

She did a spin and the dress floated around her long legs. "This is my IKE campaign dress."

He didn't get it. "Why?" Not that she didn't look great. Hell, she looked great in everything. But a dress with IKE printed all over it seemed a bit different.

She smoothed down the flouncy skirt. "I wanted to invoke a bit of nostalgia. Besides this dress is a true bit of American history and when I'm done I'm donating it to the town museum."

Merrick shook his fork at her. "It so...so...conservative."

She tossed him a saucy grin. "Only on the outside. Besides, I'm pairing it with my Naughty Monkey shoes." She flipped the lid of a box and held up a red and white checked stiletto with a red and white flowers decorating it. "Don't you love that name--Naughty Monkey."

Yeah, he did. What did that say about him? "Those shoes make my monkey want to be naughty."

Elle gave him another saucy grin. "Really?"

"But only with your monkey."

"Well since I'm not wearing panties under all these crinolines that might be workable." She flipped up the hem of her dress showing him layers of white material, but not anything fun.

"Ann-Elizabeth, I'm shocked. Turned on, but shocked." He reached for her so he could verify she was pantyless.

She slapped his hand away from the hem of her dress. "If you're a good boy, after the shindig is all over, I'll let you take me up into the library and bend me over my mother's brand new Hepplewhite chair and do me dirty."

He didn't know a Hepplewhite from La-Z-Boy and didn't care. But to get between those mile long legs, he'd learn. "You gonna keep the dress on?"

"Yes."

"And the shoes?"

"Of course."

He reached into his pocket and pulled out his never ending supply of Grandma Elizabeth donated condoms. "I'm in."

She put the back of her hand against her forehead. "I knew you would be."

"Can I get little taste now?" He jiggled his eyebrows.

"No, you'll knock the starch out of my crinolines."

He sat back in his chair. "You are such a tease."

"Only with your monkey." She blew him a kiss and then bent over to put on her shoes. Again not enough to verify her no-panty-wearing statement.

"Have you got your problem all solved with the reporter?"

"Phil Blackstone came through." She put on a wide brimmed straw hat decorated with a red ribbon and grabbed a red straw purse. "Hang with me, Sugar, and I'll show how the hackers have fun."

"You're going to annihilate that woman aren't you?"

"But I'm going to be nice about it."

"Exactly what did that mean? He didn't want to know. "I have bail money."

"No blood will be shed." She batted her eyelashes at him. "I promise."

"Yeah. Right. Sure."

A maid knocked at the door to babysit Mojo. Her mother had requested that Elle leave the pig behind for the press conference. Merrick had surprised she's agreed.

Elle laughed as she slipped her hand into his. She tugged him out of the pool house to the lawn where her father had set up his press conference. "Look, I've spotted my prey. Let the non-bloodletting begin."

In that moment, the fog in his brain cleared. He had everything figured out. He was in love with Ann-Elizabeth 'Elle' Walker.

❧

Elle plastered her big fake, I'm-a-debutante smile on her face and headed for Angela the reporter, Vanessa's partner in muckraking. In a group of people surrounding Darrin, Elle saw Vanessa glance at her and then frown when saw Elle bearing down on Angela.

Angela was a pretty woman with very white teeth, a café-au-lait complexion and slightly slanted eyes. She wore a cream colored silk suit that hugged her bone thin body. Her hair was pulled back into a neat chignon. She blended in as though she belonged to the rich and restless crowd.

"Hello Angela," Elle said sweetly, aware that Merrick had stopped a dozen feet away to watch her in action. "I don't know if you remember me, I'm Ann-Elizabeth Walker, Darrin's sister. We met when at his and Vanessa's wedding. Vanessa was telling me you're a TV reporter these days. Nice career move."

Angela looked her up and down, her pale brown eyes appraising and cold. "You've changed. Where's the Morticia Adams dress?"

Elle splayed her hand across her chest. "I wanted to go classic for this occasion."

Tanya seemed to force a smile. "With an IKE dress?"

"They have one in the Smithsonian." *This bitch had no class and no appreciation for an icon. I'm historic.*

Angela stuck a microphone in her face and rolled her finger at the camera panning around to take in Elle and the dress. "What does your father think of your sense of style?"

Okay, this was going to be easier than she thought. She was almost disappointed. "Did you want an interview with me? I'd be happy to answer all your questions." She grinned at Merrick standing just out of the range of the camera watching her, a grin on his face. He gave her a thumbs up sign.

"Vanessa has told me all about you, being the black sheep daughter and all." She gave Elle a superior smile as if she knew something Elle didn't.

Elle shook her head and gave a fake titter. Damn she was good at this swapping sugar shit. "I've grown up. You can't hold the past against me now, can you?"

"Always nice to know someone who learns from their past mistakes," Angela said with a cool smile. "Shall we start?" Angela nodded to her camera man. "Dan, ready to roll?"

He nodded and adjusted his camera on his shoulder to a more comfortable position.

Angela smiled at the camera. "Today we stand with Walker heiress, Ann-Elizabeth.

Blah Blah Blah, Elle thought to herself. Angela liked to hear herself talk.

Angela shoved the microphone in Elle's face nearly hitting her in the nose. "Ms. Walker, you had quite a reputation as a rule breaker a few years ago. How does that relate to your father's strong family values stance?"

Elle forced herself to smile and remain calm. She really wanted to slap the bitch upside the head, but with the camera rolling she restrained herself. "First of all, my father's running for mayor, I'm not. And we were all young and dumb at one time. It's not as if I have a porn film lying around anywhere just waiting to be exposed, like some people I could name." *Like you.*

Angela's lip twitched. "Well, Ms. Walker—"

Elle plunged on, "He's never slept with his boss, like some people I could name, but good taste forces me not to." *Like you.*

"Thank you—," Angela said and glanced sharply the cameraman the look on her face telling him to stop the camera. Dan didn't seem to hear. He kept the camera square on Elle's face with a silly grin on his face.

Elle grabbed the microphone from Tanya. "...Or has a pharmacist on speed dial."

Angela's café au lait complexion turned beet red by this time as she grabbed the microphone from Elle. "I have prescriptions."

"From seven different doctors!"

"I think this interview is over." Angela turned away.

Elle stepped in front of the woman, blocking her retreat. Dan lowered the camera, but the look on his face told Elle he knew what she was doing. "You know something, Honey. When you trade in secrets, you better make sure your own are buried deep. You hurt my family in any way, I will rain down hell on your narrow behind. You get me?"

Angela couldn't even look at her. "Dan, let's go."

Run rabbit run. "Toodles, hon." Elle waved at Angela's hastily retreating figure.

Merrick came up to her. "That was not nice."

No, but it was efficient. The newshound was no longer a threat. One down and one more to go. "She was going to hurt my dad. I didn't need to be nice."

He slid an arm around her shoulder. "I'm proud of you Elle."

"Really?"

"Yeah, me and the pig." He leaned down and kissed her on the cheek.

Elle put her hand on her cheek. Her skin burned from his touch. All she could do was stare at him realizing how thrilled she was that he was proud of her. As a matter of fact, she wanted him to be proud. She wanted him to love her. Because she loved him. Elle blinked. Oh my God. She was in love with Merrick. "We have to mingle." With that she headed straight into the crowd of people milling around.

10

FOR THE FIRST TIME IN HER life, Elle called a family meeting. Usually she was the reason they were having said meeting so she tried to avoid them at all costs. Didn't she felt grown up. After the long day she knew her parents were tired, but she needed to get this off of her chest.

Elle glanced around the living room, aware that her mother had moved the Hepplewhite chair from the library. She must be trying it out in different rooms to see where it worked best.

Vanessa was the first to enter the living room and Elle could tell she'd already had a few too many martinis. Her parents were about a minute behind and then Darrin sauntered in with a curious look at her. She grinned and he grinned back. She did love her brother, as stodgy as he was.

When everyone was settled and eyeing her with curiosity, Elle stood up and announced, "I just want everyone to know that I know about your secret."

Her parents looked surprised. Despite the long day, her mother still looked elegant. Her father was filled with suppressed excitement. Elle could tell he was going to love being a politician. She was pleased for him and now she made sure nothing bad would stand in his way.

"And," Elle continued, "why didn't either of you tell me? Why did something like your marriage have to be kept a secret from me?"

Her mother had the grace to look guilty. "Frankly, Ann-Elizabeth, we didn't think you'd care."

Elle told herself she deserved that remark and she wasn't going to be hurt by it. "I understand I haven't been exactly the kind of daughter you wanted, but I am still your daughter and what concerns you, concerns me. It's not like you all committed a crime. Or even did it on purpose."

Her father rubbed his hands together. "Ann-Elizabeth, that's not the kind of thing you'd want to get out. Not everyone would understand and it could make the entire family suspect. Not to mention bad P.R. for the company."

Hello Paris Hilton. Elle rolled her eyes. "Well Daddy, it could have cost you your chance for political office. Trust me I deal with secrets all the time."

Elle's mother rubbed tired eyes. "I know such a thing wouldn't bother you. You would thrive on the idea, but you're father and I were ashamed. We didn't want people to…"

Elle let out a long breath. "You were worried about gossip? That people will start thinking Darrin and I were illegitimate?"

Her mother sighed and fidgeted as she ran her hands along the arm of her new Hepplewhite chair. Her mother actually sat in that incredibly expensive chair? Didn't it belong in a museum or something? "Yes, and because your father has taken a strong family values stance, we felt that if the knowledge got out it would undermine his campaign."

"Relax, mom, nothing you do will embarrass me. And Daddy stop throwing stones. The meaning of family isn't just one thing."

Her father tilted his head and stared at her as if she'd grown another nose. "Why are we having this talk, Ann-Elizabeth?"

Elle hitched a thumb in Darrin and Vanessa's direction. "Because we have to settle something. Darrin here is miserable. He's staying married to a lying cheating 'ho who is blackmailing him."

Vanessa looked up from examining her very expensive French manicure. "Why you—"

Elle held up a hand. "Shut up. You can't blackmail me, too. I had a little talk with your reporter friend today. I found a few things out about her. You see, everyone has secrets. I thought you'd like to know your little reporter friend is high-tailing it back to her hole and your threat of revealing everything to the press is over."

Darrin rubbed his forehead. "What did you do, Ann-Elizabeth? And when is it going to bite me in the ass?"

Elle chuckled. She was gloating and knew it. "I found out every little dirty secret Angela had and I informed her that if she utters one nasty word about my parents or family, her career was over."

Vanessa pushed unsteadily to her feet and walked across the room to stand in front of Elle. "You're lying."

Now it was time to drop her Vanessa bomb. Elle lifted her chin and eyed Vanessa. "Think what you like, but I hacked into the security cameras and have some lovely footage of you in several compromising situations that with a little encouragement from you could end up on the Internet. Which might make you star, but you'll never get your children in a custody battle."

Vanessa balled her fists at her side, her face twisted in anger. "You bitch."

"So what's your point?" Elle stood praying Vanessa would take a swing at her. "Go find yourself a good divorce lawyer. You're going to need one."

Vanessa stood in front of Elle, indecision on her face and then tottered out of the room sobbing.

Elle rubbed her hands together. Another problem solved. "Daddy, just come clean. People will forgive you. Especially all the other people that 'pretend' minister hoodwinked. Once you reveal what happened, others will too, and they'll back you up and make you seem human."

"You have been busy, haven't you?" Her father rubbed a hand across his face. "I don't know how you found out about the reporter and don't want to know how."

Elle simply smiled. "Daddy, learning secrets is what I do best, don't ask questions. Plausible deniability is always a good choice."

Her father took several deep breaths. "Are you enjoying knowing about your mom and I not being married?"

Pain gripped her heart. That hurt. The way truth usually did. "Maybe the old Ann-Elizabeth would, but not the new one." She paused to think about her next words, she wanted them to be right. "This trip has been an eye-opening experience. And I'm only going to say this once." She stopped again and took a deep breath before plunging onward. "I'm sorry I've been such a pain in the ass." She probably wouldn't have been if they'd been less concerned with appearances, but she'd come to realize that if they had to accept her as she was, she had to accept them for what they were.

Her mother looked taken aback. "Ann-Elizabeth, looking back I realize I could have been more accepting of you as you were. You really have nothing to apologize for."

Elle laughed. "Mom, I know I didn't come with an instruction manual." Rebellion just seemed to be branded into her soul. She couldn't be any different than what she was, but she could be a little less blatant about it.

Her father rose and hugged her. "What has brought on all of this?"

She saw pride in father's dark eyes and she felt a little dizzy knowing she'd finally made him proud. She felt good. "Daddy, I think I'm finally getting comfortable in my skin."

"Does a certain man have anything to do with this?" His eyebrow rose.

"Maybe? We'll see." She kissed her parents goodnight and nudged her brother as she passed him. He looked relaxed and happier than she'd seen since she arrived. She hurried through the house and outside. She couldn't wait to get back to Merrick.

⌒⌢

Merrick held Mojo close to his chest. The pig was almost asleep. He was a former Delta Force commando rocking a pig to sleep. If any of his buddies could see him now, he'd be the object of every joke from now until he died. But damn, he'd fallen in love with a pig. He might never eat bacon again.

"Where is a camera when I need one?" Elle said as she walked into the living room. She'd removed her hat and let her hair down. The curls fells about her shoulders like a waterfall.

Merrick grinned at her and said, "Shhh! Don't wake the baby."

Elle placed her hat and purse on the table. The IKE dress swished around her, the crinolines crinkling with their own unusual sound. "I thought she was my pig?"

"We've bonded." Merrick was no dummy. Win the pig's heart and the woman's would follow.

"Kind of like you did with my family." Elle put her hands on her hips and studied him.

Mojo gave a final snuff and finally dropped off, her eye closing. "Does that bother you?"

"We are leaving Sunday. What are the chances you're going to see them again?"

Merrick walked over to Mojo's bed and gently put the pig down. "Did you know your mother knows the president of the

University of Florida?"

"I wouldn't be surprised. Why is that piece of information important?"

He suspected now that she'd buried the hatchet with her family she'd probably want to move back to Florida. He was letting her know in an off-handed way that he was willing to move with her. "Good vet school in Gainesville."

"And this has what to do with you seeing my parents again?"

Merrick noticed the slight smile on her face. She knew what he was talking about, but she wasn't going to give it up easily. That was okay, he liked working for what he wanted. That made the prize so much sweeter. "I've received a personal invite to apply."

Her eyebrows rose. "How nice."

He settled Mojo on her blanket and pulled the edge over her. He went to the kitchen area to wash his hands. "It seems we're dancing around the subject."

Elle followed him and stood in the center of the bright white room. "What subject?" Her eyes widened.

"You know, Ann-Elizabeth, I really like you."

She tiled her head at him, a coy look on her face. "I'm easy to like."

That was the understatement of the century. Nothing was easy about her. And that's why he liked her. "Not really."

Her bottom lip poked out. "Oh."

Did she have any idea how hot she was? "You have a hot body and face like an angel, but that mouth."

She walked up to him and he caught a whiff of her subtle perfume. "What are you saying, Merrick? Just spit it out."

He pulled her into his arms and she gazed up at him with something he thought was more than 'like.' "When I first agreed to come with you—"

"For the money," she interjected.

"Right, for the money." Merrick couldn't help but laugh. "Don't get me wrong, the money is going to come in handy for school, but I was more interested in seeing what made you tick."

She leaned into him and he pressed his hands against her butt. The crinolines rustled beneath his hand. He wondered if they were scratchy, but at the same time, the thought of taking them off her one by one made his suddenly go hard.

"And what did you find out?" she asked.

"That you are a complicated, fascinating, sexy woman." He pulled her tighter to him. Her skirt belled out behind her as the front crinolines flattened against his legs.

"So?"

That was the question. "I had a goal. I had a plan." Until she rocked his world, he'd known exactly what he was doing, where he was going, how he was going to get there.

"You still do," she whispered.

The heat of her skin burned into his. He rubbed himself against her to let her know how turned on he was. "You are the monkey with the wrench that jumped into my plan."

"And that means what?"

He nipped her ear. The moment of truth was here. He was going to lay it all out for her. "I'm in love with you."

"You are? Why?" Her voice was causal but he felt her stiffen against him.

"I have no clue." Merrick smiled.

She started to tremble. "That sucks."

Closing his eyes, he buried his nose in her sweet pea scented hair. "I knew what I was doing, until I met you."

"Well since we're being all honest," she said, her voice trembling. "I'm in love with you, too."

Merrick brushed her cheek with his lips. Her skin was so soft, like molten silk. "So what are we going to do about it?"

She gave him an arch smile. "What do you want to do about it?"

"I want to buy you a French maid's outfit, be a daddy to your pig, and marry you."

She gave a low, throaty laugh. "That's a messed up proposal."

The musical sound warmed his heart. Love was… Hell, he didn't know, except that he liked it. "I thought a rebellious-Goth-chick-hacking-into-the-NSA kind of girl like you would appreciate it."

"A French maid's outfit," she mused, putting the tip of one finger in her mouth, a wicked look in her eyes.

He nodded at her surprised expression. "With a feather duster and no panties." He nibbled on her ear. She had perfect, shell-shaped ears. He loved them. He loved everything about her.

Elle glanced back at Mojo, still sound asleep on her blanket. "Well, my pig loves you."

His heart pounded so hard, he barely heard her. "She does."

"And my parents adore you."

Always a good thing. In the back of his mind, the plan he didn't even know he was working so well. He was cool with that. "That they do." He smiled. "Am I still too alpha male for you?"

"I've re-evaluated my opinion somewhat."

"And that would be?"

She glanced at him, her eyes filled with a promise. "You're not so bad in real life."

He liked that she was making him work hard for her. "Is that your messed up way of saying yes?"

She grabbed his hand and pulled him from the kitchen to her bedroom. Once inside, she pushed back and he willingly fell on the bed. She lifted her skirts and he saw she wore no panties. After climbing on top of him to sit on his thighs, she leaned over and she kissed him, long, hard and sweet, with a promise in her voice and a tantalizing look in her dark eyes that told him they were going to have a great future and a highly, thoroughly unpredictable marriage.

"Yes, it is."

He was good.

❧

To find out the skinny on Georgina and Dante check out Going Commando in Parker Publishing's Solider Boys Anthology.

Author Bio

J.M. Jeffries is the award winning writing team of Miriam Pace and Jacqueline Hamilton. Authors of romantic suspense and romantic comedies, they can't decide if they like killing people more than the like making them laugh. Miriam and Jackie have been writing together for six years, though it seems longer on occasion when they are on deadline. Miriam thinks Jackie is a master manipulator. Jackie knows Miriam is a bulldozer. Miriam has a deep and passionate love for shoes, amber jewelry and purebred cats. Jackie collects red lipsticks, Animaniacs memorabilia and steals pens.

Together they've written nineteen romance novels including the award winning Cold Case Crime Unit series for Genesis Press and the critically acclaimed Cupid series for Amber Quill books. They have also appeared in three anthologies.

Miriam and Jackie live in Southern California.

Continental Divide

By

Dyanne Davis

Books by Dyanne Davis
The Color of Trouble
The Wedding Gown
Misty Blue
Let's Get It On
Forever And A Day
Two Sides To Every Story
In The Beginning (As F.D. Davis)
Many Shades of Gray
Another Man's Baby
The Critic

Dedication

Barbara Keaton, my friend who gets me. I'm glad we're both on the same guardian team.

Acknowledgments

To God as always for the continued blessings of life.

To J.M. Jefferies who invited me to be in this anthology. Thanks ladies.

To Parker Publishing, I continue to wish you well and thank you for the opportunities you've given me to give life to my characters.

As always Bill and Bill Jr. You're both the best. Much love to you.

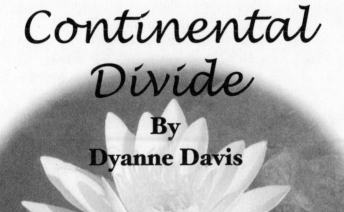

Continental
Divide

By
Dyanne Davis

1

CHUBBY ARMS CURLED AROUND Tanya Reed's neck while wet sloppy baby kisses were plastered on her face. Tanya held baby Jo Jo, aka Joseph Jermaine Warren tightly, wishing that he were hers — that she didn't have to turn him over to the waiting arms that were stretched out reaching for him. But she did. The baby didn't belong to her. He was a ward of the state and the woman standing in front of her waiting for the baby was a foster mother that Tanya had begged to take the baby in temporarily. Still it wasn't right that he was less than a year old and she'd had so much contact with this baby that he knew her and cared for her and gave her kisses and hugs each and every time he saw her. It wasn't right at all. It damn sure wasn't right that each time she turned him over to someone that her heart broke again. One of the dangers of the job. She'd been taught empathy, not sympathy, not in her job. As a social worker she couldn't afford to get emotionally involved. There were far too many children that she was responsible for.

Yet somehow Tanya's head must have been absent on the day that particular lecture was given. How could she not get involved? How could she not be angry that at this ungodly hour one of her charges would without warning need a new place to live? It made her angry at the birth parents, at God, at the system and even at the foster parents who sometimes turned out to be

worse than the biological parents. Sure the department did what
they could in the screening, but if they were really good at their
jobs then this precious baby would not now be slobbering over
her.

"Miss Reed, are you ready to hand me the baby?"

Tanya looked into the face of the woman who would take Jo Jo.
She looked pleasant enough. She had three other of the state's
children in her care. She was nice to the kids. Actually she seemed
to care for them.

"Miss Reed?"

Tanya found herself rubbing the baby's back not wanting to
release him. That was the problem. Mrs. Glass was a good foster
parent. She'd adopted two of the state's wards and who in their
right mind wouldn't adopt Jo Jo when the state terminated his
biological parents' custody? That would be years down the line,
but as sure as she was standing there, one day it was going to
happen. And as much as she wanted Jo Jo to have a good loving
home and stable parents she wanted him for her own. She sighed
heavily knowing that was one dream that more than likely would
never come true.

Suddenly the baby's head lifted from her neck where he was
slobbering and he pulled back to stare into her eyes. He gave her
a smile before gently patting her cheeks. If she didn't know better,
she'd think the baby was comforting her, trying to let her know
that it was okay, that she could hand him over. Still, she didn't
want to. She brought him back close to her and hugged him,
trying her best not to cry.

"Okay, big guy," she said at last. "I guess it's time you go to
meet Mrs. Glass. It's way past your bedtime, Jo Jo." She kissed
him one last time and handed him over. "He's such a sweet little
guy. He's a good baby and he loves to be held. I know you have
other kids, but if you could make him feel safe, just give him extra
hugs for me, I'd sure appreciate it." Tanya ran her hand down the
baby's back and Mrs. Glass pulled him away from her. For a
moment Tanya stared at the woman.

"I give all of my babies' hugs and love," Mrs. Glass replied
with a distinct coolness in her voice. "If I didn't, you wouldn't
have brought him to me at," she looked behind her at the wall
clock, "at four in the morning."

Tanya had offended the woman. That had not been her intent,
but the baby wasn't even a year old and he'd seen way more in
his young life than he ever should have. A chill hit her and she
wondered if in worrying about Jo Jo she'd made things worse for

him. *God, please, no don't let that be the case.* She bit her lips trying to find the right words to soothe, to assure. She'd had parents take out things against her and the department before on their precious little charges. She didn't want that to be the case for Jo Jo.

"I'm so sorry. I didn't mean to offend you," she smiled at the woman and shrugged her shoulders to acknowledge that she'd been in the wrong in the words she'd used. "I've grown so attached to this little guy. He's had it harder than most, but he's a fighter. And you're right. I called you because you're the best foster mother that I have. I know how much you do for the kids." Tanya smiled again. "It's just harder with this one." She moved closer and rubbed the baby's back. This time the woman didn't move away. "I find myself wishing he were mine," Tanya admitted. She wasn't surprised when the truth brought out the smile from Mrs. Glass that her words didn't.

"That I understand. Ralph and I fall in love with all the kids you bring to us. We never want to let go of them, even though we know it's best if their parents get their lives together and raise their babies themselves. If we could afford to, we'd adopt every single child that the state would allow us to."

She smiled and Tanya smiled back at her. "I know you would," Tanya admitted knowing that was the truth. "Listen, it's really late and I want to thank you again for always taking my calls. I know some of my foster parents ignore my late night calls, so thanks again for not looking at your caller ID and ignoring me." Tanya grinned. "I'll let you and Jo Jo get acquainted." She walked to the door, determined not to give the baby another glance, but he started laughing and when she turned back he waved at her and said, "Bye-bye." Tanya laughed also; she didn't know he was making words. "Bye, Jo Jo," she said. "I'll see you in a couple of days."

Walking out into the still dark morning Tanya sucked up her tears. In one more week she would finish the classes for being a foster parent. The department played no favoritism that way. Social worker or not, she still had to take the classes if she wanted to take children into her home. But Tanya was going for the bigger picture. She was investing in the dream of a friend of a friend. A woman with clout, Sara Combs.

Tanya had met her at a charity event several years ago and had seen the woman many times since. She liked her and for a millionaire she didn't have airs. In fact she was always trying to find a way to give back. She considered her money a blessing and was always trying to help those less fortunate. Knowing Tanya was a social worker she'd eagerly told her of her plans to build an entire community of brand new homes where foster children would live with parents. It was a kind of utopia. Tanya knew that the idea hadn't been all that original considering that SOS had been doing that for years. It was Sara's enthusiasm for the project that had swept Tanya up into wanting to be a part of it. She'd already donated her time and money to the project. She'd been saving all of her money to give to the organization to buy more land as soon as all of the plans were approved for the village. In fact, one home had been built and furnished. With political clout and financial backing from a major university, Sara had pulled some strings and had become affiliated with several agencies that were willing to allow the children to live in the homes.

She hadn't asked why the state had approved their plans but Tanya wanted in on this project. All of the participants had undergone background checks and had all taken the foster care training classes. They were ready. The homework had been done. The plans laid out would give these children a stable neighborhood and a family. They would go to ballet lessons, learn to play the piano, ski, play tennis, go skating, all the things kids with two sane loving parents would do. Tanya was all for that. And every spare dime was going into a fund to help finance the building of the next home. She'd already saved a little over twenty-five- thousand dollars. She thought of Heaven and Hamid. If she ran short, she knew she could count on Heaven.

A twinge of regret hit Tanya. She was taking advantage of her friend and they both were aware of it. Still, she'd never asked Heaven for money for herself, only for the kids. Putting her key in the ignition Tanya's gaze landed on the dashboard. Almost five—much too damn early to be up, and definitely much too early for a baby to be roused from his sleep. Jo Jo couldn't help it though. He was at the mercy of adults, poor little thing. In a way Tanya couldn't help it either. She just didn't trust that anyone else would go in at whatever ungodly hour to answer the calls. She's heard the complaints and she knew for a fact some of the workers waited a few hours to do their jobs when it was more convenient. It didn't mean that there weren't a lot of dedicated social workers out there. But it did mean that there weren't enough. And there were far too many abandoned, abused kids without enough caring people to tend to their needs. The job was that much harder if one had a family. Thank God, Tanya didn't have a family.

At that thought she felt an unexpected twinge to her heart. She wanted a family and she wanted one badly. Ever since Heaven had left Chicago for Pakistan Tanya's own biological clock had begun ticking. At the least she'd thought she'd be able to share in her best friend's pregnancy. But noooo, Heaven had talked some mess about following Hamid halfway across the world to Pakistan to make her husband happy.

At her crazy thoughts, Tanya couldn't help but smile. She didn't blame Heaven one little bit. If she had a man who loved her as much as Hamid loved Heaven, she would follow him also. And one that was that fine. Damn. Then to add to the pot, Heaven got to Pakistan and found out her husband was loaded--, filthy rich, a damn millionaire. If it weren't that Heaven was constantly sending her money when she asked for it to help out with the kids, Tanya would have been even more jealous than she was. Sure, she wanted her friend to be happy but she would be a liar if she said she didn't want the same things for herself. She'd day dreamed more than once about having a millionaire husband. She knew exactly what she would do with the money. She'd build a community for her children without Sara or anyone's help. She'd make sure they never wanted for anything.

◌

'It don't matter if you're young or you're old,' Tanya sang along to the words for, *The Cupid Shuffle*. This was exactly what she needed a night out with her girlfriends. She needed to dance and maybe please God, meet a decent guy. She was tired of sleeping alone.

Five dances later, Tanya was dragging off the dance floor. "I must be getting old. I'm tired."

"So am I." Ongela turned and smiled, and they both watched Peaches who remained on the floor.

"Sassa, we didn't expect to see much of you and Isha once Hamid left the country. I'm glad to see that we can all be friends still." Tanya smiled at Hamid's cousin then turned to include his wife, Isha in her smile.

"Of course we can. Why wouldn't we?" Sassa questioned, his look one of curiosity.

"You know? We hung out because of Heaven and Hamid."

"That may have been true, but both Isha and I enjoy going out with you. You're all so much fun."

Tanya sighed. "We do have fun, but I miss Heaven. I'm still pissed that she didn't tell any of us she was pregnant before she left. That was so wrong. We didn't get to throw her a baby shower or anything. And we haven't even seen the baby."

"You could all go to Pakistan for a visit. Heaven has a very large home and would welcome a visit from friends," Sassa piped in. "Hamid told me that she's a bit homesick, that she misses all of you."

"She missed us so much that she didn't ask any of us to be godmother to her baby. That was the plan we'd all talked about it. It was decided long ago that we'd choose from among us for godparents."

"Yes, Tanya, while that might be true Fatima is her sister in law." Peaches chimed in.

It had to be her internal clock ticking. Why else would she be angry with her friend for being happy, for having a baby? Surely it couldn't be jealousy. Tanya pushed the thought away and glared at Peaches. "So what? We're her friends, her family, she should have asked one of us."

"Which one?" Sassa asked. "Which one could she have asked and not had the others feeling bad or angry? I think she did what she did to prevent any feelings of jealousy amongst her best friends."

Tanya thought about that for a moment. Maybe that was what Heaven had done. She didn't know. But she was still ticked at her that she hadn't asked any of them to be godmother. She frowned at Sassa then looked first at Ongela then Peaches making her way from the dance floor. Yeah, they would have been fighting over it.

"I need a break," Tanya announced. "I think maybe I will go to Pakistan and visit Heaven. I want to see the baby."

"Just the baby?" Sassa asked.

"Just the baby," she pouted, knowing Sassa didn't for a moment believe her. "Forget Heaven and Hamid. They could have come back for a visit already. They're the millionaires."

Sassa smiled. "Perhaps if you go to Pakistan one of my cousins will fall in love with you and marry you. Just think, Tanya, your dreams would come true in an instant."

And just like that an idea was born. Tanya looked at Sassa, he was kidding but the words were true. One of Hamid's brothers would be perfect. She smiled. She would give Heaven a call and make arraignments to go to Pakistan. Surely if Heaven had found her true love, Tanya could find hers. She thought of Hamid's gentleness and generosity. His brothers had to be like him, right? The idea grew deep roots. She rubbed her hand along the side of her neck remembering the feel of Jo Jo's chubby fingers. He would be the first baby that she'd make sure got a good home.

He'd want for nothing.

✑

The scream of joy from Heaven was so loud that it forced Tanya to hold the phone away from her ear. She was glad to know that Heaven really did miss them and that the invitation was not just something that one issues. The giddiness in Heaven's voice made Tanya laugh. Now for the test. "Heaven, you know I have a hard time keeping my opinions to myself. How do you think I'll go over in Pakistan?"

"Listen girl, if they can take me, they can take you."

"I want to party. I'm not coming there fore six weeks and being stuck in your home not being allowed to do anything unless Hamid comes along with us. You know I'll go crazy."

"Tanya, you make it sounds like I've changed, that I'm not fun anymore. Believe me, Hamid and I have lots of fun." Heaven laughed.

"I'm not talking about that kind of fun, unless you're willing to share."

"You'd better get that idea outta your head fast or I'll whip your behind the minute the plane lands. Now cut it out. You're making it t sounds like we have no life. Sure, we love spending time with each other and the baby, but please, Hamid and I go out."

"Right. When was the last time?" Tanya laughed and waited for an answer.

"We went to the family for a party just two nights ago."

"That's not going out, Heaven. I'm serious. Tell me something, are any of Hamid's brothers looking for a wife?"

"Not that I know of."

"And none of them care that you're black right?" Tanya held her breath. As much as she wanted to have what Heaven had she wasn't about to become involved with anyone who had race issues.

"Of course not."

"Then what about me? Do you think they'd welcome me into the family?"

The hesitation on the line didn't bode well. "Heaven? Be for real. Tell me, do you think one of Hamid's brothers might fall in love with me?"

"You're serious. What is this about?"

"I want a husband," Tanya said. "I want a rich husband. I'm tired of the slow train to helping my kids. I want an express train."

Heaven laughed then sighed. "Listen, Tanya, you can't come here expecting to go home with a husband. It doesn't work that way. I'll help you with the down payment on the house you're trying to buy. You know that. I already told you that I would."

"I know, but I want to do it on my own."

"No, it sounds more like you want to do it with a rich husband."

"Whatcah trying to say, Heaven? Are you calling me a gold-digger?"

"I'm calling it as I see it. You sound like a gold-digger."

"You know why I'm doing this." Tanya swallowed back the pain of having her best friend call her a gold-digger. If Heaven felt that way what would others think? "Heaven, you know I've always wanted to do something to help the kids I work with."

"I know it's for the kids, but your methods are crazy. You can't just come here, make one of Hamid's brother fall in love with you, and expect to marry them and have them finance your dreams. They have no desire to live in America. They visit, but that's about it."

"They should want to leave. There's a war in that country."

"I know, but this is their home and they have no plan on leaving it so you'd better take that into consideration."

Tanya was silent. She knew her friend was right but still she wanted to try, she had to try. "Listen, Heaven, I've being playing the lottery, twenty dollars a week. I haven't won a dime."

"I'm sure you haven't. But if you'd put away that twenty dollars, look how much fatter your bank account would be now."

For some reason Heaven's attitude was pissing Tanya off big time. "You're talking that way because you can. Hamid's a millionaire. You can have anything you want. Are you jealous that I might be able to have the same thing?" The moment the words were out Tanya regretted them. "Heaven, I'm sorry. Listen, I really do want to come out and visit you and Hamid. I want to see that baby of yours."

"And?"

"And I want to make one of Hamid's brother's fall in love with me. Dag! Why did you make me say it? Heaven, help me okay. You can talk me up to the brothers before I get there. If you put in a good word for me then who knows."

"Don't you want to see which you'd prefer? Who lights your fire?"

"They're all millionaires, right?"

"Right."

"And they're all handsome right?" Tanya held her breath and waited.

"Yes."

"One last question," Tanya said. "Are they nice?"

"Yes," Heaven laughed. "They're all very nice."

"Then, Heaven, either one of Hamid's brothers will do. So go ahead and talk me up to all of them and let me pick the one that picks me."

"This is so crazy. If Hamid finds out what you're coming here for or that I knew anything about your crazy plans you're going to make problems between us."

"Please, Heaven, Hamid adores you and you know it."

"Yeah and I want to keep it that way." Heaven laughed. "Maybe part of the reason my husband adores me is because I've never done anything to trick his brothers. He can trust me and that's important in a marriage. Tanya, I know how much you want to help the kids but what about love?"

"What about it?"

"I have a better idea. Hamid has a cousin I think will be perfect for you."

"Is he a millionaire?"

"No, but...he's such a nice guy."

"And broke."

"Tanya."

"Don't Tanya me. I can love a rich man as well as a poor one, so start working on Hamid's brothers. I'll start preparing for coming and I'll let you know." Tanya ignored the long sigh from Heaven. She was doing what she had to do, the same as Heaven did what she had to do in order for Hamid to be happy. No one had complained when she'd just up and followed him to Pakistan. Well they had but it hadn't done any good. And Heaven's badgering her about finding someone to love wasn't going to do any good. Besides, if Hamid's brother were anything like Hamid she didn't think there'd be any problems. She thought of baby Jo Jo. He deserved a better life. While it was a long shot at best that she would ever have him as her own it was a real possibility that she would one day be raising her cousin Lettie six kids. Lettie was fighting cancer and Tanya had promised her that if God forbid she didn't make it she would step in. For now she didn't want to tell Heaven that.

"Tanya, stop ignoring me. Your plan is crazy. Just come and visit me and have a good time. Forget about Hamid's brothers."

"Okay, Heaven, enough. I have to go," Tanya said deciding to end the conversation.

"Don't forget to go to the health department for shots. Your insurance won't cover everything, so I'll pay for the things that it doesn't.

"Dag, Heaven, I'm not a beggar. I can pay for the shots myself. You're already paying for the ticket."

"You can get mad at me for offering to pay for your shots but you tell me outta your own mouth that you're going to come visit me so you can get a rich husband. And I offended you? You're crazy," Heaven laughed. "You'd best be glad you're one of my best friends and that I love you. See you soon."

Heaven disconnected and Tanya stared for a moment at the phone. She shook her head. Yes, what she was planning was crazy but if she worked it right it could be the perfect thing.

৵

Tanya glared at Sassa as he gave her his wrapped gift for Heaven's baby. "Sassa, you've already sent a ton of gifts to Pakistan. You even went to see the baby. Why are you giving me more packages?" She looked around the room at her friends. "If I have to pay for over the limit you all are going to pay me back." She glanced at Peaches. "I thought you guys wanted me to pretend to snub Heaven's baby."

"We do, but just for a minute," Peaches explained as though Tanya should have already known what they'd meant. "Then we want you to give her our gifts. Tell her that she was wrong for not naming one of us as the godmother."

"Hey," Ongela chimed in. "Tell her we all hate the baby's name that she should have given him an American name."

Tanya couldn't help laughing. They all missed Heaven and wanted to see the baby and be a part of it. She'd decided like the rest of them to razz Heaven and Hamid a bit. It might be fun. "Don't you all forget technically Heaven's a black belt in karate. What are you all going to do if she decides to kick my behind all over Pakistan for talking about her son?" When everyone shrugged and started laughing Tanya gave them a look and an 'I-thought-so' and laughed with them.

The blowing horn of the taxi didn't stop last minute messages everyone wanted her to give to Heaven and Hamid.

"Enough," Tanya said hugging each of them. "I have to go before I miss my flight." She waved and blew more kisses at them as the taxi took off for the airport. Then she settled back to think about what she was doing. A two month leave of absence...burn out, she'd cited and not a peep was made. It happened a lot in her field. She had gone to check on Jo Jo who was doing well. She'd also called all of her kids letting them know she would be gone for a time telling them who their new social worker would be and telling each of them that she would bring them back a gift from Pakistan. She had thirty kids. That was a lot of money, but she was determined to keep that promise.

2

HAMID'S BROTHERS HAD BETTER be worth it, Tanya fumed
silently after her third trip from the tiny airplane lavatory. At
least the thought of thinking of it as that, made Tanya smile. Her
idea of a lavatory was something a lot bigger than what she'd
been using to puke her guts out. That was one little piece of
information Heaven had managed to keep to herself—the side
effects of all the medications she'd needed to make the trip to
Pakistan. If she didn't leave the country with one of Hamid's
brother's falling madly in love with her Tanya just might not ever
speak to Heaven again.

Luckily, when the plane landed the rumbling in her stomach
dissipated. Grabbing her bags from baggage claim she made a
mad dash through the airport heading through customs, ignoring
the way the custom agent looked at her gaily painted fingernails
in varying colors and moved his gaze over her in disapproval.
Forget him and what he thought about her clothes. She was
American, baby, and she was going to let everyone in Pakistan
know it. She had no plans to wear anything other than what she
wanted to. In her opinion Heaven had gone soft since she'd
moved to Pakistan. Tanya plans didn't include living in the
country she was there strictly to 'bag em and tag em.'

Retrieving her passport Tanya admitted that she did like
traveling and if she were being honest she'd have to acknowledge

that she'd always wanted to visit a Moslem country. She glanced around the crowded airport and finally spotted Heaven and Hamid. Tanya squealed and raced toward them.

"Look at you two. I can't believe it. Heaven, you're a mommy now. And, Hamid, you're a daddy." She lunged herself at Hamid knowing that within second Heaven was going to pull her away from her husband.

"Down girl," Heaven laughed. "This one's taken."

This time when Tanya hugged Hamid it was more sedate. She grinned at him as he smiled at her then looked at Heaven, his look clearly saying, 'Pakistan is not ready for your crazy friend.'

With a bold gaze she appraised Hamid. Tall, drop dead gorgeous, long, black, curly hair, eyes that sparkled, and a behind that was perfect for the black jeans he was wearing. She then turned her gaze to Heaven, short, beautiful and stacked. She grinned and touched her hand to her friend's hair. "You're not wearing your twists anymore," she said looking at Heaven's ponytail.

"I haven't been able to find a beautician here who can do it. Maybe before you leave you'll twist it for me." Heaven turned pleading eyes on Tanya and put her hands together, bringing them under her chin in a sign of supplication.

"We'll see. Besides, I like you in braids and your hair has really grown since I last saw you. I did bring you a gift though, something for your hair. I kinda thought you'd need something to help you out." Tanya smiled at the couple, their happiness something she envied and wanted for herself.

"Come on show me to this paradise you claim to have found. Then I want to go and meet Hamid's brothers." The look that passed between the couple didn't go unnoticed by Tanya. "What's wrong?" she asked. "Doesn't Hamid know why I came?" When Heaven groaned she knew he didn't.

"Do you think you could have given me a chance to make introductions to Hamid's brothers and see what happens? Dang, Tann. Could you be a bit more blunt?"

At that remark Tanya stopped moving and planted her hands on her hips and did a head roll. "What are you talking about? You know I love the culture. I love learning new things and I could have easily fallen for Hamid if he hadn't been so gah gah over you." She stopped and smiled up at Hamid. "Now you're fronting, you've got me all the way here, made me take shots which we both know I hate. I've been sick as a dog." She pushed Heaven's hand away as she tried to shush her. "No, you're not going to stop me from talking. I get it. You don't want Hamid to know. That's your deal; he's your husband, not mine." Ignoring the blazing fury in Heaven's eyes Tanya turned toward Hamid.

"Hamid, Heaven has been trying to get me to come here and when I kept refusing she dangled your brothers in my face. She told me they weren't married." She tilted her head toward Heaven and gave a smirk. "And she told me that they were as fine as you. Now I've been on a plane for what seems like a hundred hours. I'm tired. I want to see this utopia Heaven told me you two found and I want to meet your brothers pronto." She swished past both Hamid and Heaven and straight out the door.

❧

"Heaven, tell me you didn't do that," Hamid turned soft, adoring eyes on Heaven. "You know Tanya is not my brothers' type. My family will never accept her as they have accepted you. She's a bit crass. My brothers are not going to fall in love with her."

Heaven turned from the door Tanya had just gone through to give her husband a look. "Are you saying my friend isn't good enough for your brothers?"

"Those are your words not mine. Why did you do this?"

For a long moment Heaven held her husband's gaze. "I was lonely for my friends." She shrugged and looked away, knowing that this would be one of the times Hamid would forget about the limited touching of her in public places. He reached for her hand and pulled her to him giving her a light kiss and a hug.

"You're given up a lot to remain in Pakistan with me. We can return to America if you want, us and our son. It's okay if you're ready to leave. I will not hold that against you." Hamid gave her fingers a squeeze. "Whither thou goeth I will go dear wife."

Making her husband feel guilty wasn't her intent. Well, maybe just a little. "Hamid, don't worry, I love having you happy and you're happy in Pakistan. I just still missed my friends and thought it would be nice to have at least one of them come to visit. Tanya is the only one of them bold enough to give the country a try. But you know how she is. I had to give her a good enough reason for doing so."

Pulling back a little Hamid looked into his wife's eyes. "So you devised a plan to use possible marriage to one of my brothers as the bait?"

"Not exactly. To be honest, Tanya came up with the crazy scheme to marry one of your brothers. I know she's not right for them but she's perfect for Imran. The two of them are so alike and they're both a lot of fun. I really do think Imran will like her. Tanya needs a nice guy," Heaven answered softly. "Will you help me get the two of them together?"

After pretending to think it over Hamid tilted his head a slight bit then turned to look toward the door and spotted Tanya waiting for them. He did like Tanya and she was a lot of fun. Imran needed a woman who was fun. That was one thing Heaven was right about; they did have a lot in common. He sighed as his wife discreetly gave his fingers a squeeze. "Yes, for you, I will do what I can," Hamid answered at last, then smiled. "But you're going to have to make my part in your little conspiracy worth my efforts." He grinned and gave her another kiss before going out to join Tanya.

৯৯

Tanya gazed at the white mansion taking in the well kept lawn and enough trees that one could easily think they were in a forest preserve. "Dang gurl, is this really your house?" Tanya asked before the car had come to a complete stop. "You never told us you were living in a mansion. I am so not going home without one of Hamid 's brothers." She laughed at the pained expression on Hamid's face. "Don't worry, Hamid, at least I'm not after you."

Tanya followed Heaven into the house demanding to look around "oohhing" and "ahhing" at the paintings, the costly furniture not stopping until Heaven stopped moving, her hands planted on her hips and a glare on her face.

"Are you never going to ask to see my son?"

"Our son," Hamid came behind her and slid his arms around her. "Well, Tanya, would you like to take a moment from touring the house to have a look at our real treasure?"

"My bad," Tanya laughed, embarrassed. She couldn't even lie her way out of this one and say that she hadn't been so impressed with the house that she'd forgotten about the baby. But she did try. "I thought maybe he was sleeping."

"Nice try," Heaven laughed, reaching for Tanya's hand and pulling her toward the nursery that was next door to her and Hamid rooms.

"Fatima, this is my friend Tanya. Tanya, Fatima, Hamid's sister. I think you two will get alone and become great friends." Then Heaven raced for her son but Hamid beat her by a step and had lifted the baby from his crib. He was looking down at the baby with awe the same kind that he had each and every time he held him. Heaven watched as Hamid walked toward Tanya.

"Tsukama, this is your mommy's friend Auntie Tanya."

Tanya reached for the baby and gave Hamid a look when he moved away from her with his son in his arms.

"Hamid, what are you doing?" she asked.

"Do you know how to hold a baby?" he responded.

"I work with kids for a living, you know that," Tanya laughed holding her arms out for the baby.

"But most of the kids you care for are older. I've never actually seen you hold a baby." Hamid held the baby closer to his chest. "In fact I've never heard you even mention that you've ever held a baby."

"Give me that baby." When he still refused she looked toward Heaven in disbelief. "Are you two crazy or what? Heaven, give me that baby before I go off on you." When she finally snuggled the baby in her arms she looked across the room and saw Fatima eyeing her warily. Damn, she'd gotten off on the wrong foot with the first member of Hamid's family that she'd met. She looked down at the baby. At least he liked her. He had a big grin on his face and was bouncing. At least she was hoping it was a grin. Either way she didn't come to Pakistan to fall in love with Hamid's sister. If she liked her she liked her, if she didn't... well if that was the case she could just go to hell. Tanya had no intention of living in Pakistan with her new husband as Heaven had done with Hamid. No, she was taking Hamid's brother right back to America.

A few moments later the grunts from the baby told Tanya it might have been something other than a grin for her. "Here change your kid," she said and handed the baby back to Hamid and walked out of the nursery. She saw the stunned surprise on all three faces. *What?* she thought. She hadn't traveled this many hours to play nursemaid, nor was she fond of watching parents change a baby's poopy diaper and go crazy over it. And the way those two behaved she could just tell they were the kind of parents to do something crazy like that. She heard Fatima mumble something and was positive it wasn't anything nice, but oh well.

"Tann, what do you think about Tsukama?" Heaven came and stood in front of her friend.

"Well, I wasn't going to say anything. But why the heck did you name that chile Tsukama? Don't you think Black men have enough problems without you and Hamid giving him a name like that?"

"It's an African name it means 'learner'," Hamid walked from the nursery.

"And I repeat, that chile isn't African. Why saddle him with a name like that?" Tanya wasn't backing down on that. It was her opinion and she was sticking with it. Besides, she'd promised everyone she was going to give Heaven a hard time on the baby's name for not making one of them the god-mother.

"Hamid chose the name long before we were ever married. In fact he chose it when he was so angry with me I didn't know if I'd ever see him again. The name has great meaning for us." Heaven stood next to Hamid and defended their newborn's name.

"It's still ugly." Tanya glared first at Hamid then Heaven. She was finding it hard not to laugh at the looks on their faces. She wondered how long she'd keep it up before confessing that the idea of giving a baby a name with a meaning really appealed to her. The baby smiled at her and the smile tugged on her heart. Maybe it was time to lighten up, just a bit. "It was an ugly name to give to such a cute little baby," Tanya smiled and kissed the top of the baby's head.

Hamid looked toward Heaven then swore softly in Urdu.

"You promised," Heaven said in response.

"Promised what?" Tanya interrupted. "And Hamid while I'm your guest you will either tell me what you're saying or speak in English." She laughed when Hamid's mouth flew open and Heaven rushed to his side. Okay she'd taken this ugly American bit too far. If she didn't stop they would more than likely be taking her butt back to the airport. "Okay, okay, the baby is beautiful, but you both knew that. With you two for parents the baby had no choice but to be beautiful. Heaven, you're beautiful and, Hamid, you already know I think you're yummy. You're super fine. I just hope your brothers look half as good." She gave a smirk. "That's why I know one of your brothers and I will make beautiful babies. Now all I have to do is pick the one which I like best."

"You're going to do what with our brothers?" Fatima asked entering the room and bringing the freshly diapered baby with her.

Tanya sized Heaven's new sister-in-law up, the woman who'd taken the honor one of Heaven's friends should have been given, the godmother to Tsukama that Tanya desperately wished she was. Fatima was frowning at her, her look one Tanya didn't approve of. When she saw her glancing in Heaven's direction as for an explanation "nasty" snapped to attention inside of Tanya.

"So you work for Heaven? Are you the nanny?"

"Tanya, stop it okay." Heaven rushed Tanya toward the other end of the huge house. "Let me show you your rooms."

When they were safely inside Tanya figured if she and her friends were going to be living together in the same house for six weeks she needed to know what was going on. They had to be straight with each other as they'd always been.

"What the heck is going on, Heaven? You're giving me looks every time I open my mouth, and I see you looking at Hamid. You told me when I asked that I didn't have to do anything any different than I did at home, that I didn't have to change to come here. You know how much I wanted to come here first hand and learn about the culture and everything. I'm glad you gave me this vacation. But why are you suddenly acting like I'm doing something wrong? And that sister-in-law of yours she has her nose all turned up in the air like she smelled something bad."

"You're being rude and you wonder why we're all giving you looks. What's wrong with you? You know better than that. Fatima is one of the nicest people that I know and if you've pissed her off I don't even know if I should introduce you to the rest of the family."

"But you told me I didn't have to change the way I behaved."

"I know that but who knew you were going to hop off the plane and call my baby ugly, threaten to hit my husband and then straight out ask my sister-in-law if she was my servant. You have more class than that and we both know it. Come on, what gives? Why are you doing this ghetto diva bitch thing?"

"Was I really that bad?"

"Yes. What gives?"

"I'm tired."

"That doesn't excuse your behavior and you know it."

"Promise me you're not going to laugh." Tanya pleaded.

"Just tell me," Heaven fumed, "before Hamid tells me to get you outta here. Hurry up."

"What if none of Hamid's brothers like me? What if his family won't accept me? And you know I'm being for real about not coming here to live."

For the first time Heaven breathed a real sigh of relief and hugged her friend. She'd hoped Tanya would love the country as much as she did and she wanted her to get alone well with her new family. Whether or not Tanya left Pakistan with a husband was a different matter. Heaven just wanted her friend to have a good time and help Heaven alleviate her homesickness. "You're crazy, you haven't even met them and you're worried about them liking you and following you to America. First, I don't think that's going to happen. But I do know you need to take it down a notch. Hamid and I will have the entire family over in three days for a party. Behave, okay. Now, for real, do you think my baby has a stupid name?"

"First, you tell me, do you really like it?"

"I love the meaning." Heaven conceded refusing to meet Tanya's eyes.

"The name." Tanya laughed, "Do you like the name?"

"I love his daddy madly."

"The name, do you like the name?"

"I adore my baby."

"Heaven."

"Well, I'm afraid I might have to live in Pakistan forever to protect him from someone wanting to beat the crap out of him because of his name." Heaven said seriously then they both fell on the bed and laughed.

Wiping the tears from her eyes Tanya asked, "If you didn't like the name why did you allow Hamid to give the baby that name?"

Heaven shrugged then smiled. "It's custom here for the father to name the baby and to be honest, when Hamid looked at me after I'd given birth I would have named the baby whatever he wanted, done whatever he wanted, gone wherever he wanted."

"You two really are happy here, aren't you?" Tanya sighed unable to hide her envy.

"Yes, it was so the right decision for us to move here. Only one thing could make it even better and that would be if one of my best friends would move here also."

"Forget it," Tanya laughed. "No way is that ever going to happen."

When they hugged again, Tanya felt better. She knew she'd made the right decision to come. Maybe she wouldn't end up with one of Hamid's brothers but it was still nice to see Pakistan and to visit with Heaven and their beautiful new baby. It was going to be a great trip and she was going to do her best to stop acting like a bitch simply because she was a little afraid and feeling as though time was running out on her for getting married and having the same happiness Heaven had found. All she was hoping for was to find a way to help build the village. "Thanks for bringing me here. I'll try and behave, I promise."

"You'd better keep that promise. Now come on out and let's eat. I have a ton of food out there for you. My mother-in-law sent

over food and Fatima has been cooking. She helps us with the
baby because she loves him and she adores Hamid. He's her baby
brother. And, Tanya, she loves me also. I love her so I'm going to
try and mend the fences between the two of you. But you have
gotten off on the wrong foot. You've even gotten Hamid annoyed
and you know how hard that is to do."

"You annoyed him all the time."

"That was my falling in love with him and making him fall in
love with me. Come on now, I'm not asking you to change. You're
open and honest and speak your mind. I know that and I love
you. I'm just asking you to take that chip off your shoulder and
be nice like I know you can be."

⤚

An hour later, Tanya was laughing and enjoying the food when
the doorbell rang and the sound of the door brought her attention
to the person entering. *Damn*, she thought as she looked up at Mr.
Tall, gorgeous, and a beautiful golden bronze. Wow! *Welcome to
Pakistan Tanya*, she said to herself. Before anyone could stop her
she was making her way toward the door sticking out her hand
and smiling.

"Hi, I'm Tanya Reed." For a nanosecond she didn't think the
hunk was going to answer her as he glanced questioningly
toward Hamid.

"Hello, my name is Imran Ahmed."

Oh, damn. The sound of Imran's deep voice had made her wet
her panties. It had a musical quality. She opened her eyes wider,
not even hiding the fact that she was checking him out. She
wondered how the men in Hamid's family could have hair that
black without using dye from the Oriental store like her and her
friends did. She liked his face. There was a smile playing along
his full lips as he watched her evaluating him. He had brown eyes
that held a mischievous glint. Tanya moved back a little just for a
better look. He was even taller than Hamid. Good. She loved her
men to be over six feet. And he was built. Nice. A nice broad
chest, she smiled, long, long legs, and…she couldn't wait to see
how he looked from behind. He had to be Hamid's brother. "You
look like Hamid," she offered. "Are you his older brother?"

This time Tanya knew it took longer than a second as Imran
gave her a look and the small smile that had played about his lips
turned into a full fledge grin.

"Wrong Ahmed," he answered at last. "I'm not one of the
millionaire sons. Sorry, but you were flirting with the poor

relation. I'm Hamid's cousin. Better luck next time." He gave Tanya another smile and moved away from her.

Did he just call me a gold digger? Tanya paused with her hands on her hip. Screw him. She didn't come to Pakistan for a cousin nor did she come for one of the 'not millionaire' relatives. So Imran could just go shimmy up a tree. She took another look at him. The man was still fine but she wasn't after him. She passed by him, stopped and batted her eyes. "On second thought you're right, Imran, you don't look like Hamid, nor do you look rich. My bad." She grinned at Heaven and shrugged her shoulder. She'd tried to be good hadn't she? She walked back into the kitchen, took her seat and returned to eating trying to ignore Imran. But every time he uttered a word she got wetter. If one of Hamid's relative that was not a millionaire could do that to her, she wondered how she'd react when she met his brothers.

3

IMRAN LIFTED HIS EYES AND stared across the table at Tanya, smiling slightly, knowing that Fatima was right. She'd thought he was one of his cousins. No Moslem woman would have rushed to meet him the way she had, introducing herself instead of waiting for a proper introduction from either Hamid or Heaven. Imran grinned. He liked that Tanya had introduced herself. He even liked the way her eyes had flicked appreciatively while she'd looked him over without embarrassment. In the moment when their eyes had met and held she'd smiled and he'd felt a spark.

He glanced once more at Heaven's friend Tanya. Besides the things he liked about the woman he'd noticed something about her that he didn't like. It was no different than when they'd been children and all of the mothers had tried to push their daughters in his cousins' directions. He'd wondered when Fatima had called him sputtering angrily about Heaven's rude American friend. Fatima had cursed, something he'd never known her to do, saying the woman had come to Pakistan to trick one of her brothers into marriage. Imran had laughed at his cousin. Heaven's friend had barely had to time to say hello let alone hatch a plan to marry one of his cousins, sight unseen.

"See, what did I tell you?" Fatima came and stood by his chair. "She's nothing like Heaven."

Imran couldn't help that his gaze swept over Heaven's friend. No, Tanya wasn't anything like Heaven. Though Heaven was very beautiful, in Imran's opinion she was much too tiny. Tanya was a tall woman, the kind he liked. He found himself smiling even more. She was at least 5' 9" or 5' 10" easy. He allowed his eyes to travel leisurely across her chest before making a downward journey. Not that he wasn't used to seeing women in jeans and sweater, but Tanya filled out her clothes rather nicely. When he brought his gaze back up to rest on her face, he met her unsmiling eyes and he smiled slowly at her, aware that she'd observed him making a pleasurable journey across her body. Well, since he was caught he didn't see any harm in continuing his perusal. Besides, she'd done the same to him.

Her glaring eyes were a beautiful brown and her long hair was healthy, soft and shiny. Her brown skin glowed, showing the red undertones. *Very nice*, he thought. Then his gaze took in her gaily-painted long nails and he frowned and fought back a shiver. The nails were ugly, too long, the paint too garish, detracting from her true beauty. With a start he realized that the brass American was truly beautiful. An unknown flicker danced about his spine and this time he couldn't stop the shiver. He had to not allow her beauty to dissuade him. The woman was also here for one thing and one thing only and that was to trap one of his cousins into marriage. He had no intentions of allowing that to happen. If fate had such plans for another of Hamid's brothers Imran was going to give fate a quick shove.

At long last Tanya leaned an elbow back on the chair and cocked her head sideways. "Did you find what you were looking for?" she asked.

"I think I found it when I came through the door." Imran answered then turned toward Fatima and spoke in Urdu.

"It's very rude for you to do that with me sitting here," Tanya interrupted him.

For a long moment brown eyes met darker brown eyes and stared then Imran gave her another smile. "Tanya, it was not my intention to be rude to you but it was my intention to have a private conversation with Fatima." He turned once again in Fatima's direction and spoke a few more words in his native tongue.

"Hamid," Heaven cautioned, "make him stop."

"Imran, Tanya is our guest. We all speak English, please let's do so."

Imran's gaze swung back to Tanya then to Heaven. Heaven

had his cousin wrapped around her little finger. All the gibberish he'd given the family about fate bringing her to him. Nonsense. Hamid lived to make Heaven happy. Imran praised Allah for his own level head. He'd never allow a woman to do that to him. An unexpected swelling in his groin and an acknowledgment of lust pure and simple hit him when he gazed in Tanya's direction.

"Imran," Hamid said again this time more firmly, "please apologize."

This time Imran's eyes sought those of his cousin and he frowned before sighing and deciding to apologize to make his cousin's life a bit easier. Heaven was becoming upset and Imran knew Hamid would never allow that. Besides, he really liked Heaven.

"Heaven, please forgive me if I offended you. It was not my intent. This is your home and I will respect your husband's wishes." He then turned his head slightly to the left and spoke again to Fatima. "Fatima, will you walk outside with me so that we may continue our conversation in private?" He almost laughed aloud at the look on Tanya's face. Had she thought all the Ahmed men could be so easily tamed by American women? He couldn't help grinning as he glanced over his shoulder and saw the challenge in Tanya's eyes and the tiny smile gracing her lips. A tiny flutter in his chest drew his attention away and he continued walking out the door with Fatima.

❧

"Don't start with me, Heaven. I did nothing wrong. All I did was go to him and say hi. That's it. He then took it upon himself to insult me."

"I didn't hear an insult," Heaven defended Imran.

"Oh it was there, it may have been veiled but it was there. Didn't you hear him say, 'I'm not one of the millionaire sons?'" Tanya did an imitation of Imran her hand on her hips twisting her body. She continued until both Heaven and Hamid were laughing. When they stopped abruptly they didn't have to tell her Imran was behind her. She groaned and turned to face him.

"Sorry," she said then turned away.

"Don't be sorry, Tanya, I find you very amusing. At first glance I had thought you ill, maybe having a fit or something but with Hamid being a doctor and Heaven being a nurse and seeing the two of them laughing I then assumed you were trying to look as though you were having an attack." He smiled and walked away.

Round one to the cousin, Tanya thought, then remembered the comment he'd made before he went out the door. No, he had two rounds. She had no intentions of allowing him to win a third. She glared at his back and couldn't prevent her eyes from sliding down to observe the way his rear end looked in the jean. What was it about the Ahmed men and black jeans? She didn't know but she was sure glad they wore them. Heck she didn't have to like the guy in order to appreciate his fine male form

For an hour or so both Tanya and Imran behaved as they sat in the foyer bantering lightly back and forth. Every time Imran looked in her direction or spoke, she felt a tingle in her southern region. She couldn't put her finger on it. Oh wait, she could. The man was fine with a capital F and he'd had the ability to put her in his place. That was a gift. Not many people got the better of her. In fact she went out of the way most times to ensure that she wasn't beaten in the word game. It was always, 'get them before they get you.'

From time to time she saw the smirk on Imran's face when he looked at her. He was sizing her. Out of the blue it hit her and Tanya blinked. He wasn't sizing her up he thought he already knew what she was about. She cringed, narrowed her eyes and glared at him and he laughed at her. Laughed. How dare he? No man had ever laughed at her. When the look in his eyes softened and he stood she wondered what had happened to change him. Her eyes quickly went in the direction he was staring. Hamid and his son. Imran wanted kids. Like dominoes, things began to fall into place. Evidently he wasn't married or if he was he didn't have any kids.

"Let me hold him," Imran said reaching for the baby and cradling him in his arms as Hamid stood close to him beaming.

For a long moment Tanya stared at the men. She'd never seen men look at a baby the way these two were doing. Yes, she'd seen them look at their sons with love, but this was something different. This looked close to adoration, downright worship. Tanya glanced toward Heaven and back toward the men, finally getting what Heaven had meant when she'd said she'd given her son the name Hamid wanted because of the look he'd given her. Tanya didn't blame her one little bit. No wonder, 'feisty, fight with anyone Heaven' was acting all soft and giddy. Damn, Heaven was truly in love.

The knowledge hit her in the chest and she heaved a soft sigh, wondering if she'd ever have that kind of love, wondering if she should just forget her plan to charm the pants off on one of Hamid's brother and marry him. Maybe she'd admit it was a bit more than materialistic. She'd even admit to being jealous. Who wouldn't be? After being married to Hamid for almost two years, Heaven had found out he was a frigging millionaire. She'd given up everything to follow him and live in Pakistan because she wanted him to be happy. Shortly after they'd returned to Pakistan Hamid had given her the news that they were almost as rich as God. None of that seemed to impress Heaven. She was more concerned with her husband getting the gleam back in his eyes that she'd said he'd lost.

Well, Tanya wasn't after putting the gleam in a man's eyes. Sure it would be nice to have a man look at her the way Hamid was always looking at Heaven. Heck it would be super fantastic to have a man look at her the way the two men were looking at the baby. But since Heaven had told all of them that Hamid had some equally fine unmarried brothers Tanya had made plans to snag one of them. She looked again at the two men and the baby and sighed. *But finding love would also be nice.*

"Hey, Hamid, what's the deal? Why did you give Tasukam to Imran to hold and I had to wrestle him from you?" Before Hamid could answer, Imran turned with the baby in his arms toward her.

"Perhaps he allows me to hold his son because I can properly say his name. The baby's name is not 'Tasukam' it's 'Tsukama.' A name is important to us, Tanya, learning it and saying it correctly is a sign of respect. I'm sure when you begin to show Heaven's and Hamid's baby the proper amount of respect, they will allow you to hold him."

Tanya actually had no words to say, no come back. She was speechless. She looked to Heaven for help but she merely shrugged. She then glanced toward Hamid who grinned liked a fool.

So this was how her friends were going to play it huh? "I can say the baby's name," she said, defending herself.

"So you deliberately mispronounced his name?" Imran tsked and tilted his head to peer at her. "And you called me rude." Then he turned his back to her and continued cooing to the baby. Imran had to turn quickly from Tanya. There was something about the woman that made him unsettled, had him wanting to kiss her full lips, to wrap her in his arms, to make love to her. He'd had to shake the image away. He was nothing like his cousin. He was not about to allow this American woman to steal his heart. But he could swear when he looked into her eyes, his heart was definitely what was in danger.

What the heck was wrong with him? No one had ever had this

effect on him. He'd never been this rude to anyone and he knew it wasn't all in defense of his cousins. They were adults well able to take care of themselves. If he were honest and he had no choice but to be honest with himself he'd have to admit that it had something to do with Tanya. From the moment he'd entered the house and she'd walked up to him his heart had beat a little faster. If she'd not been so obvious in her greeting that it was one of his cousins that her warmth was for, he'd more than likely be trying to figure out a way to ask her for a date. But she had wanted the cousins and Imran wasn't anyone's second choice. He could never compete with his cousins on a financial level—at least not yet. He had yet to make his own fortune and he was still hopeful that he would. No, if Tanya was to notice something different about him that set him apart from the millionaire brothers it was this. He'd seen it in her eyes. She enjoyed the verbal repartee and he had every intention of seeing that she continued enjoyed it. He gave her a smirk and smiled down at Tsukama.

Tanya saw Imran's smirk. Round three had now been lost and the man had turned his back on her. She had to be tired. That was it. Her game wasn't as sharp as it should be. She put her hands on her hips and gave a deep neck roll before realizing with his back turned to her Imran was missing it all. She wasn't wasting her annoyance on Heaven who was almost laughing at her. Marching up to Imran she was determined to put him in his place. When she stood in front of him she held out her arms. "Give me the baby."

"He's not yours," Imran said.

"He's not yours either."

"You don' show him the proper respect."

"He's a baby," Tanya fumed

"Precisely. Show him that respect and show him the respect of being Hamid's son."

"Well, he's Heaven's son also," Tanya bragged and pointed toward Heaven, hoping to have Heaven back her up but all she got was Heaven bending over with laughter. "Give me my friend's baby."

"The baby belongs to my cousin. I am the child's blood. I have more right than you to hold him. Besides, you don't look as if you've ever held a baby. Perhaps, you don't like children. What if you allow him to fall?"

Don't like children! Don't know how to hold a baby. Tanya was getting angry for real now. The entire reason, well, almost the

entire reason she was in Pakistan was because she did love
children. She did know how to hold a baby. Jo Jo could vouch for
that. Her hands went immediately to her hips and she was
sputtering trying to get her words out. The man had her
practically speechless for the second time, something that never
happened to her.

"Time out." Heaven said moving to stand between the two of
them and took her son from Imran. "My son is not in this fight.
He's too young for your squabbling." Laughing at the two of
them she and Hamid disappeared toward their bedroom with
Fatima following and laughing loudly.

"Why are you judging me?" Tanya asked. "I've been in this
country just a few hours and both you and Fatima have treated
me rudely."

Imran frowned at her. "From my vantage point it is you who
have been rude since arriving. You are in my country yet you
have been rude to my country, to my cousin Fatima, to Heaven
and Hamid, to the baby and even to me. I have not attempted to
judge you but if you see something of your bad behavior reflected
in my own and wish to make a change then I am happy to have
been of service."

"You're an arrogant piece of work aren't you? How do you
know that I did all of that?"

"Fatima called me."

Ahhh now Tanya knew why he'd behaved the way he had
when he'd come into the room. "So Fatima told you what I said
about wanting to meet one of her brothers?"

"Wanting to marry one of them."

"Okay, so what? I said it. What's wrong with that?"

"That's not the way we do things."

"You use matchmakers here. Heaven told me."

"You're not a matchmaker. Besides, you can not make a match
for yourself."

"Who said? Are there rules?"

Imran didn't want to but he was finding that he liked the
verbal fighting with the American. He liked American women, he
looked at Tanya and grinned. And he really loved beautiful
American women. That Tanya was without a doubt. But she was
still a greedy American woman who didn't like babies all that
much and didn't think before she spoke. It would be rather nice
to teach this American a lesson in manners. Maybe he'd find the
location of one of the many minefields being planted and take her
there and not bring her out until she could correctly pronounce

the baby's name. Though he had to admit she'd almost gotten it correctly that last time she'd tried.

"There are rules in everything," Imran said at last. "There are rules in the way a man takes a wife. Rule one; a woman does not come and stake a claim."

"Look, I have no plans to hit your cousins over the head and take them back to America. It worked for Heaven and Hamid," she shrugged. "Why can't fate be on my side?"

"But you're trying to navigate fate. You have no idea if you will even approve of my cousins. You want to marry them because they are wealthy. They are much older than Hamid. They are wise and will not be fooled by you or your antics. Besides that, Fatima will warn them. How do you plan to accomplish getting one of them to want to marry you?"

"They can come and live in America."

Imran burst out laughing. "Are you offering citizenship in exchange for millions? They don't need you, Tanya. We can come to America and live legally. What else do you have?"

"I'm a woman," Tanya glared at him and tried her best not to flinch while Imran took a couple of steps back and appraised her, smiling and frowning when he looked at her chest. She took it until his frown deepened.

"Why are you frowning at me?"

"How old are you?"

Tanya coughed as her eyes widened in surprise. "Excuse me?"

"Your age, how old are you?"

"Why?"

"You are getting on in years. Your breasts appear to be firm. That indicates you've not yet suckled a child. Is that why you do not know babies should be respected?"

"My breasts? Babies?" She was muttering. "You're crazy, Imran, and I'm too tired to fight with you right now."

"Would you like for me to return tomorrow and continue this?"

There was a twinkle in his eyes but he wasn't smiling. Tanya wondered if he was serious. If he was she was definitely going to take him up on this. She hadn't expected the fight to go more than three rounds now it looked like it would be at least a ten round match. So far she'd not won a single one and that wasn't going to continue. But right now she needed some rest.

"You know what, Imran, I would love for you to come back tomorrow. But right now I have to take a long bubble bath," she said slowly and gave him a look and watched as he swallowed.

Bingo, she thought, score one point for the American. "Let's continue this tomorrow." She walked quickly toward the room that would be hers for the remainder of her stay. She almost ran not wanting Imran to take a parting shot and take away her small victory.

Imran laughed and shook his head. "Then tomorrow it shall be." Once again the flutter filled his chest and he looked downward, then at Tanya's retreating back. He liked her.

&

Imran turned from clearing away the dishes as Hamid and Heaven came back into the room. "Your friend went to bed," he said.

"Who won?" Heaven asked.

Imran smiled but didn't answer for a moment. Then he said, "There was no contest."

"Ha. You two sounded like it to us," Heaven pointed out. "Could it be fate is once again working in the Ahmed family?"

"I have no such belief in fate and I have no intention of doing anything to get your friend to notice me. Besides, your friend is here looking for a millionaire. That I am not. Could you please tell me why that would matter so much to her?"

"Tanya's not as bad as she appears. She's rough around the edges but she's a good person. She's a social worker and she always wants to find a way to take care of the children she works with. She's always saying if she had the money she would build homes and put loving parent in them to take care of the children. She's even working with a private organization in one of the Chicago suburbs to do just that. They have actually already purchased land for a village and they've built one home. They're trying to raise money to build and fund the other homes and to take care of the families.

"So she's not a gold digger?"

"No, she's not. She doesn't want the money for herself. From the moment she found out Hamid had money she's been hitting us up for donations for some of the children in foster care."

"But she doesn't even like children, she doesn't like your son."

"Please, she's fronting." Heaven flicked her hand in a dismissive fashion.

"Pardon?"

"Acting, pretending," Heaven explained. "She loves kids. She just has to play it hard you know. She doesn't remain in the kids lives that she helps so she can't become attached. As for my baby

I know all of my friends were a little hurt that I didn't name one of them as godparent. We haven't talked about it but I'm sure she's trying to pay me back for that."

"Are you sure she really likes your son?"

"I'm sure." Heaven paused and tilted her head to peer at Imran. "Why are you so worried that Tanya likes kids? Is fate talking to you?"

Imran looked over Heaven's head a very easy thing to do and grinned at Hamid. "Don't play matchmaker, Heaven. Your friend is not my type and for that matter neither is she my cousins' type. She will go home disappointed, I'm afraid."

"But at least she can have a nice time while in Pakistan. She loves to party and frankly you're the party animal. Hamid and I rarely leave the house so we're a little out of touch." Heaven gave Hamid a sly glance then turned all of her charm on Imran. "I just thought of a great idea. This would be perfect. Imran, would you do me the biggest favor, please? I'll be indebted to you. Would you help us entertain Tanya? She really wants to learn about the culture. You would be the perfect person to accompany here while she's here."

"She didn't come to visit me, Heaven."

"No, but she came to visit your country. You're a part of the country, don't you want her to think well of the people of Pakistan?"

"I'm not an ambassador for Pakistan," Imran laughed.

"But you could be an ambassador for the family," Heaven insisted as she turned pleading eyes on Imran.

"Hamid said you were lonely for your American friends, that you wanted the company now it seems as if you're not so happy to see her. Is that it," he teased. "Your friend has already worn out her welcome and now you want to throw her to me?"

An indignant grunt came out of Heaven and she glared at Imran. "Of course I'm not tired of Tanya. I just want her to have some fun while she's here and I know just hanging around us," she pointed her finger at Hamid then herself, "is not going to be all that much fun." She shrugged. "If you don't want to help me…"

Imran wasn't fooled by Heaven's act of having hurt feelings. He was very much aware of her scheme to set him up with her friend and truthfully he wasn't averse to spending time with Tanya while she was in Pakistan. There was just one little problem. Well, not so little, the problem was 5' 9" and had a mind of her own and her mind wanted a rich man. Sighing Imran leaned back into the chair and cradled the back of his head in his hands.

"Heaven, you're aware that I would do anything for you. Your friend came to this country seeking a rich husband. Even if her reasons are honorable I am not who she's seeking and your hopes for that to change will not make it so. I'm a writer. I have no money."

"That may be true but you're an excellent tour guide. Even Hamid has never heard of many of the places you've taken us to. You've done so much research you're better than the guides who get paid to take tourist around. We both know that it's true, so don't deny it. What better person to show her around Pakistan?"

Imran didn't miss the way Heaven's eyes took on a mysterious glint. She was plotting a relationship between him and her friend. Tanya would go home single. He wasn't even in the running and he was going to make sure that his cousins wouldn't fall for the woman's manipulating ways. A smiled struggled to come out but Imran prevent it. At least Tanya was honest. He'd have to give that to her. The smile he'd resisted came out. Tomorrow he would come back and resume their fight.

"Imran, you didn't answer my question. Will you help us show Tanya the country?"

"I'll think about it, Heaven, but for now I think it's time to say goodnight." He walked away toward the nursery as was his habit and leaned over the crib. He rubbed the baby's head asking for Allah's blessing on the child. With a sigh of longing at last he walked out and said goodnight to Heaven and Hamid ignoring the way they were both smiling at him. "Come, Fatima, I'll take you home."

◈

"Heaven, Imran's aware of what you're trying to do. You may as well give it you your little scheme isn't going to work.

Heaven turned from the door a grin on her face she shook her head at Hamid's telling her no. "What? I'm not doing anything."

"Except trying too hard to match Tanya and Imran."

"I didn't do anything."

"You gave Imran Tanya's bio. You never told me about Tanya's desire to help build a community for orphans."

"I told you every time she asked for a donation. I never sent her money without asking you and telling you what she wanted it for."

Hamid shrugged. "I can't say that I remember all of those

conversations. I do remember you kissing me while asking and we both know that when you kiss me I can deny you nothing."

For the moment Heaven was soothed as she moved into her husband's arms. She wrapped her arms around his neck and whispered in his ear. "Wouldn't it be wonderful though if Tanya and Imran fell in love? You'll have to admit there was a spark there. How many times have you seen Tanya speechless. This six weeks is going to be fun."

"I hope so. Tanya already has Fatima upset with her. You do know that she's the one that called Imran over here. From what Imran said I gather he plans to make sure that Tanya will not get one of my brothers to fall in love with her."

Heaven couldn't help laughing. She doubled over shaking her head as she did so. "Your sister should have been an actress."

"Heaven, tell me you didn't ask Fatima to help you in your crazy scheme," Hamid scolded.

"All I did was get Imran over here before Tanya has a chance to meet your brothers. There's nothing wrong with that." She nibbled her husband's lips as she ran her hands down the side of his thighs. "For now let's not worry about Tanya and Imran. I think we can find better ways to spend our time." When the look in Hamid's eyes changed to lust Heaven smiled and reached for her husband's hand. For now she could leave the matter. The seed had been planted.

4

THE SUNLIGHT STREAMING THROUGH the windows woke Tanya. She stayed in bed for a moment to adjust to the sounds of the household to see if she could smell breakfast cooling she was hungry. Opening her bag she dumped the gifts for the baby on the bed grabbed for clean clothes and rushed into the bathroom to shower and get ready for her first full day in Pakistan. She hoped Imran kept his word. She'd dreamt of him the night before. As she lathered her skin and rinsed off the suds she shivered as she remembered the feels of Imran's fingers on her body. It was only a dream she tried to remind herself and a dream more than likely brought on because she'd been tired had enjoyed fighting with him and dare she think it, yes, she'd lost to him on her own turf and she very much wanted to rectify that.

Dressed and ready to face anything Tanya reached for the stack of gaily wrapped gifts and carried them out of the room. She took in a deep breath. That was coffee she'd smelled. Thank God, she thought, she needed her caffeine.

"Good morning, Tanya."

The deep sexy voice snuck up on her, startling her, making her jump, dropping the presents in the process. When she bent to pick them up, Imran was already on his knees retrieving the packages. Reaching out at the same moment for the last wrapped box, they both stopped their fingers inches apart. Their eyes connected and they both smiled.

"What do you think would happen if we touch?" Imran asked.

"I don't know, but I'm wondering if I want to take a chance on that right now." Tanya's eyes were focused on his lips, they were slightly parted, moist, and looked so kissable and dang it all, she wanted to kiss him. She didn't know the man but she sure wanted to kiss him. She found her body swaying moving toward him. *What the heck*, she wondered.

Imran moved barely an inch in Tanya's direction their lips nearly touching. He searched her eyes and found confusion. He could feel the heat from her body her unpainted parted lips begged to be kissed to be suckled. She was a stranger he couldn't do that, it wasn't proper. What if Heaven or Hamid walked in right now? What of Fatima? Still he didn't move. He wanted to touch her see if her skin was as soft as it looked. His glance fell on the base of her throat at the tiny flutter he found there. She was afraid. He brought his eyes back to meet hers wondering what it was she was afraid of. He didn't want her to be afraid of him.

"Are you afraid of me that I would take advantage of you if fate were involved and gave us a jolt?" He grinned. "Or are you worried that the jolt would be so strong that it would waylay you from your plans of marrying a rich man?"

"You really are annoying, Imran."

"But correct," he said grasping her hand in his own. "See, no electrical charge, no sign that fate has brought us together. You're free to do whatever it is you came to Pakistan to do. You're free to try and pursue one of the cousins." He rose bringing her gently up with his movement. "But be warned, Tanya, I have every plan to prevent you from being successful with my cousins. So I do hope your tricks are many for we've been well trained to the ways of women by some of the best courtesans in the world." He laughed at her surprised look. "Maybe while you're here you'll allow me to show you where they plied their trade. Just in case you're interested."

Oh hell no! He didn't just call her a prostitute. "Imran, you had better tell me and tell me quickly that you didn't mean what I think you meant by that remark."

"What do you think I meant?"

"That I'm here to sell myself and you want to show me a place where I can do it."

Imran shrugged. "If you're here with the intent that you stated then yes that was what I meant." He saw anger burning in her eyes but he saw sadness also and softened his reproach. He had pushed her too far. "Heaven asked me to show you around the country. I'm a writer and I've done extensive research on my country. If you'd like I can show you things you'd never see with Heaven and Hamid as your tour guides."

"Like this place you think I belong?"

He held her gaze staring deeply into her brown eyes. "Now there you have me wrong. I do not think you belong there. I think you dishonor yourself with your plans but some part of me admires you and believe your plans are honorable."

"That's a contradiction."

"I'm filled with contradictions." He looked down as their hands still joined, "and so are you," he said. "By the way I felt the tremble when we touched. It wasn't a jolt of electricity but there was the tremble. Do I make you nervous?"

"A bit but I felt your hand shake also, just barely but I still felt it." Tanya dropped her hand. "So are you here to fight with me today?"

"As I promised."

"You went for the jugular." Tanya hesitated and bit on her lips, she rather liked the way Imran was gazing at her, the warmth of his eyes making her feel soft and feminine. But he'd also made her feel trashy. She didn't want him to think she was some kind of loose unmoral woman who'd jump into bed with any man for the right price. She nearly groaned aloud. Was that how she'd sounded like last night? No wonder Imran was insulting her as he was.

"I don't have sex for money, Imran."

He lifted a brow but did not speak.

"I don't. I'm not going to lie to you about who I am. But I don't have sex for money."

"If you marry a man for his money then you would be having sex for money."

"I would be married."

"I don't see the difference."

"I haven't done it yet."

"Then maybe you should rethink your plans. I don't think you'll be able to handle the results. You don't like the comparisons that I've made and we're here alone in this room. I've not shouted the words at you or said them in anger yet they hurt you." He stared hard at her. "I know of your dreams, Tanya. But you will kill your soul if you pursue it. Then what use will a fulfilled soulless dream be?"

"You don't know what you're talking about, Imran. I didn't come to sell myself. I came to fall in love," she ignored his raised brow and his smirk. "I came to see if one of Hamid's brothers would fall in love with me. I'll admit to that," she said softly not liking the bitter taste in her mouth. "I don't see what's wrong with that. You said you know of my dreams. If you did you wouldn't continue looking at me like that."

"I'm sorry if my looking at you makes you uncomfortable. If I'm staring at you it's because I find you interesting," he stopped, his lips curved into a smile. "You're a brave, woman. You're honest with others but not yourself. I believe you want love as much as you want to give a stable home to these wards of your. You're afraid to admit it because you believe it will make you appear weak. Could it be possible that you'd feel guilty for having love when those you want to help need so much of you? You come to Pakistan and behave badly in case the people here don't like you. You play it tough to insulate yourself from the world. Hamid told me that Heaven had done much the same thing. I suppose that as a woman you feel the need to do this. Maybe it's as an American woman."

"How do you think you know so much about me? You only met me last night. We fought I wasn't at my best and now this morning we're fighting again. You don't know me, Imran, how do you think you can judge me?"

"Judging?" he stopped and cocked his head. *Was that what I was doing?* He shook his head as though to clear it of something. "I'm sorry if that's what you thought I was doing. I was merely pointing out my observations. Remember, I told you I'm a writer. That's what we writers do. We observe, we study humans and we write about it. You speak volumes without talking. It's all there in your eyes. I see your pain, your anger, your sadness and your need for love, your great need for love," he said softly. "Someone has hurt you deeply. Perhaps you'll tell me of it. I'd like for us to be friends."

"I thought you came to continue the fighting."

"Not today," he laughed. "No, today I'd enjoy learning more about you, about the children that you care for. I want to observe you with my cousin's child and see which is the real you, the gold digging American or the concerned social worker." He gave one last smile and walked toward the kitchen.

"Wait up," Tanya yelled. This wasn't going well at all. How the heck did he think he was going to just put her on trial? And who did he think he was to say it or to intend to do it? She didn't give a darn what he thought. Imran stopped walking so abruptly that she walked into his back and her stomach clenched. She moaned softly as her body came in contact with his. A moment of burning hell fire heat zapped her right in her private area and she had to stumble back. She fought off a breath and coughed to cover up her frustration. If she'd had even water to drink she'd swear she was drugged. That was how she was feeling—disoriented and hot, very hot. Her eyes met Imran's and for a long moment they stared. She was too close to him everything about him screamed out masculine overpowering male. He smiled slowly making her breath catch in her throat. When she saw him swallow she went weak. What the hell?

Coffee, Imran repeated the word over and over to himself. Heaven and Hamid had asked him if he'd make coffee for Tanya and then bring her to their clinic. What they hadn't asked him to do was to stand there and devour her with his eyes. Maybe it was the conversation he'd had a moment ago with Tanya about fate and feeling a jolt when he touched her that was almost making his toes curl now. He wasn't sure but he was sure that he wasn't standing as close to her as he wanted. He could feel the heat from her body, he could smell the tantalizing scent of pure woman mixed with some kind of fragrance she'd used in her bath.

The ever increasing tightening in his groin became almost unbearable as he remembered how he'd heard her running her shower and an image of her naked, wet and luscious came to him, an image that he'd not bothered to erase. And now as he stood so close to her that the image returned and he could now count the lashes in her eyelids as they fanned her soft skin he was fighting a shudder of desire pure and simple. As much as he shouldn't as much as everything that was right and sane in his world was screaming at him that it would be wrong there was something in her that called to a primal part in him, his erection jerked, a *very primal part*.

He'd touched her hand when he'd lifted her up now he wanted to caress a finger down the side of her face, slip his hand into the tight jeans she was wearing cup her round buttocks that looked so luscious and he wanted to kiss her full and sensuous lips. He was praying she didn't look down right now. He shouldn't be having a massive erection but he had one anyway. It was the hardest thing he'd ever done when he tore his eyes away from her chest as she'd shuddered and drew in a breath. No woman had ever dared to show that honest of a reaction to him before, it was heady stuff, no wonder his cousins loved so many women. He stared into Tanya's deep brown eyes nearly groaning as she absentmindedly swiped her lips with her tongue. What was he thinking of? His cousins would fall all over themselves to bed Tanya.

That thought stopped the smile and the erection. He'd have to double his efforts to make sure his cousins weren't interested in Tanya. It would be for their own good he tried to assure himself. Then she gave him a lopsided grin and the now ever present flutter filled his chest. By all rights he shouldn't want this woman. She smiled more fully, but he did. She was so wrong for him, loud, rude, he pulled himself up and moved back from her to peer at her horribly long blue painted nails again. *Tacky*, he thought, not at all what he wanted. His image of the woman he wanted had been firmly planted in his mind for years. Quiet, that was the main thing. He didn't want to bicker with a woman the way Hamid did with Heaven, he didn't have time for that. He was a writer. He needed things to be quiet. He needed a woman who wouldn't require much attention and he definitely didn't need a woman he'd have to keep under lock and key to keep her from tempting any that came in contact with her. He'd no doubt have to do that with Tanya. He shook his head slightly, this was crazy. *Coffee*, he thought again, *get the coffee.*

"Coffee?"

"Excuse me?"

Her breathy whisper went all through him and caused him to shiver in want. He cleared his throat. "Tanya, Heaven and Hamid asked if I would stay until you woke and make coffee for you." He headed for the kitchen, "Heaven said to tell you she's sorry but she'd promised Hamid she would go in and help him out today. I'm to take you there as soon as you're ready."

Tanya's eyes widened as she realized that she and Imran were home alone. Panic rushed in suddenly. "Are you telling me that Heaven got me to Pakistan and dumped me and left me in bed sleeping, and left a strange man in here? She could have had the decency to wake me and tell me that." Her voice went shrill and she moved a step away.

A flash of annoyance crossed Imran's face and she saw a twitch along his jaw line. As he poured the coffee he didn't speak, neither did he speak as he laid out dates, sweets, an assortment of bread and rolls, butter and jam. His annoyance seemed to kick up a notch when he went to the stove and poured boiling water from a pan into a sieve spilling boiled eggs. "This crazy woman is rubbing off on me and is making me crazy," he nearly grunted, talking aloud to himself.

When he'd placed the eggs in a bowl and carried them to the

table he sat the bowl down. "Eat," he ordered.

"I would have preferred my eggs scrambled or maybe even an omelet if you'd bothered to ask." Tanya stared at Imran then at the bowl of boiled eggs.

Imran decided it was time to confront the issue head on. Of course he wanted to spend time with the beautiful but rude woman, what man in his right mind wouldn't enjoy admiring her beauty? But her acid tongue...now there was a problem. Instead of thanking him for breakfast she was complaining that he was there. He sucked in a breath.

"I was here to do a favor for Heaven. I have done as she asked and more. I prepared breakfast for you, but since you prefer to be alone I'll leave." He started for the door his steps quick and sure.

Snap out of it, Tanya commanded her body. She turned watching him walk toward the door knowing she didn't want him to leave. She knew she had to say something quickly. "Imran..." she called and her voice faltered. It was his voice it had done something to her. She had to fight to concentrate "Imran, wait, listen. I'm sorry," Tanya said.

He turned toward her leveling her with a look. "Did you want me to stay or go, Tanya? It's your choice. I have a ton of other things I could be doing."

While he stared at her Tanya had to catch the back of the chair for support. *Oh God*, she thought as the deep musical sound of Imran's voice played over her spine. She'd swear she could...she could...

"Well, Tanya, which will it be?"

"Drop the attitude and stay if you want. Either way I don't really care." *Liar.* She brought the coffee mug to her lips and took a sip. "Thanks for the coffee. It's really good." She turned back toward the spread Imran had laid out and gobbled one sweet roll. By the time she had finished her second one Imran was handing her a peeled egg and was once again smiling at her.

"I see you were hungry," he said with a slight smirk.

"Famished," she answered, reaching for the egg. The tips of their fingers touched and zap, like that Tanya knew what had just happened. Fate was trying to intervene in her life and mess up her plans. Besides wanting a gorgeous hunk that made her shiver just by the sound of his voice she wanted a man with more driven than Imran, one more like she was. She wanted a man who believed in her dreams and who could understand the dreams would take up top priority. She did not want a teacher slash struggling writer. What the heck did she need with a man she'd have to no doubt end up supporting? And she was not into that. She bit into the egg. "Imran, are you sure you're not rich?" she asked as he peeled a second egg for her and placed it on her plate.

"No, I'm not." He smiled and sipped his coffee. *But my father is*, he thought but didn't say. "Would that make a difference?" She didn't answer only gave him a tiny smile. But she didn't have to answer. He knew it would and didn't like it. He didn't want a woman who wanted only the gold in his pockets. He wanted a woman who wanted to struggle with him, to know that his dreams were important and would come first. He wanted a woman who wasn't so driven to succeed but one who could enjoy the simpler things of life.

❦

Tanya walked around Hamid's office looking in wonder at the sentimental objects Hamid had built into a shrine. She smiled at the movie theater ticket stubs, a menu, a playbill and other worthless trinkets and laughed. She remembered Heaven's complaints about constantly misplacing things. Looks like she'd found where they were. An unwanted ping of jealousy zapped unexpectedly at Tanya making her wonder if anyone would ever love her the way Hamid loved Heaven. For all her big talk she wanted that kind of love and to love a man that way. She wanted to be school girl goofy the way Heaven was. She glanced at Heaven and watched her for a moment while her friend's eyes sought out her husband. She saw them smile at each other and they both went all soft and mushy. For a second Tanya wondered if that was how it started for her friend. If she'd been all hot and bothered when Hamid looked at her. As a smile curved Heaven's lips, Tanya had her answer. Hamid still made Heaven hot and bothered. Then she glanced over Heaven's head and her gaze landed on Imran who was watching her with a very curious look on his face.

"I like your office, Hamid. But still I'm wondering why Heaven would have to help you when she had my visit planned for weeks. It was kind of rude, don't you think, to just leave me in your house alone with a man I just met? How did you know that he wouldn't take advantage of me, or that I wouldn't take advantage of him? That was so not cool, Heaven." She was putting a bit more mean into her words than she felt because frankly it was bothering her how Imran was watching her and it was bothering her even more about the reaction she was having to him. He was ruining all of her plans. If he were one of Hamid's brothers or even rich she'd stop her search but he wasn't. And besides having the ability to make her hot and being able to go toe to toe with her, he seemed darn boring. She turned her back toward Imran wanting to block him from her line of vision. "Well, Heaven? Is this how my entire vacation is going to be?"

"Hamid needed to be at the clinic early and you were sleeping so soundly I didn't want to wake you and I didn't want to leave you alone. So I called Imran. I was looking out for you."

There it was again. Tanya hadn't imagined it. Heaven and Hamid were giving each other looks. Then it hit her like a lead pipe. *I have one of Hamid's cousins who would be perfect for you...oh no she didn't.* She was being set up, so not cool. Okay, if that was the way the two of them wanted to play it, she'd just call them on it right here, right now, right in front of Imran. It would be good to let everyone get their cards on the table.

"Imran, have you realized yet that these two are playing matchmakers?" She put her hands on her hips. "What do you think about that?"

"I like it," Imran grinned.

Now she was taken aback. What the heck? "Don't play with me, Imran. You don't like me. You said I'm rude and a gold digger."

"And you are. But I find it ironic that you traveled all the way here to Pakistan to find yourself a millionaire husband and your friend has plotted to set you up with the one member of the family that everyone consider a failure."

"Imran, cut it out. No one considers you a failure. Teaching is an honorable profession," Hamid defended his cousin's career choice

"And the writing?" Imran stopped teasing Tanya to look at Hamid. "What about that? You were there when my father practically disowned me for wanting to write." He shrugged and looked toward Tanya then back to Hamid. "He doesn't think I'm a man." Imran shrugged again. "He thinks writing is demeaning and not so manly," he shook his head. "It doesn't matter how many well known authors I point out to him who are married." Imran's voice went soft and for a moment he didn't speak. "You wouldn't say all of that makes me the family failure?" he asked Hamid quietly.

For a long moment Hamid and Imran stared hard at each other both communicating silently. Then Hamid sighed heavily and spoke. "Parents are sometimes very foolish. You know that. Your father loves you and is angry that you won't come into the business with him." Hamid paused and glanced toward Tanya deciding not to talk of family business in front of her.

Hamid's discretion wasn't lost on Imran. Family matters were never discussed in front of strangers. He also glanced at Tanya. There was something about the way that she was looking at him that made him want her to know all about him and his family, to know that he was the shame of the family. He didn't want her to have any wrong perceptions of his place in the family. She might as well know that he was going to continue his pursuit of his dream. "Of course my father worries. He worries that I'm being as foolish as he had been. He wishes that had he followed your father's advice sooner. He would also be a millionaire and I would be one of the millionaire cousins. I do not care about money, Hamid, nor do I care what the family thinks. Look at you. Look at Sassa, neither of you did what the family wanted." He glanced toward Heaven. "Yet you're happy. I'm happy as well."

For a long moment Hamid and Imran merely stared at each other talking in the secret way of men and of family. Hamid's hand slid around Heaven's waist and he pulled her close. He placed a kiss on her forehead quieting her worries. "No power on earth could have kept me from marrying Heaven. Besides, the entire family loves her now. Family eventually comes around, Imran. They loved me and wanted me happy. The family also loves you and wants your happiness no matter what path that might take."

"You hold the position of favored son, Hamid, even if you disappoint that will still be your position and you have brothers who will be able to redeem the family name. I on the other hand have the position of only son. My father wants great things from me. He wants me to make up for the mistakes that he made." Imran gave a brittle laugh.

"If uncle truly thought that, he would not have bought you a home and furnished it. He would not make sure that a woman comes in to clean and cook.

Imran shrugged again. "Those things he does so that the community does not say his only son lives as a beggar." Imran grinned. "Who cares?" he rolled his eyes. "I am an adult and I will do what pleases me. My father's displeasure will not prevent me from pursuing my goals. If I fail, it is still my life, my decision. If my father wishes to disown me then he will have no son and I will have no father. But I will still do what I want." He glanced away from Hamid and his gaze connected with Tanya's. Her soft brown eyes looked a bit misty. She was smiling softly a hint of pity in her eyes. He'd said maybe a little too much. As he stared, her look of pity became more pronounced.

"Stop being so melodramatic," Hamid spoke up, glaring at Imran. "Uncle has no such plans and neither does any other member of the family. You're a writer and you're imagining things, trying to make a story where there is none. As for uncle thinking you're not a man. Please. He does that because he wants grandsons." He stared across the room at his son then back at Imran. "They all want grandsons, the next generation."

There was nothing in Imran's future plans that even hinted that babies were in his near future. But he did want them. His gaze slid over to where Tsukama slept and he acknowledged that desire. Glancing up he found Tanya's gaze had remained on him. This time it made him a little uncomfortable. She was looking at him as if ….as if she thought… He wondered if she was thinking he really didn't like women. He narrowed his eyes, not like women. He'd have to stop that nonsense immediately. Hamid was right. He'd been a little melodramatic.

"Tanya," he began making it clear that she was the one he wanted to understand what he was about to say. "My father is wrong about many things and he's most assuredly wrong about my not being a man who wishes to one day marry and have beautiful babies." When she grinned he grinned also. "I love women," he said in an almost whisper.

"I know," Tanya teased him back, "just not greedy Americans."

"I might make an exception if it were a truly beautiful American woman," he held her gaze.

"I do understand about parents not supporting your dreams not because they don't love you but because they think you're choosing a path that will be hard." She tried unsuccessfully to prevent the sigh that escaped. My parents don't like the idea that I've made a promise to someone they think if I have to keep that promise I won't have a family of my own. They don't think I should put so much time and money into trying to help build the community. But they're my dreams and I have a right to go after them like you have every right to go after yours. I admire you for trying no matter what your family thinks. Dreams are what makes us who we are, they're important. Your dreams are important, Imran. I hope they come true. Have you at least received a sign that things might go well for you?"

"I think I just did," Imran gave her a full grin,

"I meant your book."

"Oh," Imran grin widened even more. "In that case it's not

book but books. I have two out with publishers and I'm working on the third. I'm thinking maybe I should add a bit of romance to this one. What do you think, Tanya?"

"Okay," Tanya finally tore her eyes from Imran. "It's getting hot in here," she said fanning herself. Then she turned to Heaven. "Come-on, now pick up the baby and lets go do something." Heaven made one step toward the crib when Hamid stopped her.

"Tanya, I know Heaven and I are being rude but could you please allow Imran to escort you to lunch today? My treat," he glanced at Imran, "that is if you don't have things to do. I'm swamped with paper work and if Heaven could just help me for a few hours, we'll be free for the rest of the week. I promise."

Tanya looked to where the baby was napping in the crib in Hamid's office and she laughed. "This is bogus. Heaven, you did not come to the clinic to work, not with the baby. Now come on and bring your behind home. Nice try. Thanks, Imran." She went to the crib to pick up the baby and Imran stopped her. "Not again," she said.

"Tanya, I really don't mind taking you to lunch. Besides, the baby is asleep and should not be disturbed. Heaven and Hamid will be home in a couple of hours. If you'd like I could take you on a drive of Karachi. I have no qualms about escorting you when Heaven and Hamid have to work. And, Hamid, I may be the poor relations but I can afford to take Tanya out for lunch." He laughed, "Tanya, we do have McDonald's here in Pakistan." He grinned. "But that's not where I plan to take you.

Tanya turned quickly, half expecting Heaven and Hamid to be jumping with joy. They weren't jumping but they were sure grinning from ear to ear.

"Thanks, Imran." She frowned at her friends. "But the two of you are not fooling anyone. I just happen to be enjoying Imran's company right now more than the two of you. You're bad hosts," she said and flounced out of the door. When Heaven grabbed her from behind pulling her into a hug she stopped walking.

"You don't mind do you, Tann?"

"No, I don't mind. If I did I wouldn't be going off with him. Nice try, Heaven, but I still intend to go after one of Hamid's brothers. Since Imran is indeed fine I won't mind spending some time with him for the next couple of days."

❧

Heaven watched at the door of the clinic as Tanya got back into the car and Imran closed the door. She turned toward Hamid and threw her arms around him. "Thank you," she whispered against his lips. "That was a fantastic idea."

"You're right about the two of them being right for each other. They have that certain look. I couldn't resist," he replied kissing his wife passionately. "But I do expect to be rewarded for having thought of it."

❦

For two days Tanya had enjoyed hanging out with Imran listening to him play tour guide. But after the first day she'd insisted that Heaven and Hamid accompany them as they'd promised. There was just too much heat between her and Imran for her to want to be alone with him. She wanted to keep the lusting to a minimal. Her plans hadn't changed. She was there for one of Hamid's brothers. Now the moment she'd waited for and had journeyed thousands of miles was at hand.

The biting of her nails was the only sign that Tanya was a bit nervous. Fatima had only warmed slightly toward her. In just under an hour this new family that Heaven had adopted would descend on them and Tanya was determined to make a better impression on them than she had on Fatima and Imran.

When she heard his voice she groaned. She should have known thinking about him would bring him around the same as it had for the past two days. They'd sparred as they had from the moment they'd met. Not that Tanya minded but she'd talked with Heaven and was determined to try and find her softer side to woo the Ahmed brothers. But with Imran around it would be darn near impossible. He brought out the need to fight and flee, to want love and fulfillment but he wasn't the one. She needed someone to help her make her dreams come true. Imran wasn't it. She turned in his direction and frowned

"The party doesn't start for an hour. It's considered bad manners to come so early."

"It's also considered bad manners to give orders in a home that's not your own. I'm family. I'm welcomed here but are you? I have heard of a saying, fish and visitors both begin to stink after three days," he retorted. "You're been here three days." He smiled at her and made his way into the nursery.

Laughter from behind her made Tanya turn. "I'm getting sick of Hamid's cousin." She leaned back and did a fake neck roll then she laughed also.

"You like him, don't you?" Heaven asked.

"Yeah I like him, but stop trying to fix us up. I didn't come here for *'no'* cousin. I came for one of Hamid's brother."

"You need to stop saying that, Tanya. At first it was cute... now...not so much. Listen if Fatima can't stand you, you have got a serious problem. I'm not kidding. This isn't cute. What's the deal?"

"There is no deal." Tanya turned away she hadn't wanted to tell Heaven she hadn't wanted to tell anyone. "Damn," she muttered.

Heaven touched her friend's shoulder trying not to scold her but to figure out why Tanya was still behaving so strangely. "What's going on with you, Tann?"

"I may have to adopt six kids and I need to be able to provide for them. You know social workers don't make that kind of money."

"Hold on. You told me about the village you're trying to help with but nothing about adopting kids. Why in the world do you need to adopt six kids?"

"My cousin Lettie has cancer and she's been given only a few months. The entire family wants to pitch in and help with the kids but no one wants to take care of all six. As a social worker I know what can happen to these kids if they're split up. I can't let that happen but I also don't have that kind of money to take care of them. You told me how big Hamid's family is on taking care of family. They have money enough to easily take care of six kids."

"Are you crazy?" A tear fell from Heaven's eyes. "While your reasons might and I mean a small 'might' be good, your logic is faulty. Even if one of Hamid brothers fell for you, how do you know they would want to raise six children and since I know you have no plans to move here, you're expecting a lot."

For the first time since she'd devised the plan and decided to come Tanya felt helpless. Heaven was right. Her plan was crazy. She felt the shudder of pain as she thought about the kids. "I know. I just want to help," she started crying comforted by Heaven's hug. "I know it's crazy. I do know that, but I wanted to give it a shot."

"I'll help you with the kids. I'm still making money from the agency. I'll ask Hamid—"

"Don't do that. I want to do this on my own. Just don't mention this to Hamid okay. The two of you have done way more than I should have ever asked you for. This was a long shot and I knew it." She shrugged. "I want to find my own way through this, Heaven. Now come-on, is there anything that I need to do? Am I dressed okay?" She tugged on Heaven's arm. "Stop looking so sad it's my problem and I'll figure something out."

෬

Imran moved slowly back into the shadows. He'd not meant to eavesdrop on Tanya and Heaven but when he'd heard the distress in Tanya's voice he'd thought he was the one who'd put it there, so he'd listened. The ever constant flutter that had begun in his chest since meeting her now beat rapidly. This crazy American woman touched something in his core. True she was crude, rude and a gold digger but she was also a fiercely compassionate and loyal woman. It didn't hurt that she was also beautiful, smart and had made him laugh more in the three days he'd known her than he had in the past month. Her tale of woe made him wish he could help her but she was right. He was a cousin, a cousin with no money.

Though he understood Tanya's need to be on her own the desire to help her overwhelmed him. He sighed knowing he could never attempt to take away her independence. He was on his own. Sure if he was in dire straits he knew his father would bail him out, but he was a grown man. He didn't want bailing out. No one believed in his writing abilities and definitely not as a means to earn money. So he taught in the university until his big break came. Though an Ahmed his father had chosen a different path from his uncle and had wanted no involvement in the oil business. He'd much preferred working the land with his hands and there had not been much money in it. Eventually his father had accepted help from his younger brother and made his own fortune, but Imran had grown up in the shadow of his cousins, the millionaire sons, as many in their lands referred to the brothers.

Imran half suspected that was the reason there were now the millionaire sons left to marry. Many women had tried to wed them but they had resisted. For the brothers not to be married with a passel of children was not the norm. Neither was it the norm for Imran at his age to not have a wife. His career choice had not made him suitable husband material. He was aware his family considered him somewhat of a disappointment. He was an Ahmed. He should be wealthy or at least working toward wealth.

He blew out a breath having made a decision. He couldn't stand the thought of Tanya's crying so he walked out wanting suddenly to stop her tears and knowing how best to accomplish that. "Tanya, are you crying because you missed me?" he asked walking up to her and standing directly in her face ignoring

Heaven's arms around her.

When Tanya's hands dropped from around Heaven, the tears ceased and she glared at him. "Imran, why on earth would I miss you?"

"Because when I'm in your presence you glow." It wasn't until he'd said it—and he'd meant it as a joke—to stop her tears that realized it was true. He watched as Tanya blinked rapidly, sputtering trying to think of something to say. The flutter in his chest was now driving him mad. He moved a little away. Could it be that they were truly meant for each other? He'd long acknowledged the attraction it would have been foolish not to. But for the past two days he'd determined not to push it, to wait and let Tanya work her magic on one of his cousins if she could. But standing in front of her he was drowning in her eyes, all thoughts of allowing her to continue her crazy plan all but forgotten. He dropped his gaze to her lips—lips that he'd wanted to kiss for days. Her pulse beat rapidly at the base of her throat. It was hard to tear his gaze away even when Heaven cleared her throat. He needed to think of something to say quickly.

"I just wanted to make you stop crying," he answered softly. "You're here on vacation. You shouldn't have tears." He reached out a hand to automatically wipe away her tears but stopped. What the heck was he thinking? What he was about to do was so improper that he didn't think even Tanya with her crass behavior would approve of such an act. He shrugged. "Okay, maybe you don't glow but I mistake your glaring at me for glowing." He smiled and saw her smile in return, obviously grateful that he'd taken them away from any mention of anything else.

In a short span of time the family began piling in. Imran watched Tanya. As she looked at each of his cousins, she was practically drooling. He'd have to admit his cousins had been spared nothing in the looks department but then again neither had he and she'd not drooled over him. He was beginning to feel a little less sympathetic toward Tanya and protective toward his cousins. Sure Tanya had a good reason for wanting a rich husband but his mission was the same as it had been in the beginning—to foil her plans.

"Ali, what do you do for a living or do you just enjoy being rich?" Tanya waited for Ali to answer but saw him frown instead.

"I am a diamond dealer." Ali tilted his head downward and smiled at Tanya. "Would you like for me to come again and show you some of my things?"

"Please do," Tanya answered coyly, batting her lashes and

talking softly. She turned away for a moment and saw Imran
glaring at her. *What's his problem?* she wondered. "Excuse me Ali,"
she said as she made her way to where Imran was standing.
"Imran, why are you glaring at me?"

"Was I glaring at you?"

"Of course you were. Now stop it and let me talk to Ali in
peace."

Imran stared after Tanya as she walked away. He needed a
diversion, anything. His cousin Ali was the most reckless of his
cousins when it came to women. They'd traveled many countries
together, many vacations, and Ali had no problems making love
to any woman. He did treat them well and he always left them
with a bauble or two but occasionally he left them with broken
hearts. Imran knew this because he'd ran interference for his
cousin to get the women to back off. As a matter of fact, they
sometimes traded identity so that if the women by chance were
able to track Ali back to Pakistan, they would only reach Imran.
Suddenly an unreasonable fury struck Imran at Tanya's actions.
He did not wish her to trap his cousin into marriage nor did he
wish for his cousin to use her and dump her as more than likely
would be the case.

He stared sternly at Ali. "Tanya is Heaven's friend. She's not
one of your…" looking around at his family he muttered softly in
Urdu to Ali telling him not to dishonor his family, his brother or
his brother's wife by playing with Tanya with his usual intents.
For a moment the cousins squared off and Ali grinned asking if
Imran were interested in Heaven's friend.

"No," Imran spat, "but I do know how to behave." He
marched angrily away feeling a bit like a fool. He and Ali had
never once exchanged harsh words, not even as children. If he
were pressed to name his favorite cousin it would have to be Ali.
Ali who was ten years older had been like an older brother to him
as well as to Hamid, taking him under his wing and teaching him
the things he should know, teaching him even about women and
how to please them taking him on countless occasions to Lahore,
Pakistan's red light district to complete his education in the art of
love making.

Walking into the nursery to spend some time with the baby he
couldn't help but wonder what had gotten into him. All he knew
for sure was that he did not want Ali using his many secrets on
Tanya. It did not mean he was jealous or that the attraction to her
was anything more than a mild attraction. His hand rubbed at the
fluttering in his chest. This was becoming annoying. He'd have to

speak with Hamid about whatever fragrance they were using in the baby's room. This annoying feeling in his chest was happening only when he was in their home. He ignored the thought that tried to come. It had nothing to do with Tanya it must be the baby.

A smile graced Tanya's lips and she cut her eyes toward the direction that Imran had gone. Of course, she thought, to the nursery. She wondered what he'd said to Ali. She'd thought at first that it was something about her being a gold-digger. Something in his territorial stance with his cousin niggled at her and the more she thought on it the more it didn't seem like the problem had anything to do with Imran thinking her a gold-digger. Even though he'd glared at her when he'd left the room in his haste she thought she'd spotted something in his eyes but it had happened so quickly she wasn't sure. But her instincts as a woman told her he was attracted to her and that he was jealous of the attention Hamid's brother was paying to her. Tanya grinned then. This would be fun. So he'd one upped her in most things now he was on her turf she would turn the charm on Hamid's brothers until Imran went up in flames. A curious flutter entered her chest and desire crested between her thighs. Damn, Tanya thought, *what is it about that man that makes me hot?*

❧

"So, Tanya, Heaven tells us that you work with children, the less fortunate. Do you find that work rewarding?"

She was about to tell Mohammed, Hamid's next oldest brother that she loved her job when at that moment she spotted Imran walking back toward them. Her mouth suddenly developed the run away disease and she said, "I love working with children and can't wait to become a mother." She batted her lashes at another equally tall and handsome man and pursed her lips before smiling. She turned toward Imran and smirked. She was well aware that she'd just baited him. He tilted his head in a mock salute to her and marched fully into the room.

"Tanya, I find it very interesting that you work with children yet do not like nor respect them."

The room became instantly silent all the laughing ceased the only warm spot Tanya noted came from the depths of Imran's brown eyes. What the heck was he trying to do to her? He smiled and she saw a dimple. He was setting her up. Her heart was racing a mile a minute. She should have been more upset than she was but all she could do was stare at him at his beautiful brown eyes, luscious oh so kissable lips and handsome face. His thick black hair unlike Hamid's or the brother was straight and cut short. She'd thought she wanted a man like Hamid with long curly locks but she didn't, she thought as a one shiver after another raced through her. She wanted a man with dark black hair cut short. She wanted a man that had a comeback for everything she had to give him she wanted a man that made her heart thump and had goose bumps crawling over her flesh making her shiver. Sure Hamid's brothers made her drool but Imran made things happen to her that she'd never experienced. She'd drooled over many men but never had one had her so gah gah that she'd lost the power of speech no matter how momentarily it was.

"Imran is wrong. I do like children."

"My mistake," Imran said smoothly, "so it's just Hamid's son you do not like or respect?"

She couldn't believe it. Her mouth fell open and her eyes went wide. "That's… that's...that's not true. I like their baby."

"So, it's his name you don't like."

Tanya looked around the room helpless then her eyes lit on Heaven and she pleaded with her friend silently that she would come to her aid.

"Imran, leave her alone she was kidding," Heaven scolded him.

"I'm sorry, Heaven, but I didn't hear your friend say she was kidding." Fatima interrupted. "She said your child would have a hard time in America with a name like that. She didn't appear to be kidding. As Imran said, she didn't even appear to have respect for your baby, our family or our country."

"Hold it everyone this is going too far," Heaven protested making her way to stand in the middle of the room and quiet the ruckus. "Tanya was kidding with me. She loves this country and the people. She was giving me a rough time because I didn't name her as the godmother to my son, that's it. I promise."

"She has never held a baby. She attempted to hold Tsukama and gave him back the moment that he needed changing." Fatima turned in Tanya's direction and glared at her.

"But she didn't come here to do that she'd been in the house for a few moments." Heaven looked helplessly at Tanya then at Hamid finally turning to glare at Imran. "Stop it," she said between clenched teeth. "Traitor," she said to both Fatima and Hamid and they both grinned. Heaven moaned. Did the two of them think this was the kind of help she wanted? Sure she wanted them to help her with bringing Imran and Tanya together. But she didn't want them to have everyone hating her friend in the process. "Imran, cut it out right now and I'm not kidding. You're embarrassing my friend."

Imran merely smiled and lifted one of his shoulders. "I didn't know this was a secret. Was it also a secret that your friend came to marry one of my cousins because she is in search of a millionaire?"

Ah damn, Tanya thought and sucked in her breath. The room, if possible, was even quieter. Heaven was livid but it wasn't Heaven's answer the family was looking for. Imran had just successfully ended her search to marry one of Hamid's brothers or anyone in the Ahmed family. This wasn't going as she'd imagined. She turned to glare at Imran and saw she couldn't believe it a twinkle in his eyes, a smile on his lips. Was the man crazy? She stared at him and saw desire. Damn! That wasn't going to happen. Imran didn't work into her plans she thought as a thump beat in her chest. It seemed forever they were locked in their staring match she mentally shook herself knowing she had to make an explanation. What could she say? She breathed out hard knowing there was nothing that wouldn't sound like excuses. So she said nothing and just tried as best she could to glare at Imran.

❧

Fate. Imran glanced toward Hamid. So this was what happened when fate entered one's life. You made a total fool of yourself. His mission had been to come and protect his cousins from the gold digging American but now he knew what the fluttering was in his heart. Desire. He desired the woman. She made him smile made him feel things that no woman ever had and there was no way she was going to be with one of the brothers. She belonged to him, fate had decreed that. He smiled as she glared at him. What of her dreams? Biting his lips in retrospection Imran couldn't help but wonder about this fate that had captured his cousin and now him. Was it always so hard? Tanya had noble dreams just crazy methods to achieve them. He had no way to help her achieve her dreams yet he knew he would want to try.

What do you think you're doing?" Hamid stormed over and between clenched teeth scolded him. "That's Heaven's friend and you know how lonely Heaven has been for her friends. What's gotten into you?"

"Fate."

"Fate? What are you talking about?"

Imran smiled at his cousin. "Fate has brought Tanya here to Pakistan and into my life for a reason," he shrugged. "She can not be with one of your brothers."

"And you couldn't think of another way to keep her from them without making the entire family hate her and embarrassing her in the process?"

"I couldn't at the moment."

Hamid glanced toward his wife. "I don't think she's going to forgive you and the fact that I'm here smiling at you instead of beating you now has my wife glaring and angry with me."

"Tell her it was fate. Besides, it was her scheme to put us together. Tell her her plan worked."

"I think I need to do more than that. I think I need to buy her a gift." Hamid's eyes twinkled. "Maybe diamonds."

"You're just looking for another excuse to give a gift to your wife."

"I don't need excuses to buy jewels for Heaven but there are certain rewards for having a gift ready after an argument."

"But you haven't argued."

Hamid hunched his shoulders. "No, but I know my wife. She's displeased with your actions and mine since I'm not pummeling you. That's close enough to an argument for me to want the joys of making up." He walked toward Heaven. "I would suggest you talk to Tanya I know her you don't. She looks ready to kill you. I don't think she's going to take likely to your saying fate made you do this.

He'd admit his methods weren't well thought out nor were they the best but he'd done it now he'd have to see what would happen. He looked around the room, his gaze landing on Tanya. He shouldn't have done it regardless of the reason. She was a stranger in a strange land and it appeared she was fighting back tears. Only Heaven and Hamid were talking to her. He walked toward them and stopped in front of Tanya.

"Do you believe in fate?" he asked.

"Are you saying that somehow it was fated that I'd come here and you'd make a fool out of me?"

"I'm talking fate bringing people together." He looked toward Heaven and Hamid. "Fate brought them together and I think it has done the same for us."

"Hamid flattened Heaven's tire. And you have told your entire family that I hate the child of their favorite son."

Imran waved his hand in a dismissive fashion. "The brothers would not have desired you anyway." He saw the moment offense was taken at his words. "Ali loves women and would have treated you royally that I'm sure of. Mohammad and Aamir have avoided marriage this long because they...come outside with me we need to talk."

Once outside Imran looked at Tanya and felt the flutter again. He wanted to kiss her, to wrap her n his arms and hold her close to his heart. He wanted to make love to her so many things he wanted that were neither proper nor could be done now.

"I want to apologize to you but you were flirting with Ali. I did not wish to see you become one of his string of women and I did not wish to see my cousins with a gold digging conniving female."

"But you don't mind a gold digging conniving female?"

"I have no gold."

Tanya sighed. Most of this was here fault. She should have acted like she had some sense and not told anyone her intents not even Heaven. She supposed she couldn't blame Imran for trying to protect her cousins. A hitch came to her throat and she closed her eyes. If only she's not had so many cases in the last months, too many abandoned and abused babies, no homes for them. She fought back tears. Yes, her plan had been crazy but she hadn't cared when the last child she was assigned to had been placed with a family member with a shit load of personal problems. Tanya shuddered. Even if she had the money she couldn't make her dreams come true. The state of Illinois had jurisdiction over children. She couldn't just take them and place them in a happy home. What if the parents she chose were no better than the ones the state chose? She closed her eyes and thought about the good she'd done, the children she had saved. A tear seeped beneath her lashes. She'd continue to do a good job.

"What's wrong, Tanya?"

"I'm not a gold digger."

"I know."

Tanya's eyes opened wide. "You know. How? And if you know that I'm not why did you just tell your family that I was?"

"Heaven told me your dreams. She's very loyal to you, even though you said you didn't like the name of her baby. I think Tsukama is a wonderful name by the way."

The man was a hunk a crazy hunk and he was definitely operating on stupid. "Let me get this straight. You did this because of what? You really think I don't like the baby?"

"Well…"

Before she could utter another word Imran had reached out his hand and was caressing he cheeks. WOW!

"Your skin is so soft." He moved closer. "I've wanted to touch you for the last three days."

"Why?" Tanya asked.

"Why does any man want to touch a woman? I have an attraction to you in spite of my plans not to. And in spite or refusing to go alone gently with my cousin's matchmaking. I find that you're constantly on my mind and I enjoy your company. I do believe you feel it also. I want to get to know you better. Heaven has asked that I assist them in showing you Pakistan I think it would please her to see we're friends. Can you imagine if her and Hamid's matchmaking scheme worked? We've both known almost from the beginning that they've been trying to set us up. This party was not for you to meet one of Hamid's brothers in order for you to charm and perhaps marry one. It was merely a party for the family to meet Heaven's friend. Be honest, Tanya, you knew this wasn't going to go the way you planned. I told you on that first day that I would stop you. You only have to look at the faces of your friends to know their true intent for you."

"Heaven and Hamid are so into each other that it's hard to know what either of them are thinking." She hesitated and held Imran gaze. "What are you after? Why are you being nice to me now? Do you think you're going to charm me and then get me into bed?"

His dark eyes smoldered with raw passion at the prospect and his lips trembled just a bit. His hand remained on her cheeks and he pressed even closer running a finger lightly over her lip, then pulling the finger into his mouth and suckling it. He smiled.

"Heaven told me there isn't a lot of public touching you're sure proving that to be wrong."

Imran glanced around. "No one can see us. Hamid made sure to buy a home that was quite secluded. He would never have survived otherwise. I don't know how he was able to keep his hands off his wife before." He laughed remembering that Hamid had used every excuse for touching Heaven when he'd brought her to visit. He noticed with satisfaction that Tanya wasn't moving away. "Do you mind that I'm touching you?"

"No, I don't mind."

"Do you mind that I've told you of my feelings?"

"I don't mind. I don't know if I believe you but I don't mind. Shouldn't we go into the house now?" Tanya asked wanting him to kiss her not knowing if he would or if they should. She moved and her lips moved into his purely by accident. A wave of want came over her and she lingered for a moment. Imran's hand caressed her back for a nanosecond before he smiled at her and pulled back.

"Would you like for me to truly show you my country when Heaven and Hamid are busy?" he asked. "I can show you some of the places that I'm writing about."

"I'd love to see some of the places that you're writing about. By the way I think it's pretty cool that you're going after your dream. It really doesn't matter if anyone else believes in your dream as long as you believe that's enough." The smile he gave her then melted her heart and her nether regions. If he didn't stop looking at her in that manner she would be attacking him. They had to remember where they were. Heaven or Hamid would undoubtedly come out to check on them very soon if nothing more than to make sure hey hadn't killed each other.

The hand on Tanya's back moved slowly along her spine and he began whispering to her. She blinked. He was singing. She didn't understand the words but from the look in his eyes it had to be a love song.

"You have a very good voice. Do all of the Ahmed men sing?" Imran didn't answer just lifted his brow. "Hamid sings to Heaven," she said by way of explanation.

"Hamid warbles."

"Before this goes any further, Imran tell me a bit more about yourself. I wouldn't mind hanging out with you while I'm here but that's it. Heaven told me you're a writer before you ever mentioned it, an unpublished writer so that tells me you're not making any money. And I don't care if you go back to thinking I'm a gold-digger or not but this has to be said. I'm also not planning on taking care of a struggling writer until he makes it. I definitely don't play that goanna help you get a green card bit, so what's your story?"

For the first time Tanya noticed the twinkle had disappeared from Imran's eyes his eyes narrowed and he held her in his steely gaze. He dropped his hand from her back and she instantly missed his touch.

"So you want to know more about me. You want to know what I'm up to. Here goes. For the past few days I have enjoyed toying with you. I felt you needed to be put in your place then I thought I saw something in your eyes, something that my soul recognized and for some crazy reason I thought I felt things for you, things that I thought you felt also. And probably from spending so much time with Hamid and Heaven and the baby I began to believe in fate, that fate had brought you into my life for a reason. Now I say this to you. Damn fate. You are not the woman for me." With those words he turned on his heels and headed back into the house.

Tanya swallowed, a moment of panic filling her. She wanted to go home. Heaven had gotten her involved in some major craziness. She should have known her plans wouldn't work anyway. Lettie's kids would deserve a home when she was gone. She saw baby Jo Jo's face in her mind and swallowed again. She'd become too attached to the baby She'd been warned it would happen. He'd been in her care a few hours after his birth how could she not be attached to him. He deserved a home. All the kids she was assigned to look out for deserved a home. Crazy that's what it was. Sure she knew that even if Jo Jo became available for adopting one day in all likely hood if she was taking care of Lettie's kids she would be unable to take in yet another baby. That thought saddened her because she didn't see any babies in her future and Jo Jo had somehow become a surrogate for her.

She'd gotten into more fights since she'd been here than she had in the last months. Sure she'd missed Heaven. The group just wasn't the same since Heaven had moved to Pakistan and sure she'd been a bit miffed that Heaven had not asked her or any of her friends to be godmother to her baby son. They would have all been honored and would have loved it but she hadn't even considered it so yes she'd made a few uncalled for nasty remarks. Heaven understood that she knew the reason. They'd squashed that but Imran had still used that against her. She'd be a liar if she didn't acknowledge that somewhere inside of her she believed Imran wanted her. But he was moving so quickly. His nearness made her lose her resolve to not have a permanent relationship. How could she? She had a truck load of responsibilities waiting for her in her future. A groan slipped from her throat. That time she'd really and truly not intended to be nasty. Imran had scared her for a moment with his directness and with his touch. He was turning her into a pile of mush and she'd needed badly to breathe. Mercy the man was working on nervous system big time. Okay, she admitted to herself. She liked him. She liked him a whole lot.

For a long moment she stared at the door. Of course she'd known Imran was attracted to her and she'd readily admit her attraction to him. The man had kept her in a perpetual state of crazy wanton need. If he'd been jealous of her talking to his cousins why couldn't he had done the sensible thing and told her instead of what he'd done. He didn't have to announce to the entire family that she was a gold digging baby hating American. That was as far from the truth as he could get. But to turn around, bring her outside and tell her that he believed fate had decreed that her life and his were intertwined that they should be together. To touch her in such a gentle manner that he almost had her begging, then to top it off with him singing to her. She'd been out of her element not knowing how to handle it. She'd known she was being rude but she'd needed to pull back to be able to breath or she would have done whatever it was he'd wanted right out there in the open. Besides, what if he were feeding her a line? Playing her? She had needed to think and being in such close proximity to him had not provided that time. But she hadn't really wanted him to storm away from her either. Ah hell! How about buying a girl a drink first? Tanya shook her head. Dang, how did he think his announce was going to go over with her? He couldn't just decide that he wanted her and that was that. And he was right she didn't come to Pakistan for a poor relation. If Imran was deliberately screwing up her chances with one of Hamid's brothers she wasn't going to take him by default. If she did, how the heck was he ever going to believe that she'd had a thing for him the moment she'd met him? Imran has issues himself and getting a woman on the rebound eventually would not set well with him. They both needed a moment to regroup.

A flutter begin in her chest and worked it's way down. Her womb clenched and wetness filled her panties. Okay so he was the only man in a long time to make her have that reaction. No matter how handsome Hamid's brothers were they had not made her have that catch

Tanya bounced around on the balls of her feet for a few moments throwing shadow punches seeing each of them connect with Imran's head. Okay so that the way he wanted to play it did he. She strutted back into the house and promptly went to the portable DVD player she'd brought and popped in *Cupid's Shuffle* and started dancing. As the room turned to watch her she laughed and put an extra wiggle in her step. She didn't care if none of them liked her. This was supposed to be a party and she was going to party. She gave Imran a smirk and saw that Heaven was watching her. She waved her hand toward her friend and in a moment Heaven was beside her doing the cupid shuffle holding her baby in her arms. Tanya laughed when Hamid came and joined in taking the baby from Heaven. So it wasn't just here that he didn't want holding the baby. Hamid didn't even want the mother holding his son. She ignored the frowns on the faces of Heaven's in-laws and wondered had Heaven never danced the entire time shed been in Pakistan. That was just wrong. She was going to have to teach her friend how to have fun again she wiggled over to Ali and grabbed his hand pulling him into the line teaching him the move smiling as the attempted to the shuffle. She was surprised he picked it up so quickly soon everyone in the room was doing the shuffle even Fatima and Imran

As Tanya kicked and turned her gaze met Imran. She moved toward him. "I'm sorry for the things I said outside, the way I acted, you're right about my feelings for you," she whispered. "I don't know if it's fate or not but I do want to believe in it."

He smiled and for a long moment she was still. It was as if the room had suddenly emptied out as if they were the only two people in world. Her hear thudded and she missed a step. '*Wow*', she couldn't help thinking. She needed to hurry and get home but she still had five weeks left. She didn't think she had five weeks of resolve in her she didn't know if she'd be able to hold out if Imran wanted to push things. Heck she didn't know if she wanted to hold out. There was no use in lying she was attracted to him. Wasn't it just like her to fall for the one member of Hamid's family that didn't have money?

≈

A breath of fresh air, a party girl, a gold digger, a woman he'd made sure his family didn't like and now what. He was falling for her. He couldn't keep his eyes from following her movements. Was this truly fate, he wondered? Shouldn't Tanya be able to pursue her dreams of building homes for disadvantaged children? It was a good thing. He thought also of her promise, her family obligation to care for the children of her cousin should it become necessary. Maybe he would not pursue her. Then she turned and smiled and told him she was sorry, that she was attracted to him. He smiled back wishing they were someplace a lot more private. As he thought about his earlier thought of not pursing her, his smile turned into a grin. Maybe he would pursue her after all.

5

A LUNCH OF TANDOOR CHICKEN, cheese, bread, fruit and bottled water filled the basket to overflowing. Imran waited for Tanya. He couldn't believe she had at last given up her fruitless search for a millionaire. He would be her chosen husband and he didn't care how old fashioned it seemed. He wanted her and she wanted him. Simple.

"Where are we going?" Tanya looked suspiciously at the basket Imran had just put into the trunk of his car. "I thought you were taking me out to show me the country."

"That's precisely what I'm doing."

"Looks like you're planning a picnic."

"If I am what's wrong with that?" He smiled. "I just wanted to have food just in case."

"So where are we going?"

"To get rid of some of your misconceptions. You think that in Pakistan there is no love or passion, that we all use matchmakers or family introductions. Sometimes it's merely that a man and woman see each other and fall madly in love. Sometimes it's just fate."

"Are you still trying to tell me that fate put us together? Listen." Tanya stopped and put her hand on her hip. "I'm not Heaven and you're not Hamid. I'm not a virgin who's waiting for the right guy. We may as well get that out and upfront. If that's what you think fate wants you to have then you're looking in the direction of the wrong woman. And I plan to return to Chicago in a few weeks so you need to know that."

"Hamid told me Heaven protested at first. In fact for the entire first year of their marriage she refused to come to meet his family." He grinned. You've already met my family."

"And they don't like me, thanks to you."

"Did you expect me to allow you to go through with your plans? You were trying to beguile my cousins."

"And instead I beguiled you, is that it?" Tanya laughed and headed to the passenger side of the car.

A smile pulled at Imran as he watched the sway of Tanya's hip he wondered what she would look like in a *lehenga*. He tilted his head. Sure she'd look good in a long skirt but the tight jeans that hugged her derrière made him hard he didn't know if the skirt would have that effect. He laughed softly and proceeded to the driver's side of the car. Once in he inhaled the smell of Tanya's perfume something exotic and spicy, cinnabar he thought. He wanted to kiss her. The thought pounded through his brain as he started the engine ignoring that Heaven was staring at them the baby in her arms with a worried look on her face. It was as though she thought he was kidnapping her friend. He was doing nothing of the sort.

"Heaven, why are you so worried? You wanted Tanya and I to like each other." He couldn't help but laugh as he glanced quickly at Tanya. I know that you elicited help from Hamid. But that's to be expected." He tapped on the steering wheel and sought Tanya's gaze before finishing with his cousin's wife. "It was a bit underhanded to use Fatima in your plans though. So tell me please why you're so worried."

"Tanya's not a toy and this isn't a game. You don't have to go out with her to get back at me for trying to set the two of you up."

Imran brow lifted. "Heaven, I am not Hamid. My world does not stop when you speak. I wish to date your friend because of me not you. And since we're both adults and do not need your mothering I would suggest taking Tsukama into the house. It's getting hot." Instead of waiting for any farther answers from Heaven he turned the key in the ignition and drove off, the sound of Tanya's laughing making him glad he'd done so.

"Imran, I swear I have to give you your props for that. Heaven looks likes she doesn't know what hit her. Thanks for giving me a chance to not be around those two for a day. Dang are she and Hamid always like this? I mean if they are how anyone can stand to be around them is a wonder. She's school girl goofy over Hamid."

"He feels the same things for her."

"I know but the two of them...yuck...yuck...they're sickening."

"Have you ever been school girl goofy over a man, Tanya?"

"No, and I have no plans on ever behaving that way. Like I said, I'm not Heaven."

"Good, I'm not interested in having Heaven," Imran said and grinned then he glanced over at her. "Are you not happy that you came to visit Heaven?"

Sure being with Heaven again was wonderful but her friend was a bit nauseating. She'd never been like that in Chicago. She didn't know if it were Pakistan or having a baby but Heaven went around constantly with a dopey look on her face, her eyes always searching for Hamid and when he went to the clinic to work Tanya saw her eyes sliding many times to the door, her ears cocked for the sound of his voice. The only time Heaven appeared not to be watching or listening for Hamid was when she was with the baby. And even then her thoughts of her husband were felt because she'd constantly croon to the baby, talking about, his-daddy-this-and-his-daddy-that. It was a godsend that Imran had invited her to accompany him as he went out to interview people and visit places for research for the book he was writing.

"Yes, I'm happy to be here but I thought it would be like old times I guess. Heaven is much too busy with her family to pay any attention to me. She's trying but," Tanya shrugged her shoulder. "I wonder why she wanted me to come so badly. We haven't spent very much time together and she palmed me off on you almost from the moment I arrived. Maybe she regretted asking me to come."

"Maybe she wants you to be married with babies. Hamid told me how much your visit has done to lift Heaven's spirits. I think she's planned your wedding in her head, possibly even your babies. I think maybe she's so involved with that that she's forgotten to be just your friend."

"Well, you can't prove that by me. Thanks for being so willing to show me Pakistan."

Tanya's voice had a wistful sadness that pulled at Imran's heart. He'd waited long enough. A mile away from Heaven's prying eyes he pulled over beneath a grove of trees. "Tanya, we should get certain things out of the way so we can enjoy the day," he said.

"What things?" Tanya answered with a snort as she looked into his eyes. He had the most sensual lips and a very strong face. He was indeed a handsome man albeit a man without money.

"I want to kiss you."

"And?"

"And I want you to give me permission."

She laughed. What else could she do? She'd never had a man ask for permission to kiss her before then of course she'd never had a man declare fate had intended they be together after hurling insults at her. Still she was game. What the heck, she was on vacation. She was going home in a few weeks and might as well have some fun if she could while she was here.

"Well?"

Tanya returned her attention to Imran. "Sure, why not?" she answered at last and moved closer to him. "Heaven told me that touching isn't done that much in Pakistan at least not out in public. And here it is the sun is shining brightly and you want to kiss me. Why?"

"Because you have the most luscious looking lips and I want to taste them." He saw her hesitate.

"I'm not looking to fall in love with you, Imran". She shrugged her shoulder. "I don't mind kissing you though." She ignored the look he gave and moved closer still.

His lips barely grazed hers as he used the pad of one finger to feather her hair and run it down the side of her face cupping her chin. He was staring the entire time into her eyes gazing at her as though she were something most precious. Tanya couldn't take it any longer she yanked his shirt and pulled him the few inches to her. Then she smacked her lips against his and plunged her tongue into his mouth. He pushed her away and stared at her.

"What?" she asked.

"You're much too forward. How many men have you been with?"

"None of your damn business. How many women have you been with? Look, you asked me to kiss me not the other way around. I didn't tell you that fate wanted us together. In fact I told you I wanted one of Hamid's brother so if you don't like that I took control of the kiss tough." He was back to pissing her off. Did he have any idea how hot he'd made her with his gentle caresses? She wanted to kiss him so she had. "Drive, Imran," she ordered.

"Not just yet." His hand again captured her chin and he

lowered his lips to hers feathering her lips with the tip of his tongue. He placed soft kisses from one corner to the next. "I love the feel of your lips," he admitted. "Open for me," he implored. "I want to taste you."

"No. You complained before about me being too forward."

"Now I'm not complaining. Open for me, Tanya."

Damn if she didn't want to kiss him so badly that to not do so would be torture. She wanted to keep her lips sealed. Instead she opened her mouth slightly and sucked in a breath. The moment Imran's tongue touched the inside of her mouth flames of desire shot through her and she moaned. *Mother of mercy*, she thought. Tanya had been with her share of men but none had ever made her feel like this, not from a kiss, not from a touch, not from anything. Just then Imran pulled her closer and deepened the kiss. He was gentle and she knew his kiss was a getting to know you kiss, a—I want to learn the taste and texture of your mouth.

Tanya had to admit it was much better than what she'd done. She'd merely wanted him and had taken him. This kiss was so sensual that she was melting. She wondered what the protocol would be for them and where, if they did, would they make love. She was a full grown woman with needs and her body was telling her that she needed Imran. When she pulled away she was pure liquid wanting the kiss to last but she sighed and leaned back into the leather seat of his SUV. "That was nice," she murmured.

"I like the way you taste," Imran said looking at her. "I've never tasted another woman who tasted quite like you."

"What's that supposed to mean?" Tanya snapped. "Are you saying you thought the kiss would be different because I'm a sister?"

"You're a silly woman. Every woman tastes different and it's never been because of their race, far from it. I've been with many women of all races but there is always something about each one that is the same, mixed in with their difference."

"You're confusing."

"Sorry," Imran said. "I wasn't trying to confuse you. I'm just telling you that I have never kissed a woman with your taste. There is something about you."

"Good or bad?"

"Very good. I like it." He lowered his eyes and ran a finger over her lips. "I like it so much that I'd very much like to kiss you again." This time he didn't ask permission just leaned down and kissed her applying a bit more pressure this time suckling her tongue caressing her jaw line as he did so. He heard her soft moan and continued, only stopping when he remembered they'd been parked under the trees long enough. He didn't want to expose Tanya to more prying eyes and the wagging tongue of gossips. She was going to be someone very special in his life and he wanted to make sure that she was welcomed in his family and his country. He ran a hand down her spine allowing the tips of his fingers to briefly come in contact with the firm globes of her encased behind. He heard her moan and barely suppressed a moan himself. He swallowed determined to bring his desire under control. He pulled away, giving a lazy smile and a small kiss on her lips, nibbling a little, at last sighing since neither the desire or erection would be tamed." I think we need to go."

Was he crazy? Tanya tried to adjust to the loss of his kisses. She glanced out the window over Imran's shoulder reminding herself that she was not in America. She didn't know everything there was to know about Pakistan but she sure hadn't come to the country to get arrested in a Moslem nation for kissing. Imran was right. It was time for them to drive. There would be more kisses later, a lot more kisses. We've been to the nuclear power plant, the army college and the McDonald's with Heaven and Hamid. Where are we going today?"

"To the city of Lahore. I want to show you the contrast in things. First I will take you to the Badshahi Mosque and Herra Mandi I thought you'd like to see it."

"Heaven and Hamid took me already to the mosque."

"I know but this trip will be different. We are going for a very different reason. Tell me, Tanya what did you think of the mosque?"

"I thought it was very beautiful, it looked like a palace, the beautiful pink tiles all of it. I guess I can see why Heaven has fallen in love with your country."

"It's not the country Heaven loves, it's Hamid. Her love for him is truly powerful. I want one day to have that same kind of love. It's hard to find a woman who will honor your dreams especially a woman who's determined to have her own, one who never wants to be school girl goofy over a man." He moved his hand to the right in order to touch her then he ran a finger down her hand and scraped the palm lightly. "I believe I want a woman to be school-girl-goofy over me. I have never envied my cousins anything until now. I envy the love Heaven and Hamid have for each other. I want that. I want it very much." His words caught and his voice had grown husky with his wants and desires. He was pushing much too hard and too soon. They had time. They had five weeks.

"What are you thinking," he whispered softly.

"That you are indeed a writer. You're writing this beautiful fairytale in your mind. Is your book going to include a fairytale, Imran?"

"Only if the things I now want come true. I do not write fiction."

"So how long have you wanted what Heaven and Hamid have?" She tried to ignore the way her heart was pounding the way his fingers entwined with hers. And she definitely tried to ignore that she wanted to rip her clothing from her body make Imran stop the car and rip his away also and have her way with him.

"How long have I wanted these things?" Imran repeated the question she'd asked. "How many days have you been here?" he smiled. "That's how long I've wanted them."

It was high time to steer the conversation to safer ground, Tanya thought as she decided to ask Imran again where he was taking her. "I hope you're taking me to a mall. I wouldn't mind doing some shopping. I have to buy gifts for my friends back in Chicago."

"Where we're going is not exactly a mall. But there are many things there for sale."

Tanya was giving him a look like she knew exactly what he was up to he couldn't help but laugh. It seemed that since he'd met her he'd done nothing but laugh. "Herra Mandi is a bazaars of diamonds."

"We're going to buy diamonds?"

Imran frowned at the glitter in Tanya's eyes. The mention of diamonds had intrigued her and brought out that greedy gold-digging side of her. The look annoyed him and he decided to tell her in a different playful manner than she'd intended. Herra Mandi doesn't sell diamonds it's Pakistan's oldest red light district." He watched as Tanya mouth fell open.

"Prostitution. Are you kidding me? I thought things like that weren't allowed in Pakistan. I don't believe it."

"Believe it," Imran said still feeling annoyed with her. "Officially you're right. Pakistan is an Islamic republic."

"I've studied some about your country and I read that prostitution is punishable by death."

"That is true."

"Then how the heck can you have a red light district?"

"We do, Tanya. Have you ever visited a red light district?"

"Yes, I went once to Holland with Heaven and we went to the red light district. We watched as the women dressed in skimpy negligees danced in the window. The windows were lit by a reddish pink glow. When a man was interested he entered the door and the woman left the window." At the look on Imran's face Tanya rushed to explain. "We were on a tour. Why are you looking at me like that?"

"You just told me my cousin's wife visited a red light district and you don't think I should look at you strangely?"

"You're taking me to a right light district yet you think Heaven is too good to go to one." This couldn't be the man who'd just made her melt from his kisses. The stupid jerk.

"From what you say it sounds as if you and Heaven went on this excursion without any male protection. You're with me, Tanya you're safe I will keep you safe. I will protect you with my life."

A catch fluttered at the base of her throat and she couldn't stop the smile at his words. He was good.

"Imran tell me how it is that prostitution can be practiced but a good many of the women still cover their faces?"

To that he shrugged. "Yes, a good many of the women still refuse to show their uncovered faces to any male except their closet relatives but a lot of that is changing also. Pakistan is changing."

"Still, I want to know why you're bringing me to see a red light district. I remember what you said a couple of days ago about me selling myself and you thought I should see the place where it's done. Is that the reason you're bringing me here?"

"I really am doing research for a book I'm writing. Herra Mandi is starting to decay but once upon a time that was not that case. There was a time when the ladies that plied their trade their were well respected. The noblemen sent there sons there to learn etiquette. A lot of the women sang and danced and aspired to be in film. In the bygone days the women that worked the are were thought to be more sophisticated that many women in the most respected and rich families".

"You know an awfully lot about the place."

"I'm a writer."

"I think it's more than that. I think it's personal. Have you been here before… I mean to use the service?"

Imran looked at Tanya and smiled. "Like you, I also am not a virgin. I went many times to be trained in the art of lovemaking."

Tanya couldn't believe it Imran was too darn honest for her.

She thought of him lying naked on a bed surrounded by prostitutes who patiently taught him the secrets to loving a woman, pleasing her, making her moan with desire.

"Imran, why are you telling this to me?"

"Because I want you to know I am a man who can fulfill your wildest sexual fantasy."

Mercy, Tanya thought and fanned herself.

⁓

The day was going as he'd planned. Imran found a private spot near the water and stopped. It was a place he and Ali had brought girls to many times. It was secluded, just the place for a man and woman to become better acquainted away from the prying eyes of aunties and uncles and gossipmongers. It was midway between Lahore and Defense. Now it was time to broach the subject of them spending the night in Lahore. He'd made arrangement for their stay at the Mirage, two rooms.

Lifting the basket of food Imran smiled as Tanya's eyes went to the basket and the grin broke out on her face. She was different in every way from the women he'd know and that pleased him. She was a woman who loved life. She had a good appetite for food and Imran suspected she had a healthy sexual appetite as well. If they would be together that was a good thing.

Once the blanket had been spread and the food arranged Tanya dug in before Imran had a chance to blink. He laughed. "Why didn't you tell me you were hungry when we stopped at the McDonald's to take pictures?"

"I didn't know that I was until I saw the food." She smacked her lips together licking the curry from her fingers. "How much farther?" she asked as she stuffed her mouth with grapes.

"Not far, an hour or so." Imran hesitated. "I was wondering though if you'd like to do a bit more exploring, you know take our time, take it slow. I thought maybe you'd like to spend the night in Lahore. They have a very nice hotel there. The Mirage is only a couple of years old and offers many amenities."

On no he didn't just go there. Damn and she'd been having such a nice time. She stood abruptly knocking over several containers as she did so, not caring that Imran was scrambling to secure them.

"Listen, Imran, I don't know what the hell you think you're doing but I will drop kick your ass and leave you here. Is that clear?" When he merely stared at her she put her hands on her hips and got ready. So be it. If she had to take him down she would. Thanks to Heaven she'd started taking karate and was damn good at it. Just let Imran try something and she'd toast him.

Imran studied her for a moment. He'd known his proposition would be met with suspicion. But threats? He looked her over, wondering if she really thought she could best him in a physical fight. Then he became offended that she'd think he'd try to take her by force.

"Tanya, tell me what it is you think I'm trying to do."

"I think it's pretty clear. You're taking me to a place that freely indulges in prostitution. You tell me how good you are and that you can take care of any of my sexual desire and now you're asking me if I want to stay in a hotel. Duhh. You do the math. I know what's on your mind."

"Do you now? Do you know that I've been enjoying your company tremendously and that I didn't want it to end so quickly? You've let down your guard since we left my cousin's home. I think now we can be friends."

"Is it friends you want to be, Imran, or lovers?" She waited, tapping her foot on the ground.

"I want to be both for you." He paused for the space of a heartbeat before continuing. "Lahore is a beautiful city, maybe not as beautiful as it once was, but you're not going to get a feel for the culture or the city if we only go in for a few hours. Besides the things I want to see don't start until after dark."

"What? The prostitution?"

"That among other things."

"You're pretty straightforward aren't you?"

Imran thought about it for a moment. He'd never been one to lie easily but he did know how to practice diplomacy he'd done it enough times with the women Ali discarded. But for some reason he found himself answering every question that Tanya asked without hesitation. He felt the now familiar flutter in his chest and knew the reason for it. Her anger had diminished and she was smiling at him and her smile was lighting a fire in his heart. Fate may have chosen this woman for him but he wanted her. It wasn't love yet… but…well there was definitely something that could very well develop into love. Imagining stretching Tanya's beautiful body out on a bed and making love to her was the easy part. He smiled at her. Yes, loving her would be easy but he was imagining them walking together, cooking together in the kitchen, taking long baths in a huge tub and family dinner and as he looked at Tanya, he imagined a baby in her arms, their son or daughter. He held her gaze, wondering if he should tell her his thoughts knowing he would. She was the other part of himself that he'd not known he was searching for.

"Would you like it if I didn't give you straightforward answers, if I gave you veiled answers instead?"

"No, I wouldn't like that but you puzzle me, Imran. You have done nothing but fight with me since I came to Pakistan well that and you've done everything in your power to make your entire family hate me."

"They don't hate you," he smiled. "They're just very wary of you." He took in Tanya's frown. "Okay, you're not their favorite person. He reached out a hand to her. "Come on sit back down. I've done more than fight with you, Tanya. I've kissed you. Twice." He saw her blush and pulled on her hand to urge her to sit when she did he moved closer.

"Seriously, I didn't mean anything disrespectful about asking you if you'd like to stay at the Mirage."

"But you've booked a room right?"

"I booked two," Imran admitted, "but that means nothing if you don't want to stay. I like this much better our talking getting alone, not fighting."

"Tell me something, Imran, are you using me for a story? Do you think perhaps you can charm me and then you'll have a chapter about how you got into the American girl's panties?" She waited while he frowned at her as she'd known he would do.

"Do you think to shock me?"

"What?"

"The vulgar talk. You behave as though you have no class. Sometimes I wonder how Heaven could have ever been friends with you. The two of you are so different."

"Are you sure about that?"

"I'm sure."

"Heaven and Hamid have had a thousand fights, vicious fights, she's even kicked his behind. When she wants, Heaven can have a tongue like a serpent and you're calling me crass. Well, all I'm doing is telling it like I see it. You're blunt but you don't think I should be. Why? Because you think women have to talk in a certain manner. You're the one who invited me out. We've been together for a few days so it should come as no surprise to you that I swear. You knew this about me when you invited me to come with you today. I think it's just that you're upset that I called you on what you want. Why don't you just be a man and admit that you want me?"

"Very well, if that's the way you want it then yes, I will admit to it. I want very much to make love to you." When Tanya sat near him with her mouth slightly open in surprise he pulled her to his body hard and then he plundered her mouth kissing her with every once of passion that was in him. When she struggled at first to pull away he slid his hand into the rims of her jeans moving it to the front unbuttoning it and caressing her smooth brown skin. He shivered as did she then he took her over the edge ravishing her pressing his mouth against the clothed breast bringing his hand from the flesh that covered her secrets and caressing her breast pulling on the nipples tweaking them enjoying the hard feel of them. She was panting so hard that Imran almost lost his sense of reason and the lesson he was trying to teach her was undoing him. Slowly he pulled away.

"When I make love to you Tanya it will not be out in the open. I will not use trickery and you will be more than willing. That I promise you. Now back to my original question would you like to spend the night in Lahore?"

She was shaking so hard that she had to clench her teeth to keep from crying out, from begging Imran to make love to her right there in the open. At that moment she didn't care that he thought she was crass she just knew that she wanted him. Still they needed to settle one little matter between them.

"I don't like that you think I'm crass and that Heaven is what? An angel?"

"You're jealous of your friend?"

"Not normally but since you're saying your attracted to me and you talk about my virtue as though it's of no worth and call me names you make me want to slug you especially when you compare me to Heaven and behave as though she'd never do the things I've done. We're friends remember.

"You're getting angry at me for things you've done and said in the five days since you've been in Pakistan. I will continue to be truthful with you. No, normally you would not be my choice for a mate, not even a date," Imran went on without pausing. "And if I didn't know that there was something more to you, if I hadn't seen it there in your eyes, I would not be telling you these things. I would escort you as my cousin asked me to do but that would be that. I would not kiss you and I would not be dreaming of making love to you. But I have seen more. And I will tell you now if a future with me is anywhere in your plans then you need to learn to behave. You say Heaven can also be crass and by that I assume you mean she like you swears like a man. I say I've never heard it and I've known her for more than a year now. And might

I remind you that it is you who keep bringing Heaven into the conversation and almost demanding the comparisons, not I. I have told you it is not Heaven that I desire. She is the wife of my cousin."

"And if she wasn't?"

"And if she wasn't she still would not be the woman I desired, though beautiful she's much too tiny." He hunched his shoulders. "I love my women big enough to…" he let it drop. "Now for the last time, do you want to stay in Lahore overnight?"

"Yes," Tanya said shaking her head. Imran made her giddy crazy. She'd never before been jealous of Heaven. Well, not much anyway but damn if Imran didn't make her confront all her own issues. She'd have to admit that she wished it had been her that Hamid had fallen heads over heels in love with. And yes, she wished that she had a husband worth millions to help her help her kids. None of that had even a tiny glimmer of happening now and if the last five days of being around Heaven and Hamid was any indication of the fun they had planned for her she would be bored out of her skull long before it was time to return home. Imran was as far as she could see her link with having a good time. And the man could kiss like no body's business. Now if they were in Chicago, she'd probably tell him to step the hell off. But she wasn't in Chicago and for the next five weeks things were going to become pretty boring if she didn't have Imran for company. She wondered what they'd see in Lahore if the women were in the window as they were in Holland. At least she'd have a story to tell she thought.

"Yes, Imran," she said again. "I do want to tour the city."

This time when his lips lowered over hers and his tongue found its way into her mouth she did nothing but wind her arms around his neck and enjoy the kiss knowing there was only so far Imran would take a kiss in public.

When the kiss ended at last Imran touched her gently. "No, I have never tasted a woman that was so wonderfully delicious. You make me burn from the inside out. It's hard for me to maintain control," he admitted, "but I do value your virtue and I will not risk it." He glanced around. "Though this spot is very secluded and not many know of it. Still, there will be time for further exploration." With a light kiss he inhaled her breath. "There will be a lot more time for exploration. That I can promise you."

❧

In Lahore, Tanya stared as they passed by the modern American looking Holiday Inn. They'd already checked into the Mirage and though clean and saying that it offered many amenities it didn't.

"If you do not like The Mirage, Tanya we can move over to The Holiday Inn."

"What's the price difference?"

Imran smiled. He liked Tanya's honest direct approach. A man most likely would always know where he stood with her. But one could never be certain; after all she was still a woman. "The Mirage is thirty-three dollars per night and The Holiday Inn one hundred-thirty five." He watched her for a moment as she whistled between her teeth. "We can still make the switch if you'd like," he stopped and grinned at her. "Or we could use the difference and go shopping and sight seeing.

"I thought you brought me here to see whores."

For a moment their gaze met and held until Imran saw uncertainty in the depths of Tanya's eyes. "Had I truly meant all of the nasty things I've said to you I would not now be attempting to make a good impression on you." He didn't see a change in her expression and sighed knowing he'd gone too far in his insults of her. "Tanya, I'm sorry for the things I said to you and for having hurt your feelings. I do not think you're a whore."

She smiled. "What are your thoughts about me?"

"I think you're a very beautiful woman that I enjoy kissing immensely, one whom I've become quite attracted to. You're always doing and saying such outrageous things that…that…we… don't have to see the whores. There are a lot of attractions I would like to show you. We could start with the beautiful Christian church."

"There's a Christian church in Pakistan?"

"And many other sights you will enjoy. I really do need to visit several places here for inclusion in my book."

"This is really for research?"

He didn't know how to answer that question until he saw the smile around her lips. "Yes, this trip is for gathering all kinds of information."

"I'd think we'd need more than a night here then."

Silence filled the interior of the car and lust permeated the air. "In that case I think we need to shop for clothes." He took a glance out of the window toward the hotel. "That is unless…."

"I have money, Imran. I can pay my share."

Not on this trip. Besides, I'm not penniless. I just chose to live a bit more frugally than the rest of my family. Still, I believe we can make this a nice trip. I think after a few days here of getting to know each other without Heaven's constant clucking over us is just what we need."

"A few days?" Tanya asked.

"At least three, don't you think?"

"I'll have to call Heaven and let her know what we're doing." Tanya couldn't believe what they were about to do. She couldn't help but laugh as she pulled her phone from her purse.

"After we shop for clothes what would you like to do?" Imran asked.

"I think we'd better find that Christian church so I can pray for strength," she said laughing as she looked into his eyes. She pushed the button for Heaven's number. "I think we're both going to need some divine intervention on this trip."

Tanya could barely wait to run from Imran's car and into the house so she could tell her friend about the days she's spent with Imran. When she spotted Heaven in the foyer she rushed to her and gave her a hug.

"Heaven, you won't believe it. I couldn't believe it and I saw it. Here in a Moslem country, a red-light district." Tanya put her hand over her mouth. "There was a lot more to Lahore than that though. It was like every few feet someone picked up these beautiful homes, palaces, and dropped them down in between little shacks, almost a part of the city. You can tell the very rich live there and then a few feet away abject poverty. It reminds you in a lot of ways so some of the neighborhoods in any inner city of American. But it was like a different Pakistan. Men and women held hands. They touched. I even saw a couple sitting under a tree kissing. It was fantastic, the hotel was very nice not as nice as let's say a Hilton or even a Holiday Inn," she stopped and giggled. "But it was nice and it was within Imran's budget," she finished.

"Slow down, Tann. Why the heck did Imran take you to a red-light district? And why didn't he mention that he wanted you to stay all night? I was worried about you. If anything had happened to you…nothing happened right? Come on you're stalling why did he take you there?" Heaven's rapid fire questions couldn't stop the relief that her friend was alive and well. She sighed several times. "Talk, Tanya."

The worried look on Heaven's face made Tanya laugh. Having a baby had changed Heaven if she thought she could tell her when and with whom she could go. That was none of Heaven's concern. She was a grown woman who didn't have to explain herself to anyone let alone a friend. But because she was so excited, this one time she would.. "I'm going to answer your questions because you're my girl but you had better seriously check yourself about the way you're asking me for information. You're behaving as though you think you're my mother or my guardian. I couldn't believe it when I called you from Lahore and you demanded that Imran return me home. Girl, are you crazy? Don't ever do that again."

"I'm sorry but I was worried. If anything had happened to you...you know me. I would have felt it was all my fault for trying to set you up with Imran. Maybe I was wrong about him. Did he try anything?"

"There you go getting all up in my business." This time Tanya laughed. "If you thought he was the perfect man for me you shouldn't now be worrying."

Heaven sighed again. "Are you ever going to tell me why Imran had to have you spend the night, correction three nights? When you called me you said one night and now you're just getting back. Even Hamid was getting worried once you stopped answering your cell." Heaven took a breath and tried to take it down a bit but she'd had every right to worry. "Tanya, you spent almost four days with Imran in Lahore. I just want to know why the heck he took you in the first place. I've been here way over a year and Hamid and I never stayed those many days."

"Imran said he wanted to knock away some of my notions and besides he's working on something for his books, some research. He took me with him to do his research."

"Is that the only place he took you?" Heaven laughed

"It was the only place." Tanya stopped and stared at her friend. "Maybe not. He took me on a journey inside myself. I love talking to him. He's so straightforward that he just cut right through all the bull. I've never met anyone like him, man or woman." For a nanosecond Tanya wondered how her friend would react to her discovery then gave a little shrug and decided to just go for it and tell her the truth. "You do know how jealous I am of you don't you?"

"Tann."

"No, Heaven, it's okay. I'm jealous that you're married to someone as wonderful as Hamid. I'm jealous that he adores the ground you walk on, that you gave up everything to come live here with him. I've never had anything like that and I wanted it.

I didn't know how much but I do. But I want to thank you for trying to knock some sense into me. I'll still take are of Lettie's kids, all six of them when the time comes. Maybe I won't be able to give them all the things that I want but I will be able to give them love. And I damn sure can make sure they get to stay together. I refuse to allow them to be farmed out to other relatives or to end up in the system."

Heaven gave Tanya a hug. "I'm so glad you've given up the idea of trying to find a millionaire. I'd hate to think when you went back to Chicago that you were still searching for a man to help you take care of the kids."

"That's over. I don't know if I would have gone through with it in the first place but for now it's over. Besides, if I am needed to take care of Lettie's kids I can get assistance and it doesn't have to come from you and Hamid. You know I'm now a licensed foster care parent and even though I'm a relative I can receive financial aid to help with the kids. It would not have been my first or even second choice. I wanted to do this without any help but I won't allow my pride to prevent me from using every means necessary to help those kids." She sighed and closed her eyes in prayer. "I'm still praying for a miracle for Lettie though."

"What about Imran? Do you have feelings for him?"

"For the next five weeks I do. He can kiss. Damn!" Tanya smiled, shook her head then covered her mouth. "He thinks I'm vulgar and should be more like you."

"If he said that then screw him," Heaven said. "You're fine just as you are."

Tanya laughed at Heaven's defense of her, wondering that no one in Heaven's new family had gotten so much as a *'screw you'* from Heaven. It was one of her favorite terms when she was pissed. She continued grinning. Imran apparently had never seen Heaven when she was pissed. Just wait until he did. Wiping the tears of mirth from her eyes Tanya decided to answer Heaven's question. "Listen, for the next five weeks I will try to clean up my act. I like Imran and fight or not we have good times together. I don't think I want to give up his kisses just yet."

"You're going to change for a man?"

"You did," Tanya said reminding Heaven of her own choices. She walked away. "Maybe I finally found a man that has my nose open, one I want to change for. But hell, what can I say. Psyche. Imran had better take me as I am or forget it."

She came back, gave Heaven a high five and hugged her friend. "I'm glad the two of us are finally going to get to spend some time alone. I swear I was getting sick and tired of looking at you and Hamid making love in front of my face when I wasn't getting any."

"We haven't done that."

"Please! Every time the two of you look at each other it's like you're making love. And I need to get home for real of go crazy over here. If you don't want me attacking your husband then you'd better send him to work for longer hours. If I'm not getting any the least you could do for a friend is kick your husband out of your bed so you won't be getting any either."

"No way is that going to happen," Heaven laughed.

"Well, could you at least stop looking at him like he's the greatest thing God ever created?"

"How can I when he is one of the two greatest things God ever created? Don't forget Tsukama."

"How can I forgot that beautiful baby with…"she leaned to the side and peered around the room then covered her mouth and whispered so that only Heaven could hear her. "How could I forget the beautiful baby whose mama gave him such an unorthodox name?" She laughed and jumped away from Heaven.

"You know there is Imran," Heaven countered.

"Oh there is that alright." Tanya sighed. "But I'm keeping my head Heaven we can only be together for a minute. I don't have time to go losing my head and my heart."

"But?"

"But he sure is fine and he sure can make my body sing with nothing more than a kiss or a touch. But we know in a few weeks I'm going home. That's that. But I do plan to enjoy him while I'm here."

When Fatima came out with Tsukama in her arms Tanya knew there was one more thing she needed to do, make amends with Hamid's sister. She smiled at Heaven and walked toward Fatima. There was no time like the present to start acting like she had some sense.

Time was winding down. Tanya didn't want to admit it but she was going to really miss Imran. So far she'd managed not to go to bed with him, just a lot of kisses and heavy breathing. He hadn't pushed and for that she was eternally grateful. She knew if he pushed she'd say yes. But it would be more than a bad idea to have sex with a man that she would never see again. She had to remember that she was going home and Imran was staying in Pakistan. She still had to return to her babies, check on them and make sure they were all doing well. Guilt moved in. She'd not called Lettie since she'd been in Pakistan. And no she hadn't forgotten her. She just had wanted to have some fun; pretend that she didn't have as many worries as she did. Even if Imran had a notion, and he didn't, to come to America, she couldn't very well saddle him with that type of responsibility. He had even less money than she did.

Tanya thought over her options as she sat waiting for him. Heaven had been a bit disappointed when she'd refused to go shopping for gifts for their friends with her and Hamid. Even if Heaven wasn't so goofy over Hamid they were bringing the baby shopping and Tanya knew what that meant. They wouldn't even notice if she were being gored by a bull in the streets. Besides, Imran had called and asked if he could come over and now she found herself thinking about him, sighing at the impossibility of a long term relationship between them.

But when Imran came into the house all thoughts of what they couldn't have vanished. She did want him if only for the next few days. If fate had brought them together as he thought then she hoped that it would make Imran open his mouth about making love to her before it was too late, before she went home. That was the one thing she wasn't going to do no matter how much she might want him. He already thought she was crass. She had no intention of having him think she was a horny tramp. Horny yes, tramp no.

Imran stood across the room watching Tanya wondering what she'd been thinking about. She'd had such a pensive look on her face. But he'd noticed as their gazes connected that a light from within lit her eyes and her skin glowed as though on fire. The flutter was back in his chest making him smile. He gave her a look, staring long into her eyes and at last he moved toward her his gaze fixed on her lips. Her lips were the most luscious things he'd ever tasted. He wanted more, needed more. Standing in front of her he leaned down and gave her a smile asking for permission by lighting feathering her bottom lip with the tip of his tongue. Her slight answering nod was all that he needed. He kissed her long and deep.

"I would love to make love to you," he whispered. "I want to feel the way we move together, to touch you in your our most secret places to have you touch me. We are adults. If we both wish this I don't see any reason why we can't."

"Try there is nothing between us."

"Nothing more than wanting, lust, attraction," Imran

answered.

"I'm leaving in a week."

"And yet you'll be in Pakistan for another seven days."

There was logic somewhere in what Imran was saying. She did like him that much she would admit. And they'd come close so many times that it seemed just plain dumb not to. If they had been anywhere else in the world they would have already hit the sheets. But then again maybe not. Imran had a way of annoying the hell out of her. One moment he'd have her wanting to rip her clothes off her body then tear away his and the next he'd have her wanting to send him home. He wasn't what she'd thought he was at all. She wondered if she went to bed with him if he would think she was cheap. She would be back in America what would she care? There was another little or not so little thing. She was curious to know what the courtesans had taught him to find out if it was all just bragging.

"Imran, I don't want to do things here in Pakistan that will make trouble for Heaven when I leave."

"Are you attracted to me?"

"A little."

"Just a little."

"Okay, maybe more than a little."

"We're alone now."

"In Heaven and Hamid's home? Wouldn't that be kinda disrespectful," Tanya eyed him suspiciously. She blinked at the naked lust in his eyes.

"To be honest, Tanya, I wasn't thinking about them. I was thinking that soon I won't see you and I will miss you when you leave. I was thinking that I would very much like to make love to you at least once before you leave."

Tanya thought of her reasons other than seeing her friend for coming to Pakistan. That shipped had sailed. None of Hamid's brothers were even the least bit interested in her. There would be no millionaire to save the day for her. It was a dumb idea anyway. From the moment she'd met Imran there'd been a connection. Why not see if he was all that before she left the country? She curled her tongue between her teeth trying to put her finger on why she was resisting taking something she desperately wanted. There was something out of place. It just seemed wrong somehow that they were casually talking about making love as though they were talking about ordering lunch. If Imran was all that good in the arts of seduction then he should realize that.

"Imran...something's off. I can't put my finger on it but I'm not sure…"

"I know what you mean it's too planned, too rushed right? It seems like a doctor's appointment. First maybe we should not consider making love here in the home of your friend and my cousins. You are uncomfortable with that. I should have thought of that. Let's forget it for now. Maybe I can cook lunch for you."

"You are a strange man. You're so modern, so Americanized."

Imran laughed. Generally Tanya's off the cuff remarks would make him come back at her with a snide comment of his on but this time he wouldn't. She was looking at him and wanting to make love with him, afraid to. That much he knew. But if they didn't make love now he had no idea when he would, if ever see her again. He had to create a bond between them. He would take her body to heights of pleasure she'd never dreamed of. He would make love to her until the only man she'd ever desire would be him.

He allowed his eyes to travel over Tanya's lush bottom. Jeans were definitely the dress for her. He loved her in them. The only other thing he wanted to see her in was luscious pecan brown skin. He didn't think he'd have to wait long. He'd never had any intentions of making love to Tanya in Hamid's home. She was right, it would be disrespectful. And besides that, he planned to make her scream out with pleasure over and over again. For that they needed complete privacy. He was going to employ every one of the tricks he'd learned. He would love her body enough to last the both of them a lifetime.

An hour later Imran had Tanya in his home and preparing lunch for her allowing her to look over his home at will. The strong smell of onions and garlic permeated the house. He was amused as Tanya looked around his home picking up first one thing then another. She was looking for tell tale signs that a woman occupied his home. He smiled she wouldn't find that. She was in fact the only woman he'd ever invited to his home who wasn't a relative.

Imran turned the fire off under the pans, eating could wait. Making love to Tanya couldn't. Before he could stop himself he had her pressed against a far wall and his hands were roaming her body his kiss fervent and urgent. He only needed a sign only a little sign. Her arms slipped around his neck and he pulled her closer. That was the sign he needed. His arms went around the curve of her hip and he easily lifted her up into his arms and started walking with her toward his bedroom. Imran was grateful

Tanya wasn't a virgin that she was a woman who liked sex. She'd
told him that. It would make it all the better. It would also make
it easier when they parted in seven days, no guilt, no
recriminations, just a man and woman finding pleasure in each
others bodies.

He walked through the flower petals he'd strewn about his
room. The he laid her on the bed amidst the orchids and gave her
a long look then sighed. "We've wasted so many weeks but I will
not bemoan that fact. I will enjoy our time together instead." He
touched her chin tilting it so that she looked up and was gazing
into his eyes. "Do you want this?"

"Yes, I want it."

"Even though we will not see each other again?"

"Even though," Tanya answered meaning it. "Though I don't
see any reason why you can't come for a visit or I can't return
here one day."

He grinned at her, just the answer he wanted. He needed to
know that for both of them this was more than a brief fling.
"Perhaps I will," he answered and begin to pull her sweater from
her taking care in taking it over her head and feathering her torso
with light kisses, feeling her tremble beneath his searching
fingers.

His hand dipped beneath the band of her jeans and he
snapped the button and pulled the zipper down taking his time.
His breathing was heavy. He was hard, wanting her more than
he'd ever wanted any woman but needing to see her naked not
just without clothing but naked laid bare, her emotions and
everything that was her. She was trembling a bit more now and
he wondered if she were nervous. He hoped not. Of course if she
demanded it he would stop but not without a lot of begging and
pleading with her to allow him to make love to her at least once.

His hand came in contact with her thighs and he lifted her hip
with one hand and pulled the black thong from her body, smiling
at the thought that he'd known she was a woman who'd wear a
thong. When she was bare, he sighed and drank the sight of her
in to keep it close, to remember her when she returned home.
Then he began to strip away his own clothing stopped by her
hand. She slid from the bed and undressed him pressing her hand
against his arousal making him shudder with lust.

"Come on," he urged pulling her hand and her behind him to
the shower. "We will prepare." She gave him a look and he
smiled. "Don't worry you will enjoy the preparation almost as
much as you will what will come after."

"Something you learned?"

"Yes," he whispered against her lips, "something I learned."

Tanya could barely stand her legs were mush. She had wondered about Imran's boast but no he was playing this just right. This was such an exotic feeling. She opened her eyes wide in surprise.

"More orchids? I thought you didn't have money. Why didn't you just try to seduce with rose petals?"

"Roses are common. You're not."

She could only swallow unable to say a word. He didn't have to try to seduce her she was already way beyond hot. She was scorching, burning, about to go up in flames. She took in a breath, anything to slow down what was happening just for a moment, give her a chance to regroup to think. She slowed her pace and took a good look at the bathroom. The two places she had ventured on her little tour had been his bedroom and his private bath.

Imran's home was modest unlike the mansion Heaven and Hamid lived in but his bathroom rivaled theirs. Floor to the ceiling windows covered almost the entire room and he sunshine made the glass sparkle like diamonds. She stopped for a moment ducking behind Imran for cover.

"Don't worry the glass in the windows is so thick that no one can see inside not even if they pressed their nose against the window. I like a lot of light but I also like privacy." His eyes seared her. "I would never allow another to view your body."

Oh he was good. He knew exactly what to say. Tanya tapped him lightly on the shoulder. "You could have warned me."

"I could have but then I would have missed having you press your warm naked body against my back." Take a good look around and assure yourself we cannot be seen."

Coming from behind Imran Tanya did as he asked and stood in the center of the room taking a good look around. She stood in front of one of the windows noticing that the glass reflected the sunlight but that she really couldn't see out. Then she noticed for the first time that the windows were covered with all manners of foliage. She glanced to her left and saw a door and walked toward it. Opening the door she gasped at the huge steam room tucked away in the corner. She couldn't believe that a bachelor would have such luxuries in his bathroom. Then she thought of his training and figured it was for the women that used it. "Very nice," she said a bit miffed, puzzled that she felt that way. There was nothing between them, no commitment or hints of any, just that they would enjoy the next seven days before Tanya returned to her own world. A happy interlude, nothing more. She glanced in the mirror and saw the way he was gazing at her in pure adoration. For a moment it was as though her heart stopped. He was looking at her in the manner that Hamid looked at Heaven. Lord, she'd never thought any man would look at her in that manner.

His hands came around her cupping her breasts and he leaned his head down to the top of her head nuzzling her. She shivered in his embrace finding what he was doing erotic beyond belief. When Imran moved slightly away trailing kisses along her spine the shiver changed into a shudder. He smiled and moved to turn on the water for the shower.

"How do you like your water?" he asked.

Considerate, very good, Tanya thought giving him an A for that. "I guess you've brought a dozen or more women in her to bathe huh?"

"Only one," Imran answered, his eyes never leaving her face. "You haven't told me yet how you like your shower."

"I like it hot, but not too," she answered smiling at him in amusement. She could have said warm but there was something about Imran that begged her to toy with him just a little. She watched while Imran fiddled with the knobs holding his hands under the running water until he was satisfied. His body was long and muscular. His hips powerful and well shaped. She turned her attention to his rear end. Very nice she thought and commanded herself not to lick her lips. She took her time observing him liking everything that she saw. Then he turned toward her a huge grin on his face.

"Like what you see?" he asked.

Allowing her eyes to travel over his front the same as she'd done his rear she took her time smiling at his massive chest downright grinning when her gaze hit the spot between his thighs. "I like very much what I see," she replied and took the hand he offered and stepped into the shower.

"I am going to miss you, Tanya."

"Let's not think of anything other than right now. I'm a big girl and you're a big boy. We're not making commitments to each other. You don't have to feel guilty for anything we do. Let's just enjoy each other okay?" She was breathing heavy.

"You're not going to think of me when you return home?" Imran asked.

"Oh, I'm going to think of you and I'm going to wish you

much success with your writing career. I hope you become even larger than Khaled Hosseini."

"From your pretty lips to the ears of Allah. And I wish you the same, Tanya. I hope that you find the funds necessary to make all of your dreams come true. I hope that all of the children you love in America find loving parents. And I pray to Allah that your cousin Lettie will live many more years so that she may raise and love her own children." He placed a soft kiss on her lips and sighed. "You know you're so much more than you appear to be at first glance. If we had a bit more time I think we would...."

"Don't say it, Imran, we don't have more time. But we can make the most of the time we have now." She sighed and decided to ignore waiting for him to make the first move instead she leaned her body into his, wrapped her arms around him opened her mouth and kissed him with all the fire that was in her. She felt him tremble as he pulled her close, felt the water pelting over them. His tongue entered the depth of her mouth and she could feel his hunger. It matched her own. Fire burned in her veins she couldn't get enough of him. Suddenly he pulled away and she watched beneath eyes that were half lidded as he poured liquid into he palm of his hands and smiled at her he washed first one breast, tenderly kissing her through the suds, lathering the next and kissing that one also, pulling on her nibbles going farther and farther down his lips trailing fires everywhere he kissed. He paused for a moment to pour more liquid as he spread her nether lips apart with two fingers. "No," she protested softly, "that'll burn."

"Don't worry I promise it won't."

He then rubbed the soapy concoctions over her tender flesh and she waited for a burn none came but the area felt highly sensitized. Imran dropped down on his knees lathering her thighs, one hand continually washing her while the other held her in place by the light pressure on her buttocks. He was coming so close but seemed to refuse to pay special attention to that spot where she craved more. She could feel his breath hot as it touched her skin. She'd never had a man bathe her before and didn't know if she'd ever want to bath herself again. This was heaven. His hand going over her wet skin, the friction, and every so often his massive erection bushed against her swaying with the heaviness. He made his way back up touching her more. His finger dipped into her, touching her spot nearly making her jump out of her skin. She groaned and reached out to press his hand more firmly to her flesh.

"Give me that," she said reaching for the bottle with the soap that didn't burn. She smiled, poured a hand full and began washing him her hand moving over his smooth brown flesh touching his flat nipples feeling an urge to suckle him as he'd done her, to flick her tongue over the little nubs and feel them throb with lust and life. She continued on her southern path going between his thighs cupping him, finding him hard as steel and soft as velvet she stroked and stroked. Enjoying the feel of him moving in her hand she smiled seductively at him and went beneath to touch and caress the rest of him. The water turned suddenly cold and she jumped back squealing realized she'd inadvertently moved the handle. "That's cold," she said breathless.

"Don't worry I'll warm you back up." He lifted her in his arms and carried her to his massive bed. "This is the last time I will ask if you're sure."

Was she sure? Was the man crazy? Of course she was sure. She was so hot she was about to pop. Dag gone. The man was good. She'd thought she'd feel self-conscious with him watching her his eyes burning her, but she hadn't. She liked it. She was glad she wasn't a virgin. She reached for Imran cupping him again running her finger over the head of his erection. He growled and attempted to pull away but she was holding him tightly releasing him slightly then increasing the pressure of her grip. Imran was big all over it seemed. Now the thing was if he knew what to do like he'd bragged. She'd soon see.

She felt Imran moving away, one hand securely around her waist as he pulled her with him. She smiled figuring he was going for a condom. Good, she thought, very good. A moment later something light touched her skin then as more pressure was applied it tickled making Tanya lose focus and release the death grip she'd held on Imran.

Moving back an inch Imran smiled down at her. "There are rules in everything didn't I tell you that? There are rules in seduction."

"But you don't need to seduce me. I'm here in your bed ready willing and able."

"Rule one. I will make love to you." He pointed at his chest. "I will bring you fulfillment over and over and then we will make love."

"But I want to participate, to touch you… you're so….so….well endowed," she finished running her tongue over first her teeth then her lips. "I think you're going to be something that I wish I could take home." Imran blinked and she saw a strange flicker in his eyes. "Imran, I'm glad we're finally together," she whispered not wanting to change the look she was still seeing in his eyes, like maybe this would go on after she left Pakistan and the truth was it wouldn't.

"Lay back," Imran said, pushing her shoulder gently with one hand while placing the pillows beneath her head with the other. "Are you aware that the soles of your feet is where every nerve center is controlled?" He smiled at the disbelief in her eyes. "I'm going to make you have the biggest orgasm of your life by touching only your feet." He laughed at her disappointment. "Don't worry; before we're done there will not be one spot of your beautiful body that I've not touched. And I will make you come for me each and every time."

"That's a mighty big boast." Tanya cleared her throat. What the heck? The man was asking to please her. "Can I have glass of water while I wait for you to begin, or maybe a book?" She laughed but stopped the instant Imran pressed a finger to the center of her foot. What the hell? She felt the pull all the way to her center. A wave of desire washed over her so strong that it almost embarrassed her. She reached her hand out to slow Imran down but he gently pushed her away.

"I thought you wanted to see everything that I've been taught." "I do but you took me by surprise."

"You don't like surprises?"

"I love surprises. But I had thought... I don't know what I thought. I just know I didn't expect that. You took me from 20 to 1000 with no preparation."

"So you require preparations?" Imran laughed. "Americans," he snorted then bent his head toward her foot and licked it from the heel to her big toe. She was squirming so much that he had to hold her foot in place.

He looked up and grinned. "Tanya, you did tell me you weren't a virgin. Is that correct?"

She didn't know how but Imran was making her wonder. Sure she'd had sex. She'd not been a virgin since she was sixteen years old. But this was so far beyond sex. It was intense, exquisite pleasure and Imran was blowing her mind.

"Give me a second," she said and sat up to shake her shoulder then her arms preparing like a fighter going into battle.

After a moment Imran gave a smirk. "Are you ever going to be ready for me to make love to your body?" he asked.

She'd thought she would that she already was, but damn.

She'd thought they would do the usual 'him inside of her' wam bam and then maybe a little south of the border action but Imran had started at the farthest end f the south pole and had damn near blown her mind. And to think he'd done it on her foot. She was looking at him wondering if he could produce that same reaction in her again. She hadn't been ready for it the first time. Now that she was she'd just like to see him try it.

"Okay, Imran, I'm ready now. Try that again," she whispered, "the touching me with your fingers first". She lay back and balled the sheet between her fingers twisting them to get ready to resist whatever it was Imran was going to do. When she realized what it was she was doing she stopped, noticing that Imran had not moved.

"What?" she asked.

"You were preparing yourself to resist me. I wanted to wait unit you got such nonsense out of your head. It's going to be so much fun loving you." He tilted his head. "I have something for you and I think you're going to like it." He rose from the bed and strolled with the grace of a lion across the room. If Tanya could see the grin on his face she'd probably get angry but she couldn't. His walk was deliberate as was his allowing her to view his nude form from a distance. Women liked watching a male body even if they lied about it. He knew his body was in good shape he took great care to keep it that way. Opening up the drawer of a bureau he brought out oils and scented candles made from some of the most intoxicating perfumes. He took his time giving Tanya a moment to view him without shame.

Tanya sat up just a little propping her arm on the pillow. She watched Imran walk across the room and shook her head wondering how she'd ever resisted making love to him for so many weeks. Only seven days left, she thought, not nearly long enough. She wanted to know every inch of his body intimately as he apparently planned on knowing her. His rear looked every bit as delectable as his front. Staring at him from across the room was so much more erotic. She wondered why for only a moment. What did it matter it was and that was that. She appraised his entire body pleased with what she saw. She could tell he worked out from the lines of his chiseled well muscled shoulders to a back that tapered into a trim waist. His butt was perfect round and high, very firm. He didn't jiggle when he walked. His long legs moved gracefully reminding her of some kind of jungle predator.

She was salivating as she watched him standing before the

huge dresser with his back to her. She could hear him rummaging and assumed he was taking things from it. She heard the strike of a match, smelled sulfur then in seconds the perfume and she took in a deep breath, enjoying it.

When Imran turned with his hands full of candles and things she wasn't sure of she sought his gaze and he smiled. She tried hard to keep her eyes on his but failed. As if in a trance her eyes lowered and she studied his chest chiseled and firm. From this vantage point he looked even better. She wanted to avoid his middle and just look at his powerfully looking long legs. But she was drawn to that spot between his thighs. A shiver claimed him from halfway across the room making it easy for her to see his immense erection. It looked as though it had increased in girth and length in the couple of minutes he'd stood with his back to her.

She scrutinized his movements as he walked, regal, his erection jutting out proudly allowing her to see his swollen twin jewels beneath. They were so large and so tight they barely moved. As he came closer Tanya could barely breathe. He was a lot more endowed than what she'd ever had and as he came near she wondered if she'd be able to stretch to accommodate him and prayed that she would. She didn't blink not wanting to miss a moment of the show that was just for her.

Then it hit her, Imran knew exactly what he was doing. He was deliberately turning her on. She smiled not caring just wanting to touch him, to taste him, to feel him buried deep inside her.

"Imran," she said throatily reaching her hand out to touch, to tease, to squeeze. She wrapped her hand around him and used a finger to caress him from his scrotum back to the tip. She felt the shudder that passed through him and he gripped her hand.

"Stop that," he said softly.

"I can't resist touching you."

"If you don't stop I won't be able to do all the things I've planned to bring you fulfillment."

For a second longer Tanya debated and then loosened her grip allowing for one last stroke. Why not? She deserved to steal some happiness for herself. One thing she agreed with her parents about and that was that she did deserve a life too. As she gazed into Imran's eyes she knew he was the key to her having that life.

"Lay back again," Imran pleaded his eyes heavy with lust his erection twitching. She sighed and did as he asked and he almost sighed with relief. If she touched him again he'd have to sheath himself in her warmth he wouldn't be able to follow thorough with pleasuring her in all the ways he'd planned, well not immediately anyway.

He poured oil into a small gaily decorated Turkish bowl then placed the bowl over the burner. For a few moments he feasted his eyes on the brown beauty that lay on his bed waiting for him. He felt the flutter in his chest again as their eyes connected. He'd had many women, had made love to them in the most exquisite ways and had been made love to in ways that had taken his very breath away. But never had a woman taken his breath away simply by watching him and never had he felt this constant fluttering in his chest. Seven days was not nearly enough, not seven weeks, seven months, nor seven years. He realized in that moment that he loved her. What he was about to do now was seduce her into loving him. A twinge of conscience pricked him. He was not what she wanted or needed to help make her dreams come true. But she was what he needed in his life what he'd been missing.

What he was about to do to her wasn't magic but it had been stressed many times that a man should only love a woman so thoroughly if he intended to keep her for life. He swallowed. He intended to keep Tanya for life. He dipped his finger into the oil feeling for the perfect temperature, giving it a few more seconds. Then he poured a scant amount into his palm and rubbed it in. He gently lifted Tanya's right foot into his lap and with slow and sure strokes he began to massage her foot going from the heels to the toes, going in between. He knew the exact moment the oil began its slow and methodical burn. He heard the moan slip from her throat and increased the pressure never leaving her foot, kneading her in just the right spot, knowing which would bring her juices gushing form her core. He pressed gently lifting up slightly then pressing more firmly until Tanya's hips rose from the bed. She screamed his name. Still he didn't stop, just changed the motion in order for her to ride out the orgasm with the most pleasure. This was the first. Before the night was over there would be many, many more and she would be irrevocably bound to him and he to her. He'd never wanted to completely make love to any woman, now he did. There was no way he wanted her gone from his life. He would go with her to America. He could finish his book there. He pressed on each toe as the aftershocks of her pleasure slid through her. He felt her body loosening its rigid hold and he smiled. He was far from done with her.

Her breathing was finally slowing down. Never in her life had she experienced anything like that. She couldn't believe she'd just had the best orgasm of her life and had not had oral or penile stimulation. It was crazy but from the very instant that Imran had rubbed the warm oil on her foot she had feel a burning that pulled at her center she'd felt a vague fullness as though Imran had entered her but was aware that he hadn't but to be sure she'd looked. As he'd massaged her foot it was as though her body suddenly had pins pricking her in her most sensitive area, every pinprick brought pleasure and every spasm of pleasure produced more and the feeling had continued until it encompassed her entire body her nipples became pebbled and hard and all over her body it was as though she could feel a touch a caressing erotic touch that filled her and brought about an eruption that she'd never known. Now she lay quietly panting, wanting to know just what the heck Imran had done and if he could possible do it again. *Wow*, she thought what a way to make love. She felt deliciously sated. Bringing her eyes finally to meet Imran she saw his grin and knew they'd just begun. She moaned in expectation as he smiled and poured more oil into his palm and began rubbing her ankle.

"Round two," Imran whispered.

With the sun streaming through the windows Tanya could easily picture herself finding her own paradise and staying on in Pakistan. She took a slow look around Heaven's home. Maybe her home would not be as luxurious but it would be very nice. She smiled as she contemplated the dream, barely hearing Hamid call her to the phone.

"Damn!" Tanya hung up the phone and willed herself not to cry as guilt assailed her. She should have called home before now. She hadn't because she knew something would happen to spoil her trip and make her feel guilty for having left. She felt a hand on her shoulder and knew that Heaven was aware it was trouble in Chicago.

"What's wrong?" Heaven asked.

"It's Lettie. She's in the hospital. I shouldn't have come. No one wants to keep all of Lettie's kids, even for the few days that she's been there. They all make it sound like it's my fault, that I did something wrong by not being at home." Anger straightened her spine and guilt sharpened her tongue. She pulled away from Heaven. "I deserve a life also. Do you want to know another reason I took this trip? Why I came here? Because I knew this would more than likely be my last chance to just think of myself. Don't you think I know with what I'm about to take on, my chances of finding a husband—A good husband are nil to zero. I came here to pretend that I could have it all, Heaven."

"You can, Tann. What about Imran? I know you have feelings for him and he likewise. I told you all along that he was perfect for you."

"Do you really think I'm going to try to start something with him knowing that I have so many responsibilities?"

"But you already started something with him."

"Grow up, Heaven, that's just sex. He'll get over it and so will I." The moment the words were out Tanya shook her head and the tears began to fall. "What am I going to do? I thought I was ready... but six kids...Heaven, how am I going to take care of them?"

"Tann, you know I'll help anyway that I can."

Tanya tried hard to keep the tears from falling. She didn't want to cry and especially not in front of anyone, not even Heaven. "This all sounds so selfish. Here Lettie is fighting for her life and worrying herself even sicker wondering what's going to happen to her babies. And I'm crying because I can't bring Imran into all of my drama. He has even less money than I do. The odds of him becoming published are astronomical and even if he does, to make a living at it or a living that would support that many kids from the off start is just about non-existent. Even if he could I refuse to ask him to do it."

Heaven hugged her tightly. "It seems you've been giving this some thought."

"Daydreaming that's all. He's made me feel so special here. He's taken me all over Pakistan. He's shown me the beauty and he's shown me the bad. He's even made me face up to my own faults," she shrugged. "I would have never admitted before Imran that I was jealous of you. He's made me feel protected when we've traveled places where we more than likely shouldn't have. And he's fought with me so much that I laugh whenever I think about it."

"Sounds like you've fallen for him no matter what you say."

"I'm not going to lie and tell you no. I have fallen for him but when I leave Pakistan I leave Imran behind. It won't take long for us to get over it. I refuse to ask him to step into this."

"And what if he wants to?"

"He's an honorable man he'll want to but I don't want him to. I have no need to be rescued by a man."

"I thought that was why you said you were coming, to be rescued, to marry one of Hamid's brother's so you wouldn't have to worry about money."

"So throw that up in my face now when I'm all sad. You're wrong for that, Heaven." The tension was broken. Tanya leaned back on her heels and rocked. "Yeah, well, that was a long shot wasn't it? Who knows maybe if I had met one of Hamid's brothers before I met Imran?" She grinned remembering from the moment she'd met Imran she's felt a connection.

"Why do you think I asked Fatima to call him to come over and stop you from your crazy plan? I knew Imran was going to be your match."

"You set us up." Tanya had almost forgotten the day Imran had first kissed her. She'd been laughing so hard at the expression on Heaven's face that she'd completely ignored his words telling Heaven that she had been wrong to have used Fatima in her plans. So he'd known all along or at least he'd been aware of it a lot sooner than she had. "You brought Imran here so he'd be the first thing I saw. You're crazy. What if we hadn't liked each other?"

"But it wasn't crazy," Heaven couldn't resist smirking. "From the moment he walked in the door you were all over him like white on rice. You liked him from the start and he liked you. I knew all along I was right. Why do you think I've been trying to get you here for more than a year? I knew he'd be perfect for you. I also knew that you were both too stubborn to do things on your own in the proper time frame. Neither of you would have made a move in time if I hadn't. We didn't have forever only six weeks and it worked. You're in love with him."

"Look, I didn't say love."

"But you are," Heaven insisted. "I see the way you are around him and all the time you've been spending coming in here with all those bald face lies. My plan almost worked," Heaven's voice trailed off as she also thought of Lettie. "Tanya, listen to me and don't get angry. I could help you take care of the kids. I can give you a set amount of money each month and you wouldn't have to worry. My business is booming. I have the money. It wouldn't be a hardship and it wouldn't be money that I was getting from Hamid."

Tanya kissed her and pulled back to look into her friend's eyes. "That is so sweet and I love you so much for it. But, Heaven, if I do not want to be rescued by a man I want even less to be rescued by a woman. You're my best friend and you know how I am about this so let it drop okay? And keep your nose to yourself. Don't you tell Imran how I feel. We only have a couple of more days. I want to make the most of them. After all when I leave here that's it for us. That's the way it has to be."

The stars blanketed the sky as Heaven and Hamid lay on the thick mattress they kept tucked in their closet for making love on the patio under the stars. Heaven's head was on Hamid's chest as she tried to think of a way to help Tanya and Imran be together.

"What am I going to do, Hamid?"

"Heaven, you're going to stay out of it. Tanya is a grown woman. She asked that you not to interfere."

"But she's in love with your cousin. She needs him in her life and he needs her. He's never been happier. He can't spend all his days coming over to play with our son looking at him as though he's never going to have sons of his own. What if Tanya is the woman for him? What if they were destined to marry and have babies?"

"Then fate will take care of it and fate will take care of it without you. I'm serious. Imran cares a great deal for Tanya he's told me so, but that would be a big responsibility for him to take on so many of Tanya's dreams."

"We could help them out, we could give them money."

"And we could take away their pride. My cousin would never consent to that. Always as a child he lived in the shadows of my bothers and I. He hated it. As a man he will not allow it. It is not that my uncle does not have money. Imran will not ask his father for money."

"But you told me your uncle bought the house and furniture for him. He accepted that."

"He's also not a fool and he had no desire to stay in a hovel which would have been what he could afford. But for day to day living he takes care of those things himself. He even cleans his home himself only having a woman come into clean and cook a couple times a week."

At that Heaven laughed knowing that Hamid thought having help only twice a week was a hardship.

"You're laughing at me?"

"Just a little. What are we going to do to help them?"

"We're going to do exactly as Tanya asked. We're going to stay out of it. You've plotted and planned and gotten them this far. Now for the rest of it they will have to take over." Hamid pulled Heaven to him and kissed her into submission pulling the covers over them. "Our bed is not the place for fights," he whispered, "but for loving. Let me make you forget Imran and Tanya."

Imran's hand lingered on her bare flesh. She was so soft, so warm. Imran pulled Tanya even closer he'd enjoyed her visit and knowing this was the last night he'd lay with her in his arms the revelation came. He didn't want it to end. He wanted her in his life. Fate had brought her to him and he would not allow circumstances to keep them apart.

Bending his head to take a puckered nipple into his mouth Imran suckled her as his fingers probed. She wiggled into position and began caressing him, each touch making him burn at his core as he thought of things he could do. He'd ask her to stay. The thought went away she wouldn't stay she had her obligations, the children of her cousin the babies of the streets. Could they make it? he wondered. Did they have what they needed to jump over the hurdle they they'd face from the moment they were together? It was an awesome responsibility one Imran wasn't altogether sure that he was ready to face. Tanya's hand closed over him and she played along his length running her finger over his tip. He moaned and shivered. He very much wanted to try.

❧

For several long minutes Imran had been pacing in his cousin's kitchen. He'd needed someone to talk to. He'd never been in love before, had never told a woman that he loved her and definitely had not expected the reaction he'd received from Tanya on telling her. Maybe it was just American women. He didn't know. That was the reason he needed to ask Hamid.

"Hamid I can't believe her reaction. I told her that I was in love with her and she went crazy, demanded that it bring her back here. Was Heaven this bad?"

"Worse. She beat me up," Hamid laughed at the look on Imran face. "I'm not kidding," he continued and told the story.

"Is it all American women?"

"I think it's women in general," Hamid admitted, "but as for Tanya she knows she's going home to face a lot of problems. Heaven told me that Tanya's cousin is in the hospital. She's promised to care for her children— six of them, Imran. This isn't a joke. Unless you decide to go into any of the many family businesses, right now you cannot support a family of that size. I think maybe Tanya is right in wanting the two of you to end things here."

"Would you have left Heaven if she had problems?" Imran cocked his head and waited for an answer that did not come. "Of course you wouldn't have left her, but then again you're one of the millionaire sons aren't you?"

"Imran, don't do this."

Glaring at Hamid, Imran walked out the door. He'd never argued with any of his cousins because of their status and it had never cut him so deeply than now that what Hamid said was the truth. Imran could not take care of a family of six kids at the moment. As for his book he'd been writing it and researching it for three years and he still wasn't done. Still there had to be a way for him to help the woman he loved. He had to find a way. Fate had brought them together with a little help from Heaven perhaps but fate would keep them together. Praise to Allah.

6

IMRAN SAT IN A CORNER observing Tanya. There was a sudden aloofness toward him that was until she turned and faced him, then the heat shimmered between them. He smiled but she didn't return it. He knew what she was doing. She didn't want to admit that she was falling for him. Her plans were what were important to her. He'd been a diversion a break from her normal life. But there was more, he saw the way her breath hitched in her throat when he'd accidentally touched her earlier. She'd jumped back as though burned it was that electrical.

For seven days and nights he'd stolen those times and made love to her worshipping her body drowning in her chocolate eyes and she'd enjoyed him. It was only when he'd attempted to tell her that he was falling in love with her that she'd cursed and jumped from his bed dressing and demanding that he take her home to Heaven's. Since then he'd tried talking to no avail, even pleading hadn't worked. She wanted no part of a relationship with him she'd hissed at him when he'd come over earlier in the day. He'd prayed and was hopeful that Tanya wouldn't give in to her fears she has such a short time left in Pakistan surely they would be able to patch things up. But now as he sat watching her knowing that the next day she would leave he wondered if he weren't a glutton for punishment. He stared at her and she stared back no warmth for him in her gaze and he winced. Could it be that she'd been telling him the truth earlier that day when she'd said she was going to tell him the night before that she didn't want a relationship with him? That was she said until he'd ruined things. Now with this wall of ice that was going up higher and higher between them it made him wonder. Perhaps it was all true. Perhaps she'd not cried as he sang to her. Perhaps he'd not seen and felt her love but he had. Imran dropped his gaze from hers and turned away.

The sound of her laugher was false the notes didn't have the right cadence. She flirted with Ali amusing him with her antics stabbing Imran with her indifference. For a moment he saw looks pass between Heaven and Hamid, a look of pity it seemed. He shrugged when Heaven glanced in his direction. He'd not admitted to loving Tanya to his cousin's wife and he'd not do so now.

Suddenly and as if by a plan all three women in the room were on the floor kneeling over the coffee table at the array of diamonds Ali had brought over.

"Tanya, I did not forget my promise to you to show you some diamonds." Since you're leaving tomorrow please pick something as my gift to you," Ali said then glanced over toward Imran and smiled.

Imran knew what his cousin was doing. Hamid had undoubtedly told Ali that Imran had confessed to being in love with Tanya. He turned to glare at Hamid who shook his head no. Then he glanced back at Ali who also shook his head no and pointed a finger toward Imran. Imran sighed and closed his eyes. He guessed the way he was behaving his cousins wouldn't have a hard time knowing what he was feeling. They'd always been close. Still, Imran wondered why his cousin would bait the woman he loved with diamonds that Imran couldn't afford to buy for her.

"What would you like, Tanya?" Ali asked again.

"Nothing," Tanya laughed and began fingering the pieces. "Listen, Ali, I'm sorry for coming on so strong to you before. I really don't want anything other than your friendship. I'm not this gold digging American that I portrayed initially."

"But I thought diamonds were a girl's best friends."

"Not even close," Tanya shook her head and moved away from Ali. "Diamonds definitely don't buy happiness." She moved even farther away from Ali and her gaze slid quickly to Imran and held for a moment. She inhaled, closed her eyes briefly and returned to looking at the jewels.

When Imran looked toward Ali his cousin had a huge grin on his face and he was motioning toward Tanya. It was Ali's way of telling Imran that he approved of Tanya that she wasn't a gold digger. Imran bowed his head slightly in acknowledgement and shrugged but didn't move toward Tanya. His cousin's proof had not been necessary. His heart had long ago told him of the character of the woman he loved. He'd have to forget her if that was what she truly wanted. In the space of a breath he knew his thoughts for the lies they were. The fluttering in his chest was so intense that it was actually painful. There would be too many things that he would be forever remembering about Tanya. How was he supposed to forget?

He sighed and devoured Tanya with his eyes trying to drink in the sight of her so he'd never forget her. At that precise moment Tanya raised to her knees and her round jeans covered derriere was starring him in the face. If only Imran hadn't remembered the way he'd pounded into Tanya's body as he'd kneeled behind her feeling the firmness of her flesh. If only he didn't get so hard while watching her rounded buttocks. He couldn't believe he'd made love to her for the last time. The thought that she didn't even want to try to pursue a more serious relationship with him stunned him into the silence he now found himself in. It would be no grand feat for them to continue a relationship. Heaven and Hamid had managed to conduct a marriage while they were a continent apart. Surely if they both wanted it he and Tanya could do the same.

Heaven's squeal made Imran look up. Hamid was kissing her unashamedly as he fastened diamonds around her neck, then put a bracelet on each wrist and handed her earring to put in. His arms went around her and the heat between them sizzled making Imran wish for those things. He felt as though he were spying on his cousin and his wife in an intimate moment. He glanced away but his gaze caught Tanya and he realized that she wanted the same things that he did. Love, for someone to have that all consuming feeling about her. Then why, he wondered didn't she take what he was offering? They had so much in common. They laughed uproariously together, enjoyed many of the same things and they fought well. His eyes remained fastened on her. And they made love equally as well. He refused to avert his gaze from her sweet lips.

Fatima ohhed and ahhed over her brother's newest jewels putting diamond bangles around her wrist and rings on her fingers. It was then he noticed Tanya's gaze hadn't moved from the pair of earrings she held in her hands. She wanted them. He saw her biting her lips before she returned them to the case. He walked over for a better look. They were pretty, he thought.

"Tanya, choose what you want as my gift to you and choose something that you believe the others will like as well," Hamid called out to her.

Imran glanced at Hamid then at Tanya. Not taking a gift of diamonds from Ali was one thing but the earrings she wanted, surely she'd take them from Hamid and Heaven. Imran waited.

"No thanks, Hamid. You've done enough for me already. I can't take anything else."

"Don't be silly," Heaven rushed over and reached for the earrings Tanya had been fawning over. "You love these. Here, they're a gift from us."

For a moment Tanya didn't move then she took the earrings from Heaven's hand and again laid them in the case. "No thanks, Heaven, you and Hamid, have done enough."

In this she had surprised him. She turned slightly and her gaze caught Imran. The look she gave him stopped his heart. It was as though she knew what their buying her an expensive gift like that would do. She hadn't taken the gift of diamond earrings she obviously wanted because of him. Why? he wondered.

He continued watching as she chose pieces for her friends while every few seconds her eyes would glide toward Heaven and Hamid as they cooed together over Tsukama. He saw her swallow then close her eyes and this time deliberately move toward him. Her look had longing, sadness, regret and yes love. She wanted what Heaven and Hamid had. She wanted love and babies. And she wanted her diamonds to come from a man who loved her as much as Hamid loved Heaven. She wanted the diamond to come from him. Imran swallowed as well. He wanted the diamonds to come from him as well.

ॐ

Tanya was going to miss Pakistan. She'd enjoyed her visit, the customs, the food and the people. Even Hamid's parents had warmed slightly toward her. When she'd figured out that Fatima had plotted with Heaven to get her together with Imran they'd become fast friends. At least that was after she'd already admitted to herself that she had a thing for him.

She was really going to miss him. Her actions the night before would more than likely hasten Imran's getting over her. She'd barely spoken to him. She knew what was waiting for her at home. And with Lettie being in the hospital the possibility of it happening sooner than later was real. It wasn't just her being stubborn. It was the right thing to do. She knew it was the right thing to do yet her heart felt heavy and a wave of sadness invaded her spirit. She did love Imran but she had to let go of that also. Out of sight out of mind right? She sure hoped so.

"Tanya, are you sure you can't have it all? You've been unhappy since Imran brought you home the other night."

"I don't know, Heaven, maybe if I hadn't gotten the call that Lettie was in the hospital. Maybe if they family had pitched in and one person had kept those kids for a few days without fighting about it. But they didn't. I promised Lettie. You know it's the right thing to do. If something happened to you or Hamid you knew Tsukama has more than enough people to love him and protect and care for him but what if he didn't? You'd want to make sure he'd be loved. I know you would."

Heaven could only sigh as the tears filled her eyes and ran down her cheeks. "I know but it's like you're giving up your chance to be happy to have a husband and children of your own. I don't want you to miss out on all of that not when you've found it. That's all I'm just worried for you and for Imran."

"Thanks, but we both know my life has become way too complicated. I have way too many problems and you know yourself it wouldn't be fair to plop Imran into all of that. She hugged Heaven. No, it wouldn't be fair to bring the things she was about take on into any new relationship. Imran had enough worries trying to go after his own dreams and trying to convince his family that his dream was worthwhile.

Her luggage had been checked all that was left to do was say her goodbyes. She hugged Hamid and flirted with him a little anything to keep it light. But when it was time to hug Heaven she lost it. She had really missed her friend. "Thanks, Heaven," she mumbled around the tears. "I really enjoyed myself. It was even worth the shots I had to take. And you have the world's cutest baby regardless of his name. He's adorable. He's going to be a heart breaker like his father," she said and smiled up at Hamid. Suddenly she blinked, her words forgotten as she found herself facing Imran. Her heart was racing. She wanted to throw her arms around him and kiss him, beg him to jump into the fire with her, to come back to Chicago and make love to her, to help her raise Lettie's kids when the time came. But she wouldn't do that. She licked her lips and bit back the things that she wanted. She couldn't have them so there was no use in hoping.

She looked first at his smiling face and her heart skipped a beat overjoyed that he'd come to say goodbye then sadness replaced it. This was goodbye for them.

"Imran, you came. I wasn't expecting you." She held out her hand for him to shake and instead he looked inquisitively at her.

"I didn't come to say goodbye." he replied.

"No? Then why did you come?"

"I came to accompany you. I don't think we should just allow us to end not without trying to find a way for us to be together."

Tears filled her eyes and a lump came to her throat. He was so sweet. She looked at his beautify honey colored skin and wanted to grasp him and hug him close. But she wouldn't do it, she'd practice modesty in public. Still, the thought was there. Imran wanted to give up his freedom to be a bachelor to follow her. A tear fell and she angrily wiped it away. Why not? She wanted to scream. She'd never thought she'd have a man love her enough to put her first. She'd wanted a man to love her the way Hamid loved Heaven, now she had it. She pulled in a breath until it hurt. She finally understood why Heaven had given up her life in Chicago and all that she'd wanted to follow Hamid to Pakistan. Hamid's happiness came first with Heaven that was obvious. It was then Tanya knew what she must do. If she loved Imran and she did she would do what as right for him. *God*, she prayed silently. I don't want to. I don't want to hurt him and I don't want to let him go. I want him in my life. I love him. I want him to come back to Chicago with me. She swallowed away her desires the same as she'd done her tears. She wiped her hands down the side of her hip praying for strength to see this through. How could she allow Imran to give up so much? She blinked, she had to do it. As much as she wanted him to come with her it was unfair.

"Imran, are you planning to live with Sassa?" Tanya asked. "I understand that he's on his way here."

"I'm not coming to Chicago to be with Sassa. Why would I plan to live with him?"

She caught the look Heaven gave to Hamid and wondered had they done anything to bring Imran to the airport. She hoped not because it would be their fault as well as hers when she ripped his heart out for his own good.

"What are you planning to do in Chicago?" She asked in the coldest voice she had.

"I will get a job, two jobs if necessary and I will help you care for the children."

Damn! Tanya stopped for a moment wondering if it would work. "What about your writing?" she asked. "You need to finish your book. It's your dream."

"Perhaps I've found a dream that means more to me. I can help you fulfill yours. Yours is a noble dream. Mine can wait. It's been three years since I began the book what's another three years?" He gave her a look wondering why all of the questions. He'd just presented her with the answers to both of their problems why wasn't she in his arms why was she instead backing away.

"What will you do until you find a job? Jobs aren't that easy to find right now in America. We're almost in a recession."

"There are always jobs for those willing to work. I'm willing to work. Why are you asking me so many questions?" he asked.

"I don't need a roommate, Imran. You should have asked me before you made your plans." He was staring at her, his liquid brown eyes that had been at first amused, narrowed slightly.

"You don't have to do this, Tanya, I'm a big boy. I'm coming with you because I love you."

Oh God. Her guts twisted. He loved her. She shook her head slightly he was making this hard on her. She loved him too. In this short span of time he'd captured her heart. She thought of baby Jo Jo and all the other kids she wanted to help. Then a picture of Lettie and her brood came into her mind. Imran didn't deserve to be settled with that. She took a deep breath and released it. "Imran, I told you before we started that we could have an affair, a brief affair, nothing more and that it would end when I was ready to leave. I don't want you to come with me."

"You're fronting, Tanya."

Fronting. So Heaven had taught him that. She almost smiled. "Imran, I'm not fronting. I mean it. It was nice to meet you but I have to return to my life. Thanks for showing me the country. Good luck with your writing." She watched as his eyes narrowed even more and anger flooded them. Good, she thought, she needed his anger. She waited for him to say something anything to make her truly glad she was leaving him behind. But he didn't. He turned on his heels and marched away.

He stole her breath when he walked away. Tanya found it difficult to swallow, her chest hurt. She swallowed again and blinked rapidly several times to keep the tears from falling. She'd done the right thing. He'd get over loving her in time. She lifted her head and saw the look of pity Heaven was giving her. Hamid was staring toward the door after his cousin. When he turned to her his look was puzzled.

"Why?" Hamid asked. "He loves you. He came to be with you why did you hurt him and in front of us?"

"I had to." Tanya shrugged her shoulders. "You both know what I'm going home to. I can't ask him to take part in that. Just don't tell him okay. We weren't together but a few weeks. He'll get over me soon."

"Love doesn't work like that Tanya. It doesn't just go away. Yes, he can get over the hurt but that doesn't mean he'll get over loving you. Goodbye, Tanya, have a safe trip." He turned and left them also, walking to where Imran waited outside.

"He's pissed isn't he?" she asked Heaven.

"Well, let's say you're not one of his favorite people right now. I guess I understand your reasons but Imran's a grown man. He knows his own mind. You should have at least taken him to the side and told him. You shouldn't have done that to him in front of us."

As if she didn't know that. Tanya winced. "Don't you think I know that? He was getting to me making me want to drag him into this mess with me. I don't think you would have wanted Hamid to have such problems not if you could have prevented it. It doesn't mean I don't love Imran. It means I do and I want him to finish his book. Maybe if he hadn't said he was willing to give up his dream in order to help me but I couldn't take that away from him. I had no choice in this. Damn. I knew what I was doing when I went for the jugular. I wounded more than his heart I wounded his pride. He won't forgive me for that." She shrugged. "It was necessary Heaven." She kissed her friend and walked toward the jet alone. Alone, she thought *more than likely what she would be for the rest of her life*. Her shoulders sagged with the weight of the responsibilities she would soon take on. She sighed. But it was what she wanted wasn't it? It was her dream to help take care of children. What did it matter if she'd never know love? She'd have the kids.

⟞⟝

For three months Tanya had been home. She'd talked to Heaven a couple of times and neither of them had mentioned Imran. It was as though she'd never met him. The only times when she couldn't pretend was in night in bed. There her body longed for him, her nipples cried out for his mouth to suckle her, her thighs craved his kisses and her nether lips wept in sorrow.

At least things were looking up with Lettie. She'd decided to take an experimental medication and the last MRI had shown that her tumors had shrunk. Of course the side effects were to be expected. Tanya kept the kids whenever things became too rough or Lettie just needed to rest. On those nights she could continue thinking her decision to not allow Imran to come to Chicago was the right one. She loved Lettie's kids madly but still they drove her crazy and she found herself praying that Lettie would live a long and healthy life for more than one reason. Sure the main one was that she loved her cousin and didn't want her to die but the second one was that she wondered if she would remain sane when the last of Lettie's kids were old enough to head off to college. Tanya laughed at the thoughts. Whenever the kids made her too crazy it seemed somehow they knew it and they would shower her with hugs and kisses reaffirming her decision and her love.

The nights when the kids were with her and driving her crazy were a thousand times easier to endure than the nights when she was alone. It was on those nights when she was alone when all she wanted to was to be able to lie in Imran's arms, to make love to him to him, to have him sing love songs to her that she understood with her heart and from the look in his eyes. She wanted to hear him tell her that he loved her and she wanted to wrap her arms around him and tell him that she loved him also. She wanted to listen as he read her passages from the book he as working on about real life in Pakistan. She wondered how close he was to finishing it. She wondered if he missed her or if he'd forgotten about her completely. She wondered if he was massaging another woman's foot and became angry.

A sigh escaped and just in time her phone rang and Tanya smiled knowing the call would be about good news on the village project. At least something was going good. She'd turned over every dime of her savings to Jonathan Sandstome, all twenty-five-thousand dollars. And the building for the second house would start any day. She's seen the finished house a couple of weeks before and knew all it needed was a family. Things were beginning to look up. Even Jo Jo was doing well. She'd known the foster home she'd placed him in would be a good fit. She'd had to force herself not to visit the baby more than she was supposed to. He wasn't hers. She had to sever the connection before it became unbearable.

"Hello," Tanya said allowing yet another sigh to escape.

"It's gone, Tanya, Sandstome took all of the money even from the first house. We've lost it all. Neither the house or the land was ever bought in the organization's name. He scammed us all. He even lied on his background check. He has a criminal record. He was good, real good that's why it took this long for the information to come back on him."

"Slow down, Sara. What are you talking about?"

"The house. The house isn't ours. He tricked us it was never ours."

"But we have keys. I've been there. We even had a party in there." Tanya's head was buzzing. "I was just there last week we've furnished the house, everything. We have a family waiting to go in there."

"Tanya, listen to me. It was all a scam. The house belongs to a realty company. He was supposed to be selling it. Oh God. It's such a mess."

"The land we were buying for the other home what about that?"

Jeannie started crying. "It was fraud all of it, even the lawyers he brought in. It seemed so real. It's all gone. We have no land, no house, no money, it's over."

"But I put all of my money in there. I gave him a check for twenty-five thousand dollars a week ago." Tanya groaned and held her belly. "I gave it to him when he was telling me that the first family had been chosen."

"I'm so sorry," Jeannie moaned. "We were all taken."

"But that was every dime I had," Tanya yelled.

"I'm sorry," Jeannie answered.

"You got me into this. You told me everything was taken care of. I never would have done this if it hadn't been for you. You're a millionaire I'm not. That was all the money I had." Tanya slammed the phone down and began rocking. God, I don't believe it. How could I have been so stupid? What am I going to do now?

∾

Imran held Tsukama in his arms, bouncing him, amused at the baby's antics, giving him a smile as the infant patted his cheeks as though to comfort him. "Imran," Heaven called to him and for a moment he thought not to answer her. If it were not for the baby he would not visit them. For a time he hadn't but he missed Tsukama.

"Imran?"

This time the voice that called him was annoyed and it belonged to Hamid.

"Are you deliberately ignoring Heaven?" Hamid asked. "She has done nothing to you."

That was true. Imran stiffened his spine and turned to face his cousin. "Your wife annoys me," he said softly in Urdu.

"Excuse me."

"You heard me. She keeps giving me these pitying looks and I've warned her many times not to mention her friend's name in front of me and to stop looking at me in that manner."

"If my wife annoys you then you should not be here in her home. Why are you here?"

"Your son does not annoy me."

"Are you saying that I also annoy you?"

"Yes."

Hamid smiled in spite of Imran's words. He sighed. "It's been months, Imran," he stopped as Imran glared at him. "Heaven wants to know if you'd like to stay for dinner."

"She doesn't use enough curry."

Hamid gave his cousin a look that meant he was going to get angry in about two seconds. "That's enough. No more insulting my wife, no more talking in Urdu either. You stay or you leave. Either way you will apologize to my wife for your rude behavior."

Imran opened his mouth to protest and as Hamid removed the baby from his arms he thought better of it. He'd been wrong to blame Heaven for Tanya's rejection. Sure she'd been the one to set them up he's suspected it long before Fatima confessed it. Still Hamid was right. That was not a good enough reason to continue treating Heaven in the cold manner he had the last few months. He glanced at Hamid knowing he was a second from throwing him out of their home and a minute from disowning him. Neither, he wanted. "Very well," he said. "I will apologize to Heaven." He reached for the baby but Hamid held him away and pointed his finger toward the door, his message loud and clear. *You will not hold my son until you made amends with my wife.* So be it, Imran thought and walked out the door and up to Heaven.

"Heaven, I'm sorry I've been so rude to you and most especially in your own home."

"You know, Imran, you're being a big baby. I've been trying to be nice because I know how it feels to love someone and to be dumped." She saw Hamid wince and immediately caressed his back. "So maybe Tanya wasn't the right woman for you. If she left you so easily she couldn't love you. Forget her. There is more than likely a woman just waiting for you to let go of the anger."

"She did love me," Imran insisted for the first time since Tanya had returned to Chicago. He'd refused since then to speak her name let alone admit to anyone how he felt about her still. Now he didn't care if Hamid disowned him. He would not stand there and allow Heaven to say that Tanya didn't love him. That was a lie that he wouldn't accept. "I know why she left me. She had responsibilities and she needs a man with money to help her."

"That doesn't sound much like love," Heaven insisted. "It sounds like she really was a just a gold digger." She put her hands on her hips. "If Tanya didn't have a better reason than that if I were you I wouldn't waste my time loving her, thinking about her or

defending her. Did she have a better reason Imran?" Heaven asked
ignoring Hamid's warning to stay out of it. This had gone on long
enough.

"Imran studied Heaven for a moment then closed his eyes as the
knowledge of what Heaven was doing came to him. "Tanya did
what she did for me. She didn't want me to give up my dream. She
was trying to protect me from acquiring her burden. Thanks,
Heaven."

"Then why have you been behaving like a jackass if you knew
this already?"

"It took your saying she hadn't loved me I supposed." He
smiled. "I am sorry, Heaven, for the way I've been treating you."

"I'm glad you said that. I was just that much," Heaven said
snapping her finger together, "from kicking your behind. Ask your
cousin." She glanced at Hamid and smiled. "Now, do you want to
stay for dinner?"

෴

Tanya sat in her lawyer's office she'd filed a complaint just as all
the donors had done. No hope was given to them. Jonathan
Sandstome had apparently left the country with all of their money
and in spite of Sara saying that she was sorry she didn't offer to
give Tanya her money back. She could well afford to lose that kind
of money. Tanya couldn't. She groaned wondering how she'd used
all of her money now she had no back up to take care of Lettie's
kids. She should have thought about that.

"Tanya, I'm sorry but you really have no recourse but to sue the
organization."

She thought for a moment of suing the organization and all the
people who'd lost money same as she had. She bit her lip trying to
let go of some of the anger and disappointment knowing that she'd
have to let it go. When you gave money for a worthy cause you
couldn't do anything else. She'd always maintained that stance
with her tithes to the church. When her friends would complain
she'd say it wasn't her responsibility to see to the spending of the
money after it left her hand. She gave for the glory of God and in
this she'd have to do the same. She gave in order for disadvantaged
children to have a shot at a more normal life. She wished now that
she'd given her money to a more established organization like SOS
village. They were doing the same thing but she'd gotten carried
away with Sara's concept and had wanted to be involved. She'd
given her money for a worthy cause. Groaning, she rocked her
body slowly back and forth and looked at her lawyer. She d given

up Imran and still didn't have the dream.

❧

"Damn! Snap!" Peaches said in disbelief. "Why the hell would you give them all of that money?"

"He told me they needed it. Sara was already getting suspicious but didn't bother to tell me. Probably she didn't think I'd give him that much money. I hadn't in the past no more than a few hundred dollars at a time."

"Why doesn't she give you your money back?" Peaches asked.

"Because she didn't take it."

"But you got into this because of her. If not for her you would have never heard of the place, never gotten involved. It's her fault."

Peaches indignation made Tanya smile and she hugged her friend. "Thanks," she said. "That's what best friends are for. You tell me I'm right even when I'm wrong and you blame others for my mistakes. I'm a grown ass woman. I should have known better. Believe me I tried to lay this all on Sara when I first found out. I said the same things that you're saying and trust me I believed I was right. But I've had some time to process it now. And I know I can't blame Sara. It's not her fault that I'm not a millionaire and couldn't afford to lose that kind of money." She shrugged. "It wasn't like I was going to ever see the money again. It was a gift. We're just complaining now because someone stole it. Damn," she said. "I should have known better but I wanted to do it. I'm mostly sad that the project isn't going to go forward. A lot of people won't bother to help out anymore and I understand why. It's the kids who're going to suffer. And me she thought, I gave up Imran for this pipe dream

"What about Lettie and her kids? You're still helping them out I know you are. What are you going to do? You have nothing to fall back on."

"I'm going to continue helping them out. And I'm going to keep praying that the experimental drugs work. One thing has nothing to do with the other."

"Dag Tann, don't you wish now you'd not told Hamid's cousin that you didn't want him? I bet right about now you could use a man's shoulder to cry on."   ·

She could definitely use a man's arms to hold her tight but not any man. She thought of the smoky look in Imran eyes before they made love and the way they changed after. She stilled herself against the hurt that always came when she allowed herself to think about him. She missed him like crazy. Since returning home she'd not had the desire to go out with another man let alone make love to one. It was almost as if Imran had imprinted himself on her body and soul leaving her irrevocably bound to him.

"Are you going to tell Heaven?" Sassa asked.

Tanya glared at Sassa and waited for the loud music in the blues club to stop for a moment. Sassa was known for running his mouth. She wanted to make sure that he didn't go running to Hamid or Imran telling them what had happened. She didn't want Imran running to Chicago to attempt to rescue her. If he did right now she might just let him. No, she still couldn't let him do that. She'd tell Heaven in her own good time. It was almost three months later before Tanya felt up to telling Heaven. She'd not told her initially because of the real possibility of Heaven spilling the beans to Imran. Then she'd not told her because she knew Heaven would want to ride in and save the day. She didn't want her friend saving the day, not this time.

"Heaven, I've saved almost five hundred dollars in the three months since it happened," Tanya attempted to soothe her friend.

"Did you tell Peaches and Ongela?"

"Yeah I did… but…."

"But what? They're your friends and I'm not?"

Tanya sighed. "You know it's not like that Heaven. But come on we both know how you are. You would have sent me a check for the money the moment I was off the phone."

"And why are you so sure I won't do it now?"

"Because now I'm not crying and stressing out about it. Now I'm just thinking that shit happens and my life isn't over, far from it. And since I'm talking with some sense I know you can respect that. The fact that I've managed to save some money tells you that I'm okay. Right?"

Heaven sighed. "Tanya, don't worry. I'll respect your wishes. I hate it though that you have started thinking you can't tell me things. If I had been home you would have told me when you told the others. I don't like that my being here in Pakistan has changed that between us."

"Heaven, that's not what changed things. And this time I'm not jealous when I say this. Your now being a millionaire is what changed things. I've used you for almost two years to help me out of jams to buy things for the center and for the kids. I told you I wanted to stop doing that. I told Peaches and Ongela because they have no money, they can't do anything but feel bad for me and that's cool. That was all that I needed. That's all that I need now. I love you, Heaven. Give Hamid a big juicy kiss for me and kiss the baby. I'll talk to you soon."

"Hold on don't go rushing me off the phone. What's happening with Lettie?"

"She has her good days and her bad days. Thank God the good days are beginning to out number the bad days. We're all keeping our fingers crossed that the experimental drugs will work. So far, so good. Just keep her in your prayers."

"I'm keeping all of you in my prayers. Good bye, Tann. I'll talk to you later."

Tanya sighed when she hung up the phone, feeling a weight lift from her chest. She'd felt bad about not telling Heaven what was going on in her life. She'd not intended that her friend feel left out but this was also something she'd had to do alone.

෴

Heaven hung up the phone and turned in time to see Hamid and Imran holding Tsukama watching her. She swiped her lips with her tongue knowing they'd heard her conversation and trying hard to think of a convincing lie.

Hamid was giving her a warning glare. She shrugged her shoulders and turned away and walked toward the kitchen.

"Heaven, what's going on? What's wrong with Tanya? What happened to her?"

She put water on for tea and fussed with the cabinets wasting time, not wanting to lie but not wanting to betray Tanya. Imran was one of the main reasons that Tanya had not told her what had happened. Heaven knew that without Tanya telling her. "Nothing's going on," Heaven said at last and brought out a bowl of fruit from the refrigerator.

"Heaven, we all heard you. You were panicked and angry and you called Tanya by name don't lie and deny it."

Oh no he didn't just call me a liar. Hell no! "Who the hell do you think you are, Imran? Don't you dare talk to me like that if you know what's good for you. You have no business listening to my damn conversation." Heaven was pissed. She threw the tea kettle into the sink making a loud clanging noise startling the baby. When he began to cry she went and took him from Imran. "Give me my son," she hissed between clenched teeth.

"Heaven, please," Imran pleaded.

"Go to hell," she answered.

Imran turned in confusion toward Hamid. "I've never seen this side of her. I've never heard her talk in this manner."

"You've never pissed her off," Hamid laughed. "I should have warned you that Heaven has a fiery temper when riled. She has quite a mouth on her when she's angry, much like Tanya has all the time," Hamid finished.

"Ah, so Tanya told Heaven what I said and Heaven told you." Imran looked toward the nursery where Heaven had gone with the baby. "Hamid, can you get her to tell you if Tanya is in trouble. I need to know."

"I thought you were over Tanya."

"Don't be a fool. I love her. I bound myself to her. Now would you please make nice with your wife and find out what I need to know?"

Twenty minutes later Hamid had not had much luck. Imran poked his head in the door. "Heaven, I'm sorry for behaving so badly and for listening in on your conversation. Please won't you forgive me and tell me what's going on with Tanya?"

When she'd finally forgiven him and told him what had happened she still refused to give him Tanya's phone number and her address.

"Stop it. This is enough, Heaven." Hamid marched to the kitchen, opened a drawer and pulled out Heaven's personal phone book holding her away as she hit at him to try and take it away. He wrote the information on a piece of paper and passed it over Heaven's head to his cousin. "I said for you to stop it, Heaven. This is nonsense and I refuse to tolerate it anymore. You started this matchmaking business when I told you to stay out of it. This is no longer just your concern. Imran loves her and he deserves to be able to talk to her and assure himself that all is well with her. I would do no less if it were you."

Imran shook his head. "I'm not calling," he said to his surprised cousin. "I'm going to Chicago. I'm going to see for myself that Tanya's well and I'm going to tell her again that I love her. I've decided that she was correct in what she did six months ago. A lot of my love was based on our passion. That is not the case now. I love her and lust has nothing to do with it. Just do me a favor and not tell her that I'm coming." He glanced at Heaven who was glaring at Hamid. "Please, Heaven," he begged.

"Don't worry, Imran. My wife will keep her pretty nose out of it this time."

As Imran left the home of his cousin he laughed. Life was really strange he decided. For the two years Heaven had been in Pakistan Imran had thought both Hamid and Heaven to be two different people. He'd thought Heaven had taken all of the fire out of Hamid because of his great love for her. And as for Heaven he'd seen this mild mannered, smiling, always cheerful woman. Tanya had been right after all. He thought of all the wrong misconceptions he'd made about Tanya. Yes, she was a loud mouth party girl and used foul language but she was his loud mouth party girl and he loved her. She'd gone though hell without him and he'd gone through hell without her. Now he was going to go and claim her, something he should have done six months before. No matter, Imran thought as the dialed the phone and made reservations.

᪣

One week later Imran was in a taxi heading for Tanya's apartment. He'd talked with Hamid and had found that when Hamid had surprised Heaven she'd been unable to hide her feelings for him. He was hoping the element of surprise would work equally as well for him also. He blew out a breath and said a quick heartfelt prayer to Allah for success. Then he rang the bell.

When Tanya asked who it was he didn't answer just rang the bell again.

"Get the hell off my bell," Tanya bellowed.

Imran pushed the buzzer again.

"Do it again and I'm going to come down and spray pepper spray in your face," Tanya's angry voice blasted over the intercom. "Now get away from my damn buzzer."

Again Imran rang the bell and moved back as he heard angry footsteps running down the stairs. Silly woman, he thought, if I were a criminal I could have a gun to counteract her pepper spray. He'd have to reprimand her about her foolhardy ways. Thinking of the pepper spray he moved to the outside door and waited.

Tanya was in no mood for whoever was playing games. She had a pounding headache and she was frustrated as hell. Her entire week had been lousy, too many kids to place, not enough hours in the day to do it. She was heading for burnout fast and this time it was for real.

"Where are you?" Tanya screamed when she reached the lobby and no one was there. She heard a soft knock on the outer door and turned her finger on the nozzle ready to let loose with a stream of pepper spray. She wasn't kidding. She saw Imran's face and thought she was dreaming. It couldn't be. The spray fell from her hand crashing to the floor and her hand came up to cover her mouth. "Imran," she said when he opened the door cautiously and came inside. "What are you doing here? When did you get here? How did you know where I lived?" she asked.

He stood before her not speaking. Tears sprang to her eyes and ran down her cheeks and she threw her arms around him. "Damn, am I glad to see you. I've missed you so much." She stood on tiptoe to kiss him wondering why he was not immediately kissing her back. "Imran, even if you're going to be mad at me please just kiss me once."

With those words Imran gave up fronting it. He'd not traveled all the way from Pakistan to not hold her in his arms. Praise Allah, he thought as he took her in his arms and kissed her thoroughly. His prayer had been answered. The element of surprise had worked in his favor.

When they came up for air Imran ran a finger lightly down the side of her face and sang to her as she closed her eyes and pressed her face to his chest. "I love you, Tanya," he whispered when he was finished with the song.

"I love you too," Tanya said against his chest not wanting to keep the words in any longer. "What are you doing here?" she asked again.

"You needed me," he explained. "You needed me and didn't tell me. I had to hear about it from someone else. I should have head about this from you. Regardless of what you said I always knew in my heart that if I need you I would call you and you would be there for me, that you would come. I thought you knew that you could call me also."

"I did, Imran, I did."

"Then why didn't you call me?"

"I wanted to. God, how I wanted to. How could I call you after the things I said to you?"

"It matters not the things we say. It matters what we, do how we feels. I will always be there for you and you must never forget that."

"Imran, you came just for me, for no one else, no family wedding, nothing?"

"Nothing but you," he answered following her up the stairs. "Why do you ask?"

"Because when Hamid returned to surprise Heaven it was because of Sassa's wedding. I just want to make sure you came just for me."

"I came just for you. I promise," he said smiling. "Does that mean more to you?"

"Yes, you have no idea how much it means to me. Here I was thinking that Hamid was the perfect man that Heaven had snared the last true gentlemen and that only she could have someone that loved her so much. But…" She gazed into his eyes. "I have you. I have my own sweet prince and you love me just as much as Hamid loved Heaven."

"If possible I love you more." Imran ran up the last couple of steps. "I can't believe we had to go through all of this to make you admit to loving me, to not throwing me out but being glad I came. You are glad aren't you, Tanya? You're not going to throw me out are you?"

"Please, Imran, the last thing on my mind is throwing you out. You have no idea how much I missed you." She shivered slammed the door pressed him against the wall and kissed him while sliding one hand between his thighs to cup him. "I have really been missing you," she admitted.

Imran grinned. "Is that the only reason you've missed me?"

"No, but it's a big part. What did you do to me? I haven't even looked at another man since I returned home."

"I bound us together when we made love."

"Come again?"

"Old secrets of love making. I bound us to each other. Do you mind?"

"Not in the least, not as long as you promise to do it again."

"There is one spot I didn't make love to. When I bring you pleasure in that manner you will never again be able to love another man even if you hate me." He grinned. "Are you ready for me to show you?" He was hoping she'd say yes. She was burning him up with her tantalizing scent.

"Show me," Tanya panted.

With a wide smile Imran pulled the lobe of Tanya's left ear into his mouth and begin to suckle it. When moan after moan slipped from her mouth he ceased his actions and looked at her sternly.

"Six months. Six long agonizing months. I can't believe you'd let it go this long that you wouldn't call wouldn't write to me."

"Can't we do this later? Finish, Imran, you've got me so hot I could explode. It's been six months since I've had release."

"It's been that long for me as well." He kissed her lightly on the lips. "Explain how you could let this much time pass then I will bring you pleasure. I'd never attempted a bond before. I never wanted to but I had thought by doing so you would not have been able to leave me. You not only left me you didn't reach out for me even when you should have. I want to know how this is possible."

"I guess you need to learn a little bit more about how that bonding thing works or perhaps you need to learn a little bit more about me. I'm a very strong woman, Imran."

"Strong enough to resist this?" he said and suckled her earlobe. When he felt a shudder of lust claiming her he looked at her just as her eyes rolled to the back of her head. "Now tell me why you didn't contact me. How you could be so cruel?"

She rubbed her hand over his fast growing erection. "But I thought about you every single minute of those six months."

"Then why didn't you contact me?"

"You didn't contact me either."

"I wasn't the one who left."

He was right and Tanya knew it. She wrapped her arms around him. "Imran," she began to sniffle not wanting to cry. "My life is such a mess. It has been almost since I returned home. Everything has gone wrong. How could I bring you into this nonsense? My dreams are dead. All of my money is gone. I lost it all I was such a fool."

Finally taking a glance around Tanya's apartment he took her hand and moved with her to a sofa, sat and pulled Tanya into his arms. "Tell me what happened."

"You're going to think I was stupid."

"Well, I already think you were not the brightest for leaving me." He kissed her forehead before she could become angry over his remark. "Tell me what happened, Tanya." Of course he knew the story but he wanted to hear it from her. He listened quietly and when she was done he stared into her eyes. "Why does this destroy your dreams?"

"I don't have any more money. Don't you understand?"

"I understand that you want to give a loving home to children. And that you want to give them two parents who will do the best they can for them and love them always. Let's start with us."

"What are you saying?" Tanya whispered. "You want us to adopt a child together?"

"That wasn't exactly what I had in mind but maybe later, yes. I want you to marry me and have babies with me."

"But what about the babies that are already here, the ones no one want?"

"They're wanted, Tanya, you want them."

"Then how?"

"Shh-shh," Imran whispered softly putting his finger again her lips. "Have you ever thought how a mountain came to be? Someone once told me when I asked the question that a mountain started out as one man's dream and that he took a pebble and every day he added to the pebble and one day he had a mountain his dream was fulfilled. Marry me, Tanya and let's start your dream with our family, our babies. Then we can extend our hearts and our home to others."

"What the heck are we going to do for money? How will we

accomplish all of this?"

"If we have to we can work three jobs each. It can be done. It will be done."

"You don't mind?"

"Not in the least, not as long as the two of us are together." He reached into his pocket and pulled out a jeweler's box. He watched as Tanya's eyes went wide and wider still as he opened the box.

"The earrings, you bought me the earrings." Her tears ran freely down her cheeks and she hugged him tightly. So he had known the reason she refused to accept the earrings from either Ali or Hamid. She hadn't wanted any gifts from any man other than Imran. She looked into his eyes and saw his love. Then she thanked God that she hadn't blown things. She never wanted to let him go, never.

"Is that a yes?" Imran asked.

"It's a definite yes."

"And you care nothing about the money, that I don't have any?"

"Neither do I," Tanya tried to smile. "Like you said we can build together."

"If you were given your money back at his moment would your answer still be yes?"

Tanya smiled and looked at him and smiled knowing she'd meant it. Her broken dreams weren't nearly so hard to bare when she had him there beside her ready to share in the rebuilding of it. "I love you, Imran. I can think of no better dream than to be your wife."

"Then show me to your shower so I can love you properly," he said standing and pulling her up. He grinned when he pulled her lobe into his mouth for the third time. He had plenty of time to tell her that he'd finally sold not one but two books that he'd sold them for an unprecedented figure and had finished the third which his agent was in the process of auctioning. They would have more than enough to finance their dreams. As her hand found his erection and began caressing him he shuddered. There would be plenty of time for talk later.

Author Bio

Award winning author, Dyanne Davis lives in a Chicago suburb with her husband Bill, and their son Bill Jr. An avid reader, she began reading at the age of four. Her love of the written word turned into a desire to write. She retired from nursing several years ago to pursue her lifelong dream. Her first novel, The Color of Trouble, was released July of 2003. The novel was received with high praise and several awards. More nominations and awards followed with preceding books.

Dyanne Davis has been a presenter of numerous workshops. She has a local cable show in her hometown to give writing tips to aspiring writers. She has hosted such notables as USA Today Best Selling erotica author, Robin Schone and vampire huntress L.A. Banks.

When not writing you can find Dyanne with a book in her hands, her greatest passion next to spending time with her husband Bill and son Bill Jr. Whenever possible she loves getting together with friends and family.

A member of Romance Writers of America, Dyanne is now serving her second term as Chapter President for Windy City. Dyanne loves to hear feedback from her readers. You can reach her at her website www.dyannedavis.com.